Narco Queen

Narco Queen

MICHAEL S. VIGIL

NARCO QUEEN

iUniverse books may be ordered through booksellers or by contacting:

iUniverse
1663 Liberty Drive
Bloomington, IN 47403
www.iuniverse.com
1-800-Authors (1-800-288-4677)

Because of the dynamic nature of the Internet, any web addresses or links contained in this book may have changed since publication and may no longer be valid. The views expressed in this work are solely those of the author and do not necessarily reflect the views of the publisher, and the publisher hereby disclaims any responsibility for them.

Any people depicted in stock imagery provided by Getty Images are models, and such images are being used for illustrative purposes only. Certain stock imagery © Getty Images.

ISBN: 978-1-5320-6148-6 (sc)
ISBN: 978-1-5320-6150-9 (hc)
ISBN: 978-1-5320-6149-3 (e)

Print information available on the last page.

iUniverse rev. date: 11/07/2018

Dedication

This book is dedicated to my beloved parents, Sam and Alice, whose sacrifice, support, and unconditional love made me the person I am today.

To my sisters, Anita and Mona, for their unwavering love and support.

To my nieces Ursula, who is my bright, shining star, and Nicole, who is in heaven.

To my stepdaughter, Lisa Fiocchi, and my grandchildren, Luke Edward, and Sarah Claire. I wish them happiness and great success in life.

To my wife, Suzanne, who has always provided me with tremendous support in designing the beautiful and artistic covers for each of my three books.

To Laurel Starkey, for her assistance in editing this book that added so much color and life to the story.

To my friend, Alvan Romero, retired IRS-CI Special Agent, who worked many dangerous assignments during his long, meritorious career. His service, integrity, and commitment to the U.S. are immeasurable. He provided phenomenal support and editing in the making of Narco Queen.

Foreword

"You have to meet Mike", said my fellow DEA Special Agent and good friend Mischa Harrington, circa 1998. I had heard many great things about Mike Vigil from Mischa and other fellow Special Agents over the years, but never had the pleasure of meeting him. I remember thinking Mischa and others who had talked about Mike had to be exaggerating because no one could be that operationally forwarding leaning, strategically and tactically brilliant, and a dynamic leader. I finally was able to meet Mike, first by phone and then in person and quickly determined everything I heard about him was accurate; he is, in fact, "the real deal!" Thus, began a friendship that has endured over 20 years and afforded me the unique opportunity to observe Mike in action from a close vantage point.

Mike, from his earliest days as a DEA Special Agent, never followed the well-worn trail or latched on to the coat tails of others to advance his career. Instead, he made his own trail in pursuit of bad guys throughout the world, in particular, the notorious Mexican drug cartels and their vicious members. No matter the difficulty or danger of the mission, Mike would let nothing stop him from pursuing drug traffickers and other criminals. There is no one more knowledgeable about Mexican drug cartels than Mike, who frequently appears as an expert contributor and commentator on national media networks to provide his insight into drug trafficking organizations and other organized crime groups. He is a true master of his craft and keeps abreast of developments in the dark, violent underworld of international drug trafficking and related crimes.

People followed Mike because they wanted to, not just because of his supervisory positions, power, or influence. Through hard work, determination and perseverance, Mike worked his way up through the ranks of DEA from a Special Agent on the streets to his appointment to the prestigious Senior Executive Service, and never forgot from where he came. Even while serving in the highest executive levels of DEA, he always thought and acted like the street agent he was, always contemplating operational plans and tactics that would result in bad guys going to jail while disrupting and dismantling the criminal organizations for which they worked. During his service as the DEA Chief of International Operations, Mike had occasion to travel throughout the world to meet and interact with heads of foreign law enforcement agencies as well as Generals and Minister level members of various countries. Mike's engaging personality quickly won over these individuals and created a level of mutual respect and trust that served as a foundation for ongoing serious discussions that concluded with bilateral agreements and pledges to mutually cooperate in criminal investigations and related matters. Many of these individuals became friends with Mike, maintain contact with him to this day, and visit with him whenever they travel to Washington, DC.

Mike is a visionary leader who practiced, in thought and deed, servant leadership long before that concept became a popular term of art. He mentored and motivated DEA Special Agents and other personnel while providing continuous encouragement for them to achieve their fullest potential. Conversely, he would not hesitate to give immediate and constructive stimulus for less than productive individuals. Mike frequently was bestowed with the highest compliment a DEA Special Agent can give to an individual who became a Special Agent in Charge, or in other senior executive level positions, and that is to call him or her "An Agent's Agent." No higher praise can come from a fellow Special Agent.

To paraphrase portions of a famous speech by Theodore Roosevelt, Mike stayed in the arena that many others were too fainthearted or risk adverse to enter. He fought the good fight while at DEA and won more battles than he lost. Mike never experienced the feelings of those cold and timid souls who neither know victory nor defeat because they never entered the arena. Mike lived in the arena!

Mike is a tough guy, but he tempers his toughness with kindness and compassion. He treats everyone with respect and dignity, no matter their station in life or circumstances. I can vividly recall one cold, blustery winter day when I met Mike for lunch. Mike arrived at the restaurant before me and as I was walking to the front door, I noticed an older, homeless man, clearly down on his luck, sitting on a bench. As we were finishing our lunch, Mike ordered for takeout, a large container of hot chicken soup and crackers. As we departed the restaurant, he walked up to the homeless man and said, "My Brother, please take care of yourself and keep warm with this hot soup. God bless you." Knowing Mike, that same type of scenario has played out many times, but he never talks about it or seeks recognition for his acts of kindness.

Following his successful career with DEA, he worked as a senior executive for several government contractors before deciding to retire for good and try his hand at being a writer. Like everything he's ever done in his life, Mike put his heart and soul into writing and made what others would find very difficult, look easy. His first two books were amazing and I know you will feel the same about this book.

The world would be a better place if we had more people

in it like Mike Vigil. I am honored he asked me to write the forward to this book and proud to call him my friend.

Mike Todd
DEA Supervisory Special Agent (Retired)

Foreword

Mike and I have been best friends since we were college roommates, almost fifty years now. Knowing Mike well, for such a long period of time has given me a unique perspective of not only his talents and attributes, but of him, as a human being. I will share some of what I believe makes Mike unique. Before I go there I want to thank Mike and tell him that I am truly honored that he asked me to write a forward for *Narco Queen.*

I spent the first 26 years in my career with IRS-Criminal Investigation (IRS-CI). While Mike adapted quite well to the international world stage, working with his foreign counterparts, identifying, locating, chasing and apprehending the most notorious narco-kingpins and seizing illegal drugs they trafficked in, I followed the money, investigating such crimes as criminal tax evasion, money laundering, drug-trafficking, public corruption, conspiracy and other financial crimes.

DEA, who Mike worked for, and IRS-CI, who I worked

for, made a perfect team—DEA took the drugs, proved the drug-trafficking crime, and put the drug-traffickers in jail for very long periods of time, while IRS-CI contributed to these very successful criminal investigations by working on the financial aspects of the case, identifying the vast amounts of ill-gotten assets and seizing them, thus putting the crooks out of operation, and often inflicting a fatal blow to their organization, so it would cease to exist.

Narco Queen is the sequel to *Metal Coffins, The Blood Alliance Cartel*. You will definitely enjoy both of these books. Prior to Mike writing his first two novels, Mike authored his autobiography, DEAL. Mike has caught worldwide attention with these recent writings. He continues to be sought out by top media outlets for his expert insight and opinion. Mike maintains his credibility with the media because he stays abreast of critical events occurring in the illicit drug world.

Mike's decades of undercover work is legendary. He faced danger many times throughout his career as an undercover operative. Mike is highly respected for his ingenious planning and successful execution of many high-profile multi-national operations, where international drug cartels were dismantled. His accomplishments across the globe, as a world leader in counterdrug efforts, are second to none.

Obviously, Mike has drawn from all his experiences in his storied career and his life's history, as he writes these most interesting novels.

I attribute Mike's unequaled success, in his career and in his life, to his tremendous *power of the mind*, his *intestinal fortitude* and the *great care he has for people*. Perhaps, better said, Mike is extremely intelligent and delivers what he promises, he has *cojones,* and he treats people right!

Mike, in his profession, has always focused on building long-term personal and loyal relationships. Over his career Mike cultivated his foreign counterparts by spending time with them outside of the job and treating them with respect. This set Mike apart, from many other DEA agents, assigned to foreign posts that basically spent most of their time in the office. Mike got out of the office and into the field where the action was!

When you read Mike's books you can be assured that they are written from the perspective of an agent, who worked in the front lines and in the trenches!

Mike was deadly calm during the dangerous face-to-face encounters with violent drug dealers. He also excelled at the international level by developing multi-national operations involving as many as 36 countries. He came up with the idea of creating global intelligence sharing strategies that are still in existence today and continue to expand.

POWER OF THE MIND – Because of what I've personally witnessed during our time together, in college and afterwards, as well as taking into account what a number of DEA Agents, who worked for or with Mike, personally related to me, I realize that Mike's *"Power of the Mind and His Capabilities"* are phenomenal! He has an extraordinary power!

One example, which I recall vividly, that clearly demonstrates Mike's powerful mind occurred in 1973. As I recall, it was towards the end of Mike's last semester in college. Mike was scheduled to take a Criminal Law Course final exam the following day. We were both studying late one night in our dorm room. I was only a few feet away from Mike, busy and quite focused on my own studies that evening, studying at my desk, in our very small dorm room in Regent's Row, a dorm at NMSU, which was centrally-located on campus and designated for upper classmen. That particular night, Mike had just about finished studying for his upcoming exam, when suddenly out of nowhere, Mike handed me his Criminal Justice textbook and asked me to follow the text in the book as he recited passages in the book verbatim from memory. He did this without looking at the book. As he recited sentence after sentence, I followed what he recited, by looking at the same exact words in the book. He did this for about 15 minutes straight. I was totally astounded and literally shocked that he could recall page after page of typewritten words, word-for-word, no mistakes, with his photographic memory!! Never in my life have I witnessed something like this! Almost too hard to believe, if not for that fact that I personally observed it!

INTESTINAL FORTITUDE AND GREAT MENTORSHIP – I will now touch on Mike's *Intestinal Fortitude and Great Mentorship*. Fast-forward forty years to the year 2013. While I was working in Colombia at the U.S. Embassy, preparing to teach two courses, a *financial investigations course* and a *money-laundering course*, to the Colombian National Police and the Colombian Judiciary, I met one of Mike's former agents, an agent who had reported to Mike in Miami during the approximate period 1989-1991. After meeting each other, we quickly learned that Mike was a mutual friend. I also learned from this agent, that since his start with Mike, he had become the head of various DEA Offices in Central and South America. He related to me that as a young agent, he was about to leave DEA for another federal agency because he wasn't enjoying his work at DEA and, consequently, it was an unfulfilling time. Mike, who had just become his group supervisor at that time, pulled him aside and convinced him to remain with the DEA. Mike assured this young agent that, soon, the job would become challenging, and fulfilling and he would begin to have fun. At Mike's encouragement, the agent decided to give it a try. As I met Mike's former agent, he was in the position of the DEA Country Attaché in

Bogotá, who oversaw the Andean Region, which included the countries of Colombia, Ecuador and Venezuela. He told me that he never worked harder in his entire career, as he did when he worked for Mike! However, he said that Mike made the job fun! He related to me that it became a well-known fact that the agents in Mike's group became the hardest working and most productive agents in the Miami DEA Office. He stated that Mike's group had the most results in Miami; drug busts, arrests, confiscated drugs and forfeitures. Consequently, because of all the hard-productive work that they did, the agents had much support from Mike and he saw to it that all his agents were promoted. He said that Mike was a *GREAT MENTOR* to both him and to all the other agents in the group. He went on to say that he would, forever, be appreciative to Mike.

During his time in Miami, while working in Mike's group, he said he witnessed Mike exhibit unbelievable courage. Mike detained a regularly scheduled passenger airliner and ordered it to be searched, after it had flown into the Miami International Airport. DEA had received intelligence that a Varig Airlines DC 10, of the Brazilian carrier, was flying into the Miami International Airport from South America, with a ton of cocaine hidden on board. As it turned out, Mike coordinated with U.S. Customs and ordered the plane to be detained. As the plane was being unloaded, Mike's agents, while performing surveillance of the plane, noticed a rental truck drive up to the plane and saw it swiftly loaded with many boxes. Almost as soon as it arrived, it drove away with its haul. Mike's agents followed the truck at a safe distance. Once separated from the plane, the agents pulled the rental truck over. When the truck came to a stop, Mike approached the truck. He received permission from the truck driver to search the truck. As a result of that operation 2,200 pounds of cocaine were located and confiscated by DEA.

Once the cocaine was field-tested and positively identified Mike ordered that the commercial airliner be seized so that a thorough search of the plane could be undertaken. A number of Varig Airlines employees, both American and foreigners, were also arrested. They were arrested for facilitating the smuggling of cocaine into the United States. That day the DEA Administrator (Head of the DEA) received significant badgering from Varig Airlines to release the plane. The White House was also being pressured by the Brazilian President to release the plane immediately. Mike refused to capitulate. The plane was not released, but was detained in a hanger, until the entire plane was searched thoroughly and the operation was complete. Only then was the plane free to go. Mike did not yield! He had *cajones*!

Mike's former agent told me that it was the opinion of the agents' in that Miami enforcement group, that if someone threw a grenade into a room and Mike was standing in it, all the agents would run and hide behind him. He said the agents knew, from first-hand experience, that when the smoke cleared, Mike would still be standing! Mike's men revered him!

Alván Romero, CPA CFF CFE
Special Agent, IRS-Criminal Investigation (IRS-CI),
(Retired)
Founding Director, Tax Fraud Investigations Division
(TFID), NM TRD

Prologue

Sometimes in the life of an agent it is the oddest things that lead to breakthroughs. Miguel Villa knew it – he'd seen it many times. Since the death of the head of the Cartel of the North, Albino Romero, and the death of La Sombra and José Atenco from the Blood Alliance Cartel, the violence had somewhat subsided in Mexico, at least temporarily. Now there were tens of corpses instead of hundreds of tortured bodies being dumped or simply disappearing. Cautious signs of civilian life, like weeds, poked through the hardened and scorched earth that made up cartel territories.

Both Miguel and his greatest collaborator, Comandante Florentino Ventura of the Federales, hoped that it would give the Federales the chance to deliver a deathblow.

The death of Albino Romero, head of the violent Cartel of the North, reverberated throughout Mexico's powerful and lucrative drug trade like a lethal bolt of lightning. Romero had been captured in Colombia in a spectacular operation of deception. Despite being under the protection of the

FARC, the Armed Revolutionary Forces of Colombia, Albino Romero had been lured out of relative safety in the jungle and taken into custody by an operation dreamed up by Villa and Ventura and executed brilliantly by General Leonardo Gallego of the Colombian National Police. As Romero was being transported via helicopter to a prison cell in Bogotá to await deportation back to Mexico, he chose to commit suicide. He jumped from the helicopter while in flight and fell two thousand feet to his death in the very jungles that he had hoped to find freedom. He jumped because of his conviction that he would not live as a caged animal again.

Smarts and cunning had outwitted the vast resources of the drug lord. Now Villa and Ventura surveyed the remnants of the cartels these deaths had left behind. Who would rise to the top?

Miguel Villa recalled the cunning and sheer intelligence of Albino's lieutenant, Lisa Rochin, a former beauty queen turned drug trafficker. Within days, the DEA had picked up information from informants that she wanted the top leadership role of the Cartel of the North and was pushing the plaza bosses hard for the spot. Miguel and Ventura had begun to interview informants and compile a comprehensive investigative file on her earlier. Now Miguel sat down to study it in earnest, to see what he might have missed.

It was times like this that Miguel missed Rafael, aka La Serpiente. He'd been a fantastic informant. Rafael had known

Lisa well from the beginning. But he was dead now, despite the fact he'd been granted protective custody in Colorado. Moths can't avoid flying into the flame and snakes can't stay hidden in their holes. Rafael was arrogant and it led to his violent death. Yet Miguel had learned a great deal about Lisa from Rafael as he'd prepped for his undercover operation they'd carried out months earlier, which resulted in a huge seizure of money and cocaine. Lisa was, by all accounts, a remarkably bright woman with a sponge-like ability to learn. She was sexy and she was ruthless – the complete package.

It was almost stereotypical: born poor in the mountains near Los Mochis, Sinaloa. Dirt floors, no plumbing, barely a house. She'd grown up with her younger sister and brother, watching those who sold opium and marijuana to the cartels to pull themselves out of the mud and into a decent life. It was no secret there wasn't any other game in town, really. Schooling was sporadic and she attended every chance she got. When there was no school – she read on her own in-between hauling water from the streams, washing clothes and making tortillas to take to her father in the fields.

She looked after her younger siblings: Armando who was always in trouble and Anita who stood off in the shadows, always watching but never saying anything. Anita had a reputation for the black arts – she looked like La Llorona with her fair white skin, long black hair, and emaciated body. She was indeed fascinated with Santeria and black magic.

Villa and Ventura both knew that despite their successful operations, the cat and mouse game would continue with new players who were more devious than those who preceded them. It was an extremely dangerous game, but they loved being in the arena. They were modern day gladiators.

CHAPTER 1

The Making of a Narco Queen

The death of Albino Romero, the head of the violent Cartel of the North, reverberated throughout Mexico's powerful and lucrative drug trade. Romero was captured in Colombia in a dramatic operation where, as a fugitive from Mexico, he had been under the protection of the FARC, the Armed Revolutionary Forces of Colombia. Rather than spend the rest of his life in prison he opted to commit suicide by jumping from a Colombian National Police helicopter at two thousand feet as he was being transported to La Picota prison in Bogota. He chose a horrible death over a long, torturous incarceration. Romero didn't want to live as a caged animal, especially after tasting supreme wealth and power. Rotting in a miserable prison for the rest of his days was not something that was appetizing to any criminal, especially him.

DEA agent Miguel Villa and his close friend and Mexican counterpart, Florentino Ventura, along with Colombian National Police General Leonardo Gallego had worked collaboratively on the sensational operation that had lured Romero from an impenetrable jungle by manipulating FARC radio communications. It was nothing short of spectacular. Villa and Ventura were smart, cunning, and adaptable. Villa was tall, strongly built with dark hair and had a thick mustache. He was born in a small, poor village in northern New Mexico. Spanish was his first language and he didn't learn English until he was old enough to start school. Ventura grew up in poverty in the heart of Mexico's drug trade, the central state of Sinaloa. Marijuana and opium poppy fields surrounded the village where he grew up. He resisted the temptation of becoming a drug trafficker, primarily because of his mother's strong influence and guidance. Ventura was tall, medium build and had jet-black hair. He had an affinity for ostrich cowboy boots.

After the demise of Romero in Colombia, both Ventura and Villa returned to Mexico City. They both felt that Romero's death had summarily eliminated one of Mexico's most powerful and feared drug lords. It also meant that he could no longer bribe or threaten government officials as he had done in the past. As the former head of the Cartel of the North, he had been responsible for the brutal killings of thousands of people. Villa and Ventura were not so naïve to think that his death would have a lasting impact on Mexico's drug trade. They knew that their work was far from over. The cat and mouse game was a perpetual one, for both the drug traffickers and law enforcement agents. To be sure, it was a deadly one. Almost immediately, Villa and Ventura begin to develop plans to finish off both the Cartel of the North and the Blood Alliance Cartel. The strategy involved the use of informants, wiretaps, undercover work, and surveillance. It was hard work that involved long hours of grueling investigation. Regardless, they were more than up to the task.

Within days, Lisa Rochin, a former beauty queen, and one of Albino's principal lieutenants put the word out that she wanted the top leadership role of the Cartel of the North. She had already lobbied hard for Romero's position with many of its leaders. Many supported her because they respected the fact that she had worked her way up the ranks. She had proven herself and had been mentored under the watchful eye of Albino. She had also displayed her ruthlessness by killing dozens of police officers and rival drug traffickers. But for every supporter, Lisa also had a detractor and she knew it. Lisa was cool, calculating, and extremely cunning. She had to be.

She was born into poverty in a small and isolated village in the Sierra Madre Mountains near Los Mochis, Sinaloa. Lisa had grown up in a rustic three-room adobe house with packed dirt floors and a dilapidated tin roof. It was devoid of running water and electricity. Lisa, along with her brother and sister, had the arduous task of slinging buckets of water to their home from nearby mountain streams. It was used for cooking, drinking and bathing.

Armando, the youngest sibling, adored Lisa and followed her everywhere. He was mischievous and would often get into fights, but could always count on Lisa to bail him out. He had coarse black hair and was extremely thin. He was bright and got good grades without studying very much. Anita, who followed Lisa in age, was very reserved and meticulous. She liked to analyze people and formed quick opinions about them. She had long, black hair, fair skin and was extremely frail. Anita was extremely independent and enjoyed studying black magic and the history of witchcraft. At night, she read her books on the black arts in the dim candlelight of her home until she fell asleep. Her favorite books were on African black magic and those that dealt with spells and potions.

Lisa, at an early age, was very rebellious, but highly intelligent and inquisitive. Although there was no school in the village, teachers would travel into the area on a regular basis and conduct classes outdoors using cheap, white plastic chairs and small, worn blackboards. All of the teachers were impressed by Lisa's uncanny ability to learn and retain information from a variety of non-fiction books that she liked to read. Many of the teachers, on occasion, would bring her old books, which she devoured quickly to learn more of the outside world. When she was twelve years old she was given an old tattered book written by Francois-Marie Arouet best known by his *nom de plume* Voltaire. The title of the book *was "The Essay of Customs and the Spirit of the Nation."* She loved Voltaire's wit, opinion and advocacy of freedom of religion and expression. Lisa would beg the teachers to bring her more of Voltaire's books in the event they came across them at bookstores.

Everyone in the area knew of Lisa's incredible intelligence and natural beauty. She was also encouraged by her family and friends to enter local beauty contests. She won several of them despite wearing old and outdated clothes. Her family couldn't afford to buy her fancy gowns and shoes for the events. Her father, Abel, was a strong, athletically built man with short-cropped black hair. He was a poor farmer who planted tomatoes, lettuce, and melons on his postage stamp size farm. Lisa and her siblings sold the fruits and vegetables to villagers or traded them for other produce or clothes. Lisa's mother, Ramona, was a highly religious person and made sure her family attended mass every Sunday at the small wooden church on top of a hill on the southern outskirts of the village. The church was poorly constructed with scrap wood and it leaned forward dramatically. Everyone was just waiting for the day it would finally roll down the hill along with everyone in it. Everyone laughingly called it the "Crooked Church of Christ." It had caught the attention of the local priest and he had given the villagers a two-hour fire and brimstone sermon against making fun of the Catholic Church.

Lisa would daydream about becoming rich and being able to buy new and fancy clothes. She also envisioned dining in the finest restaurants and enjoying the various cuisines and delicacies the world had to offer. This helped her cope with her choking poverty.

When Lisa was eighteen, a handsome young man in his mid-thirties moved into the area. He was tall, of slender build and had dark brown hair and hazel eyes. Always dressed in immaculate blue jeans and expensive ostrich cowboy boots, the women swooned over him when he passed. His name was Juan Fernandez and he told everyone he was a wealthy rancher from Culiacan, Sinaloa. Everyone affectionately called him Juancho. He built the largest and most opulent house in the area with a beautiful Spanish tiled roof and gleaming white marble columns. It looked like a castle from a fairy tale in comparison to the rickety shacks that dotted the village. Lisa first saw him walking near La Aguila Dorada Cantina. She was immediately smitten and could feel her heart beating like a war drum. Lisa melted and could feel warmth rushing through her body when he smiled at her. She blushed and felt embarrassed.

He spoke to her and said, *"Mi Amor,* how are you? I had no idea that such a small town could produce such a beautiful girl! You're absolutely hermosa! What is your name?"

Lisa responded, "Yo me llamo Lisa and I have lived here all my life. I can assure you there are many beautiful girls who live in this village. You just haven't seen all of them yet!"

He smiled replying, "It is my lucky day meeting you. You are very special! I would like to invite you to my house for dinner tonight. I'll wait for you and please dress informally. It is not a formal affair."

Lisa looked down, "That will be fine. Thank you for being so kind. I look forward to dinner and I'll be there early. Until then."

Lisa was elated and glad that dinner would be very informal since she didn't own a stitch of decent clothes. She ran home and heated up some water on the rustic, wood burning stove and poured it into a small laminated metal tub so she could bathe. The soap was made of lye and was very harsh on her skin, but she was focused on something much more important, love. As she soaked in the warm water, Lisa daydreamed and thought of Juancho, her knight in shining armor who had arrived to take her to live a fairytale life. She smiled and her heart fluttered with incredible joy. She dressed in her best dress, which went out of style at least three decades earlier. Regardless, her beauty and personality greatly overshadowed her outdated clothes. Her parents, when told of the dinner invitation, insisted that she take her aunt Dorotea as a chaperone. It was not acceptable for a respectable young girl to be alone with a man. What would the neighbors think?

An hour later, she and her seventy-year old, white haired aunt dressed in a black dress and dark shawl left the house and walked excitedly to Juancho's large mansion. It looked like a forbidding castle. It was made of large chiseled rocks that were neatly stacked and anchored with copious amounts of concrete. The entrance featured twenty-foot high wooden doors adorned with large iron discs in the shape of suns. Lisa lifted the heavy metal knocker and let it fall back on the door. It made a loud thud and Juancho, dressed in in a bright red western shirt with black embroidery, quickly opened the door.

He smiled, "Querida, I'm so glad you came. Welcome to my house, mi casa es su casa. I hope you enjoy dinner. Please come in."

Lisa blushed bright red, "Thank you! I'm happy to be here and I have to say you have a beautiful house. It is so big! It seems so out of place with the poor houses in the village. You must be a very successful businessman. Oh, and please forgive me this is my aunt Dorotea. My parents insisted that she accompany me."

He laughed, "The house is great, but it's too big for one person. I should have built a small one that would be much cozier. I just got carried away designing it with the architect and somehow it got larger and larger."

Lisa walked in and was breathless when she saw the large hand-woven Persian carpets that covered most of the floors and some of the walls. The rich red, blue, and yellow colors overwhelmed her senses. The large chandeliers were spectacular and the crystals looked like glittering diamonds under the bright lights. Her aunt kept her head down and didn't notice anything other than the tips of her shoes and the floor. She followed Lisa and remained nothing more than a shadow since her only mission was to ensure that old world cultural values were adhered to and act as a silent witness that Lisa's virginity remained intact.

Lisa said, "In all my life, I have never seen such beautiful things. Nobody in town has anything like this and even if they had the money the shops here sell only things needed for the villagers to survive day to day."

Juancho chuckled, "Everything is possible with hard work. I fought for the things I have and continue to move forward in life. But let's eat before the food gets cold."

He escorted her and her aunt into a cavernous dining area, which had a long wooden table that seated eighteen people. Aunt Dorotea took a seat at the end of the table and was completely ignored. She was a ghost to Juancho and Lisa who were completely focused on one another. The ceiling and floors were made of inlaid teakwood in the shape of dragons. Over the table was a beautiful multi-colored chandelier made by the famous artist Dale Chihuly.

Lisa commented, "That's the most beautiful thing I've ever seen in my life. I could sit here and look at it all day."

Juancho refrained from telling her that he paid over ten

million dollars for the work of art. He knew that it would lead to several questions and he didn't want to open that door just yet. Besides, he was interested in Lisa and didn't want to scare her off from the very beginning. That would be very stupid of me, he thought.

A maid served an exquisite dinner consisting of fresh lobster smothered in melted butter, rice, and for desert, a six-layer chocolate cake with fresh strawberries on top. For the first time in her life, Lisa was introduced to imported French champagne. It only took two glasses to make her feel giddy. Lisa had the best time of her life and hated to leave, but she knew that immediately showing her intense desire for Juancho was not a good idea. It was about maintaining her respect and dignity as a woman and not making Juancho think that she could be easily seduced. Laughter and flirtations continued until midnight and finally Lisa said they had to leave since her parents were probably worried. Walking her to the door, Juancho grabbed her in a firm embrace and kissed her passionately. It took all her will power to be able to pull away. Staggering out into the dark night and the biting cold mountain air, Lisa didn't feel the chill as her blood was running red-hot and her heart was pounding wildly. She was madly in love. Aunt Dorotea scolded her about kissing a man on the first date. She commented, "Men are nothing more than cabrones and they will think you are easy."

Soon, Lisa and Juancho became an item in the village and

seemed inseparable. He took her on shopping trips to Rodeo Drive in Beverly Hills and bought her designer clothes and expensive jewelry. He also took her to have her hair done by one of the top hair stylists in downtown Los Angeles. Juancho was transforming her into a flamboyant and sophisticated woman. Lisa felt like the Queen of England. Her sense of self-esteem had been lifted beyond the ionosphere. Later, Juancho surprised Lisa by taking her to a renowned plastic surgeon and paid top dollar for a breast enhancement. Heads now twisted around as she walked carefree through the opulent streets of Beverly Hills.

A year later, Juancho got intoxicated on Don Julio tequila and told Lisa he wanted to tell her a secret. Fueled by over ten shots of the cactus juice, Juancho's inhibitions were short-circuited and his discretion went out the window. Nervously, he explained that he was not a rancher, but a trafficker of cocaine, heroin and methamphetamine. He justified his criminal activities by saying that they were the only options available to him growing up in extreme poverty. Shock quickly numbed Lisa's brain, but her love for him overpowered the emotional warnings of extreme danger. She told him that her love was so intense and passionate and she didn't care about his criminal activities. However, she didn't mention that she had become intoxicated with the power and wealth that came with it.

Two months later, Lisa and Juancho got married in a

lavish wedding attended by all the villagers. A dozen pigs and several goats were slaughtered the day before and roasted on spits over hot charcoal. Beer and the finest tequila flowed like water and the loud music from a twelve-man mariachi group blared into the early morning hours of the following day. It was the greatest celebration the village had ever witnessed and they were all sad when it ended. Everyone staggered, or had to be carried, home. The next day the streets were completely deserted as everyone remained in bed nursing throbbing hangovers. Lisa and Juancho also slept late. Early in the afternoon, they enjoyed seafood cocktails loaded with lots of juice from fresh limes and chipotle hot sauce. In Mexico, this was considered the best remedy for hangovers and it was appropriately called "reviving the dead."

Lisa was happy with her life, but being an ordinary housewife was not enough. She was overly ambitious and wanted more in life. A few months passed and one day at dinner she approached Juancho about helping him in his drug business. He chuckled, "Mi Amor, this is a man's business and women are too compassionate and afraid to engage in the violence that comes with it. Besides, men don't respect women and will take advantage of them. You will need to have bigger cojones than the men in order to compete and survive."

She responded, "That is so unfair for you to say such a sexist thing. Just give me a chance. You will not regret it. Por favor!"

Lisa's opportunity came two weeks later. Juancho had promised to deliver ten kilos of heroin to one of his important customers in Phoenix, Arizona, but his courier had been involved in an automobile accident and was in a hospital with two broken legs. The delivery date was the next day and Juancho had always been a man of his word when it came to his drug business. Hesitantly, he asked Lisa if she was willing to step in for the injured courier. She immediately accepted and that night they stuffed high quality black tar heroin contained in clear plastic bags into false compartments of two large Samsonite suitcases. The next day, Juancho had Lisa dress in a very short black skirt and a revealing orange silk blouse. He drove her to the airport in Los Mochis in his shiny, black Mercedes Benz with plenty of time to catch her flight. He kissed her passionately, smearing her bright red lipstick and waved as she walked confidently into the terminal. He watched as men turned to look at Lisa like ravenous wolves. It made him jealous, but he knew she would never stray and he trusted her completely.

Lisa strutted up to the airport security area and smiled seductively at the old gray-haired man in the blue polyester uniform with a white stripe running down the sides of his pants. She could see saliva running down the corner of his mouth. She smirked and intentionally bent over so he could see her voluptuous breasts. Lisa was not wearing a bra and the man began to sweat profusely. The two suitcases passed through the x-ray machine without a problem. All eyes were fixated on Lisa. She could have been carrying a nuclear device and no one would have noticed or cared for that matter.

After checking in her bags, Lisa boarded the plane and sat in the first-class section. Before takeoff, she had the petite, blond flight attendant with bright pink high heels bring her a glass of red wine. When the attendant placed the wine on the seat tray, she asked Lisa for her autograph thinking she was a famous actress. Lisa chuckled and played along scribbling an undistinguishable signature on a paper napkin. Lisa couldn't drink the wine fast enough, as the attendant was jolly on the spot continually refilling her glass.

By the time the aircraft started its descent into Phoenix, Lisa was feeling rather tipsy. Regardless, the wine helped alleviate her nervousness. She thought about how she could best flaunt her sexuality and use it to distract Customs officials. She knew they were usually men who were bored with the monotony of their jobs. It wouldn't take much for her to get their blood flowing and brighten their dull, monotonous day. She unbuttoned her blouse even further and used a small mirror to touch up her makeup. Even Marilyn Monroe would have been envious of her stunning beauty.

She contemplated the risk involved and the fact that she would forfeit years of her freedom if she were caught with the heroin. But life is full of risk and she was of the opinion that the monetary rewards made it worthwhile.

The flight attendant announced on the intercom, "Please fasten your seat belts and make sure your seats are upright. We will be landing in ten minutes. Make sure your customs forms are completed and that your passports are handy since you will be going through Customs and Immigration. Thank you for flying with us today and we hope your flight was enjoyable."

A minute later, the flight attendant approached Lisa and handed her a bottle of wine from Napa Valley that she could enjoy later that evening. Lisa thanked her and would use it to celebrate if she was able to sneak by the ever-vigilant U.S. Customs officers.

When she exited the plane, Lisa lagged purposely behind the other passengers in line. The noise was rather loud as mothers struggled to herd their kids and fish for passports and other documents in their oversized leather purses. A female immigration officer yelled repetitively, "next line, next line" but few people spoke English so they ignored her. Lisa selected a line that had an older, overweight male officer who seemed disinterested as hell in what he was doing. When her turn came, she walked up to him, smiled and brazenly flashed her breasts. The officer almost fell off his stool and slowly stamped her passport without taking his eyes away from Lisa's amazing physical attributes. He continued to look at her as she walked away swinging her hips from side to side. They sure don't make many like that anymore, he thought.

Lisa walked over to the conveyor belt that was already spitting out the suitcases from her flight and retrieved hers. After putting her two suitcases on an airport cart, she walked quickly to the nearest male Customs officer. He was young and good-looking. He smiled, broadly revealing a mouth full of sparkling white teeth, as Lisa approached. He asked, "What is the purpose of your visit?"

Lisa replied, "I am here on a short vacation, nothing more than a tourist."

He responded, "I can see from your Customs form that you have nothing to declare?"

To that Lisa smiled and said, "No, I plan to do some shopping while here. The clothes in my country are dreadful and are poorly made. I bought this skirt here and you can see how nice it is." She deftly pulled it up to show her long, gorgeous legs.

"OK, you can go through. Hope to see you again, soon. My name is Lou."

Lisa seductively brushed back her hair and smiled as she left the Customs area. Outside she hailed a taxicab that took her to the Galaxy Hotel. She generously gave the cabdriver a hefty tip and called a nearby bellboy who quickly placed her bags on a small cart. Lisa moved slowly through the spacious lobby, which had oversized couches more suited for a masculine taste. The colorful cushions and bright floral arrangements made the ambience more palatable and refreshing. After checking in, Lisa entered the large, wooden paneled elevator and took it to the fourth floor. She quickly dumped all her clothes from the suitcases onto the king-sized bed and carefully removed the heroin from the hidden panels. She could smell the strong vinegar odor emanating from the plastic bags. It was the caustic acetic anhydride, an essential chemical used to convert morphine into heroin hydrochloride. She carefully placed the heroin under the bed and sat and waited patiently.

An hour later, Lisa received a call on her cell phone from an individual who identified himself as Felipe. In a gruff voice, he stated he was in the lobby and asked for her room number. After she gave it to him, he chuckled and whispered, "I will be right up."

A few minutes later there was a soft knock on the door. Lisa looked through the peephole and saw a man with an unkempt beard and gray disheveled hair. She cautiously opened the door and the man introduced himself as Felipe and shook her hand. He was towing a gaudy, orange colored suitcase in his left hand. He quickly stepped past her and suspiciously surveyed the entire room as he walked in. He glared menacingly at Lisa and asked, "Did you bring the merchandise?"

She looked squarely into his eyes, "Well, did you bring the money? If you have the money, then I have the product."

Felipe lifted the heavy suitcase with both hands and threw

it on the bed and moved away from it. He told Lisa, "A total of $700,000 is in it. You can count it if you want, but it is accurate to the penny."

Lisa smiled broadly and quickly unzipped it. Bundles of five, ten, and twenty-dollar bills were packed tightly into it. She flipped through some of them. She grinned and said, "It appears that it is all here and if it isn't then you will be hearing from us."

He smirked and waited until Lisa pulled out the bags of heroin from under the bed. She handed them to him, one by one, and Felipe put them up to his nose and smelled each one. Lisa gave him one of her suitcases to use in getting the heroin to his car. Felipe firmly shook her hand again and told her nonchalantly, "I'm sure we will continue doing business and making money together. Until next time." After he left, Lisa used her cell phone and called Arturo, a money launderer that Juancho used in the U.S. Lisa had never met him. Arturo was abrupt and asked Lisa the name of the hotel and her room number. He told her that he was twenty minutes away and would see her soon. Lisa got the bottle of wine she was given by the flight attendant and looked at the label. It was Napa wine. "It can't be that bad," she thought. She loudly popped the cork with a cheap hotel corkscrew and poured herself a healthy portion into a Styrofoam cup she found on the nightstand. She reflected on the day's events, "So far so good," she mumbled to herself. She took off her shoes and slumped into the brown, fake leather love seat. Her feet were killing her and she desperately wanted to crawl into the bathtub and take a long, hot bath, but she knew business was a priority so it would have to wait. She began to contemplate the risky profession of trafficking drugs. Yes, it was very dangerous because you had to fend off the government and even more deadly were the rival criminal groups who were willing to kill anyone standing in their way. It was not an easy career choice, but she knew the profits made it worthwhile, especially for people like her who had no other opportunities available to them. And to hell with the gringo pendejos who had nothing better to do than get high. "It was their fucking problem if they died," she whispered to herself. Lisa was already addicted to wealth and power that came with this new life. Her humanity and morality were eroding rapidly. She wanted more power and knew instinctively that in the drug trade a strong foundation of vicious violence and intimidation were needed in order to survive. Lisa, psychologically, was now very committed to doing this and more.

Half an hour later, there was a barely audible knock. Lisa opened the door slightly and saw a short, bald man in a three-piece gray suit with Ralph Lauren designer glasses. In a soft whisper, he said, "I am Arturo. Mucho gusto."

Lisa stepped aside and allowed him to enter the room. Arturo sat on a chair and she on the bed. She told him that the money was in the suitcase and pointed to it with her red nailed, index finger. Lisa was eager to learn every facet of the drug business and asked Arturo, "How will you launder the money?"

Arturo frowned and replied, "I use many ways, for example, I take the money and deposit it into dozens of bank accounts that I have opened using false names. The deposits have to be less than $10,000 otherwise the bank is obligated to report it to the IRS on a Currency Transaction form. I put it into checking accounts and then send the checkbooks to Juancho in Mexico. He can then sell the dollars, at a profit, to local businessmen who need them to buy equipment or materials in the U.S. since the peso is virtually useless. I also buy commodities such as gold and diamonds as a long-term investment. I have also established several front companies and launder the money as legitimate profits made during the year. I will teach you all you need to know about laundering drug money. It is easy to launder it and very difficult for the authorities in the U.S. to unravel it all."

Lisa smiled, "You and I will get along very well, gracias. Take the money and we will be in touch very soon. Hasta la proxima."

Arturo handed her one of his black and white business cards with his telephone number and then grabbed the handle of the suitcase and dragged it out of the room. He said, "See you soon. Fue un placer."

CHAPTER 2

Deadly Opioids

It was a hot day and the smog in Mexico City was as thick as pea soup. Villa was sitting in his office on the fourth floor of the U.S. Embassy preparing a cable to DEA headquarters requesting additional operational funds. Headquarters was always slow to respond to the needs of the field and that pissed off Villa to no end. With the flurry of drug investigations that the DEA was conducting throughout Mexico, the operational money used for travel, lodging, cell phones, and fuel for their cars was running dangerously low. Even worse, funding to pay informants for information was also almost gone. Informants didn't work for free and Villa knew they were mercenaries and would switch to another agency, such as the FBI, that would pick them up in a heartbeat. The information provided by informants was the foundation of most of the investigations initiated by the DEA. It was at times highly invaluable depending on the credibility of the informant.

The abrupt ringing of his telephone broke his concentration. It was the marine guard at post one located at the front entrance of the embassy.

"Sir, I have a gentleman here who wants to talk with someone from the DEA and he says it's urgent. I checked his identification and his name is Salomon Ortiz."

"Ok. I will be right down," Villa responded. With a deep sigh, he knew that he would end up doing the rest of his administrative work at home. It never failed. What the hell, too much free time was boring for him anyway. He slammed his black Mont Blanc pen on the desk and walked down the long, narrow corridor and out to the bank of elevators. He waited for several minutes and heard the loud creak of the elevator cables just before the doors opened. When Villa arrived at post one, the thin blond marine pointed to a short overweight man wearing oversized glasses. Villa pushed open the heavy armored door and shook hands with Ortiz who smiled, revealing several gold-capped teeth. Villa had Ortiz sign the visitor log and obtained a visitor's badge for him. On the way back to Villa's office, Ortiz began to talk about himself. He stated that he had been born in Chilpancingo, Guerrero and proudly boasted that his mother was a schoolteacher. He lamented that his father had been a drunk and womanizer, eventually abandoning the family when he was ten years old.

He worked on a coconut farm, the state's main agricultural crop, for ten years to make ends meet.

By the time they reached the DEA office, Villa knew everything about Ortiz's life and more. Grabbing a legal pad, Villa took him to a small interview room and they both sat at a large, oval wooden table. The walls were adorned with framed black and white photos of Aztec and Mayan pyramids. Ortiz had a perpetual grin that slightly annoyed Villa.

"Bueno! Why did you want to meet with the DEA?", asked Villa.

Ortiz's grin now disappeared from his face as he said, "Esta bien! I have some information that will be very valuable to you. But first, I want to know how much money you will pay me since I will be putting my life on the line."

Villa glared at him, "Amigo, how can I possibly even give you an idea of how much you will be paid when you haven't even told me anything other than your life's story."

Ortiz grinned again, "Muy bien! There is a man by the name of Agapito Candelaria who is involved in the trafficking of drugs, but he is different than the other drug capos. He has made a lot of money, millions of dollars selling a drug called fentanyl. He gets the drug from China for less than $10,000 dollars a kilo. I don't have to tell you, but I understand from reading that this fentanyl is fifty times stronger than heroin. Candelaria imports at least two hundred kilos a month, which is smuggled through the Mexico City International Airport.

He has corrupt officials at the airport who help him bring it into the country.

Ortiz now had Villa's full attention. Villa replied, "I have never heard of Candelaria! What else can you tell me about him?"

Ortiz continued, "He has a small group of traffickers that work for him and he is loosely connected to the Cartel of the North. He gives them a little of his product and they in turn give him protection."

"It is a smart move," said Villa. "As he is building his criminal organization, he needs the protection that only a super-sized cartel can give him. That tells me that he is cunning and not a run of the mill moron. Where did you get this information?"

The grin on the face of Ortiz got even broader. He replied, "One of my cousins grew up with him and they were best friends in school. My primo, Gerardo, is a braggart and he got drunk at my house and started telling me about his amigo. I didn't push him for a lot of details because he would have gotten suspicious. He is not a pendejo."

Villa instructed Ortiz to get more information from his cousin and if alcohol loosened his tongue, he should invite him over to drink as much tequila as would be necessary to do the trick. He then documented Ortiz as an informant. He took his photo, fingerprints, and filled out a personal history report. He also had him provide exemplars of his signature.

The DEA required the signatures for comparison in order to avoid allegations by informants that they didn't receive the money. It was a check and balance mechanism. After processing him, Villa paid Ortiz a couple of hundred dollars, which was all that remained in his budget. He promised him more once he obtained additional information. Before Ortiz left, Villa provided him with his cell number and told him to call him after he made contact with his cousin again.

After Ortiz left, Villa logged on to the DEA's Narcotics and Dangerous Drug Information System (NADDIS) using his personal access code. NADDIS was a data index and collection system, which had millions of DEA reports and records on individuals. It was one of the initial steps taken by intelligence analysts, agents, and others to retrieve reports and valuable data during the beginning of an investigation. Villa found hundreds of listings with the surname of Candelaria, but none with the first name of Agapito, at least not anyone in Mexico. One name did catch his eye. There was a José A. Candelaria with an address in Polanco, one of the most affluent suburbs in Mexico City. The only entry stated that he was believed to have started his criminal career as a sicario and then transitioned into the wholesale trafficking of drugs. Not much to go on.

Villa decided to call his friend, Comandante Ventura, on his cell phone. Ventura answered on the first ring. "Bueno, habla Ventura."

"Mi Amigo! How are you? I am calling to see if you know anything about a trafficker by the name of Agapito Candelaria who, allegedly, is smuggling large quantities of fentanyl from China. Apparently, he is not a member of the Cartel of the North, but provides them with some of his product and they, in turn, give him protection."

Ventura replied, "I can't say that I do. When I get to the office in five minutes, I will check our files to see if he is in there."

Villa stated, "If he does in fact exist, it will be an interesting twist to drug trafficking here in Mexico. Given the fact that fentanyl is fifty times stronger than heroin, one kilo of fentanyl can produce the equivalent of fifty kilos of high-grade heroin. Several millions of dollars can be made from an initial investment of less than ten thousand dollars. Amazing, but true."

Ventura gasped, "Dios mio! That is a lot of money for sure! I can see where that could be the new trend for drug cartels. They would no longer have to take the risk of their opium poppy crops and clandestine conversion labs being destroyed. They won't even have to screw with the smuggling of precursor chemicals needed to manufacture the heroin. This is really disturbing."

"It truly is," said Villa. "We are already having an opioid epidemic in the U.S caused primarily by the greedy pharmaceutical companies that keep pushing opioid drugs in collusion with doctor's and pharmacies. Tens of thousands of Americans are dying each year. We lose more people in one year to overdose deaths than we lost in the entire Viet Nam War! If the cartels here start to push tons of it up north, I hate to even imagine the devastation it will cause. We need to nip it in the bud, for sure."

"A la chingada! You are right!", quipped Ventura. "I will call you if I come up with anything. Let's have lunch soon. We have a lot to catch up on. Cuidate."

Villa reached out to other U.S. intelligence and law enforcement agency representatives in the embassy to see if they had any information on Candelaria. He struck out with all of them. "Fuck.", he thought. He was still committed to pursuing this one.

Villa stayed late at the office and cranked out the Teletype requesting more money and finally forwarded it to headquarters. He followed it up with a barrage of calls the following morning and the next day a large chunk of funding was finally approved. Villa was relived, but fucking pissed off at the same time. He hated the bureaucrats at headquarters that were such impediments to everything. The empty suits, as they were called, had never accomplished anything in their careers, but were delusional and walked around like they knew better than those who risked their lives. A pathetic bunch to be sure!

Three days later, Villa was in bed going through one of

his violent twitching episodes in which his whole body tensed up and then relaxed in quick spasms. He always had restless nights and tonight was no exception. The loud ring of his cell phone was a welcome relief. He pulled back the covers and reached over to the small wooden nightstand and picked up the phone. Lo and behold, it was none other than Ortiz!

"Tengo buenas noticias! I got together with my primo and got him drunk on tequila and scotch. He is a virtual drinking machine, but he eventually started talking and boy did he talk. I finally almost punched him out for talking too much. If you can imagine, he talks more than me! Pinche pendejo!"

Villa finally interrupted, "Okay! Okay! Tell me the good news that you have."

"Well, we met at the El Chingon bar in the Zona Rosa and after a couple of hours my cousin, Gerardo, who is a skinny bastard, staggered to the restroom. He left his cell phone on the table and I was able to look at his contact list. There was only one Candelaria and the first name was José. I wrote the number on a napkin before he came back. The puto had pissed all over his pants. It is 15563454498."

Villa asked, "Did he say anything else about Candelaria?"

"Claro, he said that he lived in a mansion in Polanco and had several expensive cars, to include a bright red Lamborghini. Apparently, Candelaria's source of supply for fentanyl is in Beijing. Is this helpful to you?"

"Of course, it is," answered Villa. "Keep pressing him

for more information. If possible, try to get info on corrupt officials that he is paying; how he launders his money; associates; and smuggling routes into the U.S. Come to the office this afternoon and I will pay you for the information and throw in a little more to pay for your cousin's bar bill."

"Muchas gracias! I will be there for sure."

Villa hung up the phone and a few minutes later called Ventura and asked him to go to the telephone company and try to determine the subscriber to the number provided by Ortiz. Not more than two hours later, Ventura called and said that the phone was listed to a José Agapito Candelaria. He listed his address as Calle Emilio Castelar # 621, Polanco, Mexico City.

Villa was very familiar with the Polanco area, which was the main urban upscale district in Mexico City. It was often referred to as the Beverly Hills of the nation's capital. Many of the ultra-rich, politicians, celebrities, and businessmen called the area home.

Villa asked Ventura, "Can you send some men to check out the address and take some photos? This is beginning to really get interesting. Very interesting."

Ventura chuckled loudly, "Hermano, I am two steps ahead of you. I sent them the minute we got the address. They should already be there. I will keep you posted."

Villa laughed, "Through the process of osmosis, you are

learning from me even though you have a thick skull!" Both howled with laughter at the remark.

An hour later, Villa called Larry, Chief of the National Security Agency (NSA) at the embassy and asked him to come to his office. Ten minutes later, he showed up in casual clothes with a bright blue and white Hawaiian shirt with colorful parrots on it. Larry was a great guy and had a mischievous personality. He was a prankster. He spoke with a Texas twang and had reddish hair parted to the side that was always disheveled.

With a smile from ear to ear he asked, "Good day to you Mr. Villa, how can I be of service to you this fine afternoon? Are you having a bad day and in need of counseling?" Larry laughed as he sat down on the brown, leather sofa, which felt like a concrete bench.

"Larry, good to see you! It's been a few weeks. I haven't even run into you at the embassy cafeteria and I know you are constantly there getting more than your fair share of donuts."

"Miguel, what would life be without its little pleasures?" Larry laughed again and lifted his arms up into the air as though giving thanks to God.

Villa then got down to business, "Larry, we are onto what appears to be a large-scale dealer of opioids, specifically fentanyl that is being imported from China. It is important to note that eighty-five percent of all synthetic opioids are produced in China and the U.S. is currently consuming about eighty percent of all opioids produced in the world," Villa continued, "and when you take into consideration the U.S., Canada, and Western Europe, that consumption total climbs up to ninety-five percent. It is incomprehensible! We have information that a José Agapito Candelaria is moving hundreds of kilos from China into Mexico and then up to the U.S. He is making tens of millions of dollars on a regular basis. Our source also indicates that he is loosely tied to the Cartel of the North. Lisa Rochin, based on our information, is the heir apparent to the throne of Albino Romero. I need you to monitor Candelaria's telephone and keep me posted on any information you develop from his conversations." Villa wrote down the phone number on a legal sized pad of yellow paper and handed it to Larry.

Larry replied, "Wow! I find it amazing, the vast amounts of drugs that Americans snort and inject into their bodies. Our politicians do nothing about it either. The other day, our idiot President paraded a couple of families that had a loved one murdered by a Mexican national. As sad and tragic as it was, he made no mention of the over one hundred thousand murders that have been committed in Mexico as a result of America's insatiable demand for illegal drugs. Never mind the thousands of weapons that are smuggled from our country into Mexico each year."

Villa commented, "Very true. Now he wants to spend between twenty to thirty billion dollars on a border wall that will be as useless as lipstick on a pig. The U.S./Mexico border is riddled with tunnels and drugs can easily be flown over any wall. Within a week human and drug traffickers will punch holes in the wall and install French doors with stained glass and gold doorknobs every half-kilometer. We have lost our logic and common sense! Sadly, insanity rules the day!"

Larry shook his head and his reddish hair fell over his forehead. "Now that I am totally depressed, I will go upstairs and start monitoring this number to wreak havoc on drug traffickers. It will help get rid of some of my frustrations."

"Thanks, Larry. If I had a bottle of tequila, we'd close the door and have a couple of shots. It would help lift the depression for a few hours. Oh well, next time."

A few minutes after Larry left his office, Villa called Ventura. As usual, there was a lot of static, so Villa hung up and redialed.

"Have you been able to get anything on Candelaria?" asked Villa. "I am pursuing some leads on my end and will let you know if they pan out."

Ventura replied, "Miguel, it is funny that you should ask. My men have been conducting surveillance on the address. They described the residence as a two-story colonial mansion. It is easily worth about four million dollars. A check revealed that it is, in fact, listed to a José A. Candelaria. A check of our files proved negative for anyone by that name. There is more. Less than an hour ago, a red Lamborghini left the residence at a high rate of speed and started heading to Acapulco. Wisely, my men had a transit cop stop the vehicle under the pretense of speeding. The cop took a photograph of the occupant's driver's license with his cell phone once in his squad car as he pretended to run the name for any outstanding warrants. We have now fully identified Candelaria. He has a DOB of March 13, 1951, is 5'7" tall, and weighs 180 lbs. He has black hair and brown eyes. The address you provided is definitely his and he has been living there for several years. I will send you a copy of his driver's license for your records."

Villa thanked Ventura, "Great! Let's stay on top of it. We don't have a lot, but now we at least have a foundation from which to launch a full-scale investigation." Let's have lunch soon."

Ventura chuckled, "Perfecto! I believe it is your turn to buy, right? Stay safe,"

Villa was now fully intrigued by Candelaria, who appeared to be operating under everybody's radar screen. It was, indeed, rare that a significant trafficker was able to operate in the shadows for so long. Villa knew that he was cunning and would be a formidable foe.

Three days went by and one morning there was a tap-tap on Villa's office door. Larry stood there with his perpetual smile. He was wearing a wrinkled light gray suit and a wide striped tie that looked more like a bib.

Like a child excited to disclose a secret, Larry rushed over to the sofa and plopped down on it. He continued to smile and rub his hands together like a television show host trying to build drama before making an important announcement.

"Miguel, we have been monitoring the telephone you gave me and we have picked up so many things. I don't know where to start. Your boy Candelaria is a busy man and he talks on the telephone day and night. We have identified his Chinese source of supply, Tong Feng, who owns Beijing Pharmaceuticals. As a matter of fact, Candelaria is expecting half a ton of fentanyl in the next couple of days. It will come through the Mexico City International Airport on a United Airlines flight from Beijing."

Villa smiled, "Wow! That was fast. Candelaria must suffer from diarrhea of the mouth. Sorry for interrupting. What else do you have?"

Larry continued, "Mario Aldana, the man who runs the airport, is being paid big bucks by Candelaria to let the fentanyl pass through with absolutely no scrutiny. He was paid a quarter of a million dollars last month for his services. Candelaria is also paying, Marco Beltran, the governor of Mexico state for protecting his shipment of drugs while they are warehoused in the area. All three have been burning up the lines coordinating the pending shipment."

"Well drug trafficking wouldn't exist if not for corrupt officials who turn a blind eye because of pure greed. Thanks,

Larry! Keep me posted. The next forty-eight hours are really critical."

"Sure thing.", replied Larry. "I will now make this a priority."

An hour later, Villa left his office and went to the DEA parking area behind the embassy. Once in his car he called Ventura and said he was on his way to see him. Villa weaved through the heavy traffic on Avenida Reforma, the principal artery of downtown Mexico City. He glanced at the life size bronze statutes of Mexican heroes that lined both sides of the street. After half an hour, he saw the purple colored high-rise building, which was the headquarters of the Mexican Federal Judicial Police. Parking on a side street, Villa locked the car and looked up and down the street. He was wary since drug traffickers had people watching the building in an effort to identify informants and DEA agents. The building outside and inside was saturated with mean looking machinegun-wielding agents who never smiled. They were dressed in black tactical outfits with gold PJF emblazoned on the back of their shirts. Villa was issued a badge and escorted up to the fourth floor. Ventura was waiting for Villa by the door to his office and gave him an abrazo.

"Good to see you, my friend," said Ventura. "What do you have that is so urgent?"

Villa briefed him on the situation and the fact that it was reaching critical mass. He also asked him to immediately have a team of agents ready to respond at any hour without giving them a lot of details. The fact that the governor and the head of the airport were involved didn't shock Ventura. He was more than well aware of the endemic corruption in his country.

"Muy bien, Miguel," said Ventura. "We will be ready. It will be nice to put all these pieces of shit behind bars. My country and yours are being ravaged by drug dealers that are driven by greed and power, but in the end they all take a fall."

Two days later, on a foggy, rainy day, Villa was in his office feeling miserable from a cold that had hit him like a runaway freight train. Just as he was starting to doze off from the medication he was taking, Larry peeked out from the corner of the door.

"Miguel, you look like shit. Are you sick? Anyway, I have some urgent news. The load of fentanyl is arriving tomorrow morning at 8:45 am. Candelaria has been on the phone with his man at the airport. He told Aldana that he would be sending a different truck than the one used before. He described it as a medium sized cargo truck with the name "Alimentos Maya" on the side panels. Aldana told Candelaria he would tell one of his cohorts working at the south entrance to let it in. The south entrance will also be used to leave the airport unnoticed once the truck is loaded."

Villa coughed and said, "Perfect! It doesn't give me much time to prepare a plan, but I will get it done with the help of Ventura. I have lost count of how many steak dinners I owe you."

Larry laughed, "Believe me, I have a ledger with all the meals you owe me and you don't have the money to cover all of them. Good luck and let me know how it goes."

"Of course! Thanks again, Larry."

Less than an hour later, Villa and Ventura met at Sanborn's restaurant a block from the U.S. Embassy. Jointly, they decided that they would use ground surveillance until the load vehicle left the airport. Surveillance by air near the airport was impossible because of incoming and outgoing flights. Ground units would follow the truck carrying the fentanyl, until it was a suitable distance from the airport and then a single engine Cessna 210 would take over the surveillance. With the congestion and heavy traffic in Mexico City, following a car was damn near impossible. Villa and Ventura would be in a UH-1D Huey with a group of Ventura's men. The Huey would provide manpower and firepower support to the ground units. It had a distance capability of 293 miles and a speed of 127 mph. Two M213 .50 caliber machineguns were mounted on each door. It had devastating firepower. Ventura and Villa would meet with all participants at an isolated parking area about five miles from the airport for a briefing at exactly 4 am. Before leaving the restaurant, Villa asked Ventura to put surveillance on Candelaria's residence, as well as on the governor and the airport manager. Once they heard about the operation they might decide to go on the lam. After meeting with Ventura, Villa called Louie Burgos, the DEA Country Attaché in Beijing, and advised him of the complicity of Tong Feng and his pharmaceutical company and the ongoing investigation.

Louie advised, "We have been looking at him for quite some time, but have been unable to get anything substantive to give to the Chinese government. Please let me know if you come up with something that I can use on my end."

Villa slept an hour and got up in the wee hours of the morning. He took a long hot shower and dressed. He got two extra magazines filled with hollow point .9 mm bullets. You never knew how things would go during an operation and he wanted to have enough ammo for his Beretta. He also retrieved his AR-15 that was in a carrying case with additional boxes of bullets, enough to start a small war. On his way to the meeting site, he called United Airlines and checked on the flight from Beijing. He was told it was scheduled to arrive on time. Traffic was light on the road and Villa ate a couple of dry Mexican cookies and choked them down with a cold diet Coke. He would have given anything for a few biscochitos that his mother, Alice, made when he was a child. They were soft, cinnamon covered cookies that were nothing short of amazing.

Half an hour later, Villa pulled into the designated meeting area and through the darkness, he could see the shadows of several cars and men milling around. His headlights illuminated them and he saw the men all carrying AK-47's. When he got out of his car, the silence was eerie. He knew what the men were thinking. They were all wondering if they would be lucky enough to return home after the operation was done. The uncertainty and the volatility of actions against violent men could lead to wholesale carnage in the blink of an eye.

Ventura huddled the men together and he and Villa briefed them on the operation; their responsibilities; and the radio frequencies that would be used so that ground and air units would know what each one was doing. An hour later they dispersed and Villa rode with Ventura and some of his men to Toluca where the Huey and the Cessna 210 had been prepositioned. It was too risky to launch out of the Mexico City airport based on the involvement of Aldana. Toluca was about an hour's drive, but it seemed longer as little was said during the trip. Upon arrival, they parked their cars in a government hanger on the north end of the airport. Everyone started pulling weapons and gear out of the trunk of the car and loading them into the aircraft. It was still early, but everyone boarded the fixed and rotary aircrafts and sat there checking their weapons and doing radio checks.

At 7:20 am, Ventura got a call from one of his men at the airport in Mexico City. He reported that the truck bearing the name Alimentos Maya had just driven into the airport with what appeared to be the driver and one passenger. Another check with United revealed that the aircraft was in the process of making its descent and would be landing in ten minutes. The helicopter pilot pushed the ignition switch and the loud pitched whine of the turbo engines filled the morning air. Villa looked to his right and saw the Cessna 210 propeller whipping through the air. Soon both aircrafts were airborne and moving rapidly towards Mexico City.

As they arrived on the outer perimeter of the airports controlled airspace, the surveillance team at the airport reported that the truck had just come through the gate. The team reported that they were getting ready to follow it. It was moving slowly, which made it easy to follow. The truck was ten miles from the airport when the pilot and the observer in the Cessna picked it up. The Huey followed from a distance. Eventually, the cargo truck got onto Mexican Highway 95 that went to Cuernavaca, Morelos. Now it picked up speed, but it was easier to follow since traffic was much lighter. About twenty minutes later, the cars driven by Ventura's men were intercepted by ten black Chevrolet Suburban's, which blocked the road. Over a dozen men dressed in cowboy hats and blue jeans leaped out of their vehicles and started to fire automatic bursts of gunfire. The loud blasts were deafening. The hot, lead projectiles raked the cars as the feds backed away at a high rate of speed. They were outnumbered and outgunned. Three feds were immediately slaughtered and several more wounded. One of the men sent a radio transmission that they were under fire.

The Huey swerved sharply to the right and dropped its altitude. In what appeared to be only seconds it came over the stretch of road where the intense shooting was taking place. On the first pass, the .50 caliber opened up and the tracers looked like a torrential downpour of fluorescent rain. On the second pass, the hot lead hit one of the Suburban's gas tanks and it exploded sending a large ball of flame and smoke high into the air. Pieces of human flesh littered the road. It was obvious to Villa that the traffickers had established counter surveillance on the road looking for a tail. He knew that the occupants of the truck were now aware they were being followed. Villa quickly instructed the helicopter pilots to land a couple of miles up the road in front of the truck's path. Once they landed, Villa and the entire assault team jumped out onto the road. Villa pulled the slide on his AR-15 and chambered a bullet. He wanted to take at least one prisoner so he could interrogate him. Minutes later, the truck came into view and it was traveling over ninety miles an hour. Villa stood in the middle of the road waving for the driver to bring it to a stop. Villa jumped to the side of the road when it became apparent that it was not going to stop. He fired several rounds that pierced the tires causing the truck to career off the road on to its side. A brown cloud of dust and dry weeds lifted into the air as it hit a tree and came to an abrupt halt, causing the truck to lay there, mangled almost beyond recognition. Seconds later, a man in his thirties, with tattoos on his face leaped out and began blasting away. In a split second, his body was torn apart from head to toe as bullets, fired by the feds, ripped through his body. In a gruesome dance with death, the man twitched and shuddered as he fell backward. He was dead before he hit the dusty earth.

Someone yelled from inside the wrecked truck, "No me maten! Don't shoot, I give-up." A pair of hands then lifted slowly from the disfigured cab of the truck.

Ventura yelled, "Pinche hijo de puta! Come out before we decide not to take any prisoners!"

The bald, stocky man with long stringy hair had to be pulled out of the truck. His right leg was broken and was twisted in a grotesque angle. He screamed and wanted to be taken to the hospital. The pain had set in and his face was that of a tortured soul who had just been cast from heaven.

Ventura yelled, "Puto! First, what do you have in the back of the truck? Then you will show us the location where you were taking the load."

Crying in pain, he answered, "There is half a ton of fentanyl in the barrels. I will take you to the warehouse, but then you have to take me to the hospital."

Ventura and Villa looked in the cargo area of the overturned truck and saw several 55-gallon barrels. Ventura left five of his men guarding the load and called his office to send reinforcements. The helicopter pilots had already called the Red Cross to send ambulances and medical assistance to help the agents who had been wounded. Villa and Ventura knew that three of their men had been killed instantly and they felt great sadness. The bald injured man was helped on to the helicopter and his loud screams drowned out the large rotors spinning violently above their heads.

In no time, the helicopter landed on a small army base in Cuernavaca. The base commander was waiting. Ventura had radioed ahead and requested support. The colonel, a tall, broad-shouldered man, smiled when he saw Ventura and gave him an abrazo. Ventura had worked with him before on several other operations. They liked and trusted each other. Ventura quickly briefed the colonel on the events of the day and the need to quickly raid the warehouse where the fentanyl was being transported. Within minutes, the colonel had mobilized two trucks filled with green uniformed men wearing helmets with camouflage webbing. The bald man was again dragged from the helicopter yelling obscenities at everyone. He provided directions and the two trucks weaved their way through a number of streets and finally came to the western edge of the city. He pointed out a small, isolated house that was surrounded by mango trees. The trucks increased speed and the ride up the dirt road was bumpy. As they were several yards away, the loud blasts of gunfire erupted from the house. It was utter chaos as everyone jumped from the trucks and took cover. Bullets kicked up clouds of dust and it sounded like a hailstorm as the bullets slammed into the trucks. Villa, in a crouch, ran behind the house with his Beretta .9mm in his right hand. Amazingly, the backdoor was unlocked. He entered cautiously and moved slowly until he reached the front. Peering from the corner of the door, he saw three men firing AK-47's. He moved rapidly through the door firing methodically. His first shot hit one of the men in the head splattering blood and brain matter against the wall. Villa fired a total of eight rounds and all three men lay dead in pools of blood in a matter of seconds. A search of the house revealed another ton of fentanyl located in one of the bedrooms. As with the load in the truck, the drug was in metal barrels.

The ton of fentanyl was left temporarily in the custody of the army. Ventura and Villa had other matters to deal with. Upon arriving at the army base once again, they boarded the helicopter and flew straight to the Mexico City airport. Again, Ventura called ahead and had some of his men waiting at the tarmac. The helicopter barely touched down when Villa and the others jumped out and entered the three dark sedans with several agents armed to the teeth. They drove around the perimeter of the airport to the administrative offices. They noisily entered Aldana's office and found him with a stunning looking girl on his lap, who was about sixteen years of age.

Aldana yelled, "Que chingados! Who are you and what the fuck do you want? Do you know who I am?"

Ventura grabbed the girl's arm and gently pulled her away from Aldana. He then punched Aldana in the face knocking him from the chair. Blood immediately spurted from his broken nose.

"Of course, I know who you are. Eres un cerdo! Get up."

Aldana broke down into tears once the handcuffs were placed on him. He knew that it was over. Villa and Ventura looked at each other and both were thinking the same thing. It was time to get the main target, Candelaria. Ventura selected six of the men with him and they headed to Polanco, which was about 30 minutes away. Once they arrived, they parked in front of Candelaria's mansion. The agents jumped out of their cars quickly and charged towards the house with weapons drawn. Ventura went to the front door and directed others to cover the back of the house. Villa covered the side of the house with the most windows. As agents were trying to open the reinforced front door, Villa heard the crashing of glass. In seconds, someone leaped out of a large window. Villa was now face to face with the notorious and shadowy Candelaria. Like western gunslingers, they smiled for a second and then fired their weapons. Villa hit Candelaria in the chest and the force of the bullet twisted him around violently. Candelaria's bullet hit Villa in the shoulder, but it was only a flesh wound. Villa fired twice more hitting Candelaria in the back of the head. The bullets erased his face as the projectiles tumbled violently tearing muscle and splintering bone. Upon entering the house, Villa and Ventura were shocked that Governor Beltran was in the house sitting calmly on the living room leather sofa.

He smirked, "What business do you have here? I am the governor and command you to leave immediately."

Ventura frowned, "I know who you are going to be, nothing more than a common criminal in prison. You are a corrupt pendejo who has sold his soul to the devil."

Ventura had his men take the governor into custody and they escorted him to one of their cars. Villa went into a large room in the back of the house and gasped at what he saw. He yelled for Ventura to come quickly. They both stood there speechless. The entire room was filled four feet high with U.S. dollar bills. It was a virtual mountain of money. No attempt had been made to conceal it. Later, it was determined that it was slightly more than 700 million dollars. It was the largest money seizure in the history of Mexico, if not the entire world. Several invoices were also found at Candelaria's house identifying Feng Pharmaceuticals as the supplier of the fentanyl. Early the next morning, Villa called Country Attaché to China, Lou Burgos, in Beijing and informed him of the operation and the evidence seized. He faxed him photographs of the barrels containing the fentanyl as well as the documents bearing the Feng Pharmaceuticals name. Louie, as Villa called him, said he would coordinate immediately with the Chinese Ministry of State Security.

Over a week later, Villa was having dinner with Ventura at the Villa Linda restaurant when he received a call from Louie.

After a quick exchange of pleasantries, Louie reported, "Miguel, the Chinese arrested Feng and shut down his operation. He had been sending tons of fentanyl all over the world and was making billions from it. The Chinese put him up before a firing squad yesterday. As you know drug trafficking here is an automatic death sentence."

Villa was most appreciative of Louie and the excellent news he shared with him. He told Louie, "Thanks for letting me know. I appreciate all your efforts and if you ever come to Mexico we will buy you all the tacos you want. Best to your family."

During dinner that consisted of excellent grilled chicken and warm corn tortillas, Ventura asked Villa about his wound.

"It still hurts a little, but what pisses me off is that it ruined my brand-new shirt."

They both laughed until they were in tears, then they raised their shot glasses of tequila and toasted to life and its twists and turns.

CHAPTER 3

Violence and Treachery

Lisa began to learn more and more of the nuances of the drug trade. She was not interested in just being a wealthy drug trafficker. She wanted to be the best and was not satisfied with status quo. More interested in innovative methods to smuggle and distribute drugs, she studied every facet of drug production, distribution, and transportation. A natural leader, she believed in strategic planning. Juancho's operation was good and they were making a lot of money, but Lisa knew they could be making a hundred times more with a little ingenuity. Juancho smuggled large quantities of cocaine from Colombia through the use of twin-engine aircraft, but based on Mexico's recent national plan to conduct surveillance on all clandestine airstrips throughout the country, it was becoming more difficult to continue with this smuggling method. Lisa learned that Juancho used the southern Mexican state of Oaxaca as a staging area to transport five hundred kilograms of cocaine every month from Colombia. He owned cattle ranches in Lopez Matias and Villa Zaachila that facilitated the smuggling activities. The Lopez Matias ranch was most often used, but he made sure to have an alternate landing area, which was the ranch in Villa Zaachila. It was important to have a secondary site in the event that Mexico's security forces were near the principal landing area. The ranches were isolated and flat pastures were used as makeshift landing strips. Lisa approached Juancho with a plan.

"Listen," she says, "although we have the municipal and state police in Oaxaca on our payroll, it is impossible to bribe all the federal police and military units in the area. As you know, they rotate them quickly to prevent corruption and it is too time consuming to get to the new personnel. Therefore, we need to create diversionary tactics when we are bringing in a load. We will use a small group of double agents who will pretend to work for them as informants, but they will actually belong to us and follow our orders. In other words, they will give the authorities false information about a drug operation taking place elsewhere. This will increase our success rate and maximize our profits. Every once in a while, we can let them seize a small quantity of drugs. It will not be much, but it will lend credibility to our people acting as informants."

Looking pensive, Juancho, replied, "That is really a great

idea, de verdad! I had not thought of diverting the police or the military away from us during an operation. La felicito, we will do that in the future. I am very impressed. Gracias, mi amor."

On a dark, rainy night, as a full moon tried to peek through the storm clouds, a short, stocky, man with heavy Zapotec Indian features approached a group of soldiers in front of the 28A Army Zone Headquarters in Ixcotel, Oaxaca. One of the soldiers wearing a green camouflage uniform with a brown waterproof poncho and a webbed steel helmet challenged him.

"Alto! What business do you have here? What are you doing out on such a miserable night? You must be fucking crazy!"

"Perdon, my name is Mariano and I have some important information for your commander on a load of cocaine that will be coming soon from Colombia. It is urgent since it will happen tomorrow."

Irritated, the soldier menacingly pointed his FX-05 Hiuhcoatl, Fire Serpent, assault rifle at his chest and yelled, "You better not be wasting our fucking time, otherwise I will kill you and feed you to our dogs. They are rather hungry tonight and will devour you like a piece of steak. Pinche Indio! Wait here!"

The soldier turned and briskly walked towards a nearby wooden guard shack, splashing loudly through large puddles with his heavy brown military boots. A minute later, he returned and ordered another soldier to take Mariano to see the commander. But, before letting him go, he quickly searched him for weapons and then shoved him violently towards the other soldier who hit him with the butt of his rifle in the stomach. Mariano moaned loudly and stumbled, but quickly regained his balance. He was marched to a large office where the commanding General sat behind a large hand carved mahogany desk filled with military memorabilia to include several gold-plated medals. The General, a large man with bushy eyebrows and odd reptilian green eyes, sat smoking a cigar. He stared at Mariano and said, "What is so critical that you have to bother me at this time of night?"

"General, I have information about half a ton of cocaine that is coming from Colombia tomorrow night and thought you should know," Mariano said nervously.

The General stared at him for a minute, making him even more concerned. Like most people, Mariano didn't trust the military or the federal police for that matter. Mariano's father, Serafin, was killed when he was five years old. An educator by trade, Serafin, was the head of a local teacher's union. He was a proud man who worked hard for his community and the children who were extremely poor. Oaxaca was the third most disenfranchised state in Mexico. The government did nothing to help the indigenous natives who lived in this southwestern state.

One hot summer in July, Serafin led a peaceful protest march down Main Street of the small, isolated town where he lived with his family. Tired of being paid slave wages, the teachers carried signs and banners demanding better salaries and benefits. As they crossed the railroad tracks, one of them yelled, "El ejercito!" A hundred meters ahead they saw at least a dozen soldiers jumping from a large camouflaged truck with assault rifles. An officer yelled orders and the soldiers immediately lined up across the narrow dirt road. Seconds passed and the officer barked another order and the soldiers quickly lifted their weapons and pointed them at the oncoming protesters. Serafin and his followers did not flinch and kept moving forward, kicking dust into the air and chanting in unison, "Mejores salarios y beneficios, merecemos mejor!" When they were about twenty yards away from the menacing soldiers, the officer lifted his shiny, steel sword high into the air and screeched, "Fuego!" Simultaneously, the rifles spit fire and lead with a heart-stopping, thunderous roar. A piece of hot metal tore through Serafin's chest completely shredding his heart and shattering his spine. For a brief second, he felt the smell of blood in his nostrils. He was already dead as he plunged to the ground with several others. The outrageous massacre left twenty teachers dead. Their spilled bright-red blood was quickly swallowed by the dry, thirsty, scorched earth.

From that day forward, Mariano grew up with an intense

hatred of Mexican politicians and their corrupt and ruthless military forces. "They are nothing more than murderers for the government," he often told his friends.

The unfriendly heavy-browed General blew a huge cloud of smoke in Mariano's direction and asked, "I assume this cocaine is coming by air? How did you come across this information?"

Mariano looked squarely into his eyes and replied, "I happened to be drinking with an old friend that I grew up with and he is the one who told me. Sadly, he is part of a gang of drug traffickers and he offered me a job, but I value my freedom and life more than money. He told me that an airplane is delivering 500 kilograms of pure cocaine from Colombia tomorrow night. As a proud citizen, I am tired of the violence and problems being caused to our villages by illegal drugs. That is why I am here. Que mueran todos los chingados narcos!"

A slight smile crossed the General's lips and he asked, "Que es el nombre de su amigo? And what is the name of the organization?"

Mariano replied, "His name is Pablo Roybal and he belongs to a gang called "Los Rojos."

The General squeezing for every morsel of information began to focus the interview on more specifics. He asked, "Where will the plane land with the cocaine? How many people will Los Rojos have providing security?"

Mariano began rattling off more details. He said, "The plane will not land, it will do an airdrop into Lake Pastoría on the Pacific side near the small village of El Corral, Oaxaca. The bales of cocaine will be picked up in wooden canoes that will be used to transport it to the shore and from El Corral will then be taken north to the U.S. border in a large commercial truck."

The General arrogantly asked, "If the airdrop is to occur at night, how will the boat crews be able to see the bales in the water? I have been to that area and it is very dark at night, even with a full moon."

Mariano looked up and said, "I asked the same question and Pablo told me that just before the bales are dropped from the plane, they will attach several glow sticks to each one. Apparently, they give a strong light when two chemicals are mixed in the plastic sticks."

"You should also be aware that Los Rojos will have a lot of security near the shore and they will be well armed. The have grenades and will not hesitate to use them," added Mariano.

"Maldito idiota! Do you think we are brand new to this business? We are the army and we have been doing this forever. No one is better at these kinds of operations than us," growled the General.

"Si, mi General! I understand, but I want you to have all of the information that was given to me," replied Mariano.

"Ok, we will take it from here. You are free to leave now

and leave a telephone number or address where we can reach you in the event we have further use of you," commented the General in a rather loud voice.

Mariano in an equally loud voice responded, "Si, con mucho gusto."

A few minutes later Mariano left the building, looked back and smiled. He then disappeared into the dark night like an eerie shadow.

At the same time that Mariano was meeting with the General another man showed up at the Federal Judicial Police Headquarters in Oaxaca, the capital city with the same name as the state. He was poorly dressed in dirty Levi's and a tattered white cotton shirt. He had penetrating black eyes and matted dark hair. He was extremely thin and very short. Everyone called him "Chapo." It was a name he hated. He preferred to be called by his real name, Antonio. He was from one of the largest indigenous groups of Oaxaca. Chapo was a member of the Mixtec tribe, one of sixteen such tribes in the state.

The young, heavyset receptionist looked up and smiled cordially. "May I help you?", she asked.

Almost tripping over the thick carpet as he approached her desk, Antonio regained his balance and his face turned beet red. He meekly stated, "I need to talk to the Comandante right away. I have some information that he will be interested in."

She grabbed a pen and inquired, "What is your name

and what is the nature of the business you want to discuss with him?"

"My name is Antonio and I have an important matter regarding drugs that are coming into Oaxaca," he responded.

The receptionist told Antonio to take a chair and she quickly walked into the room behind her. A minute later she returned and told him, "Pase por favor."

"Gracias," he said and nervously entered the large spacious room filled with oversized, expensive mahogany furniture. Antonio observed a large man with an Emiliano Zapata style mustache playing with a large gold-plated handgun. His feet were on the desk, displaying beautiful, well-kept black rattlesnake skin boots.

The Comandante reached out to shake his hand and squeezed hard. Antonio grimaced in pain and began to sweat slightly. Introducing himself as Roberto Castillo, he wasted no time in questioning Antonio.

"My secretary mentioned that you have some information to give me. What is it that you have?", he asked. He looked pensively at Antonio, which made Antonio even more nervous. Antonio swallowed hard and regained his composure.

"Si, mi Comandante! I have a cousin, Alberto Cantu, who was contracted to help with a load of cocaine being smuggled to the state of Oaxaca. It will be dropped from an airplane coming from Colombia into Lake Pastoría near El Corral. Alberto told me that he is being paid forty thousand pesos to help retrieve the packages from the water. He said that canoes would be used to fetch the packages and take them to land very close to the village of El Corral. He also said that they have a lot of armed security protecting the drugs."

The Comandante inquired, "Why would you turn in your own primo? I find it hard to believe you would betray flesh and blood?"

"Comandante, you have to understand that our family is very poor, but we are honest, hard-working people. Alberto has always been a criminal who has shamed us all and I want to put a stop to his insanity. That is why I have come to you," responded Antonio.

The Comandante replied, "Bueno! What time is this drug operation supposed to take place?"

"It will happen tomorrow night under the cover of darkness," replied Antonio.

"Perfecto! I will take all of my men and we will be ready when they bring the cocaine to the shore of the lake. We will catch them by surprise. Hijos de puta," proclaimed the Comandante.

Antonio wished the Comandante well and shook his hand once more. He pulled it back quickly to avoid having it crushed. He walked out the door and said goodbye to the receptionist who winked at him.

The following evening two uncoordinated and volatile forces gathered to form the perfect storm, which would have horrific consequences for the Mexican government and its prestigious security services. The army General deployed forty soldiers armed to the teeth near the poor, isolated village of El Corral. It was completely dark and storm clouds were forming in the skies. Not even the moon was out to provide some illumination to the area. The soldiers left their two military transport trucks several miles from the village and slowly marched through the dense vegetation. The jagged tree branches, weeds, and large shrubs caused painful scratches on their faces, arms, and legs. One of the soldiers nearly lost an eye as he ran into the end of a protruding branch. He let out a piercing howl that startled the rest of the soldiers and they all instinctively dropped to the ground. Once they realized what had happened they stood up somewhat embarrassed that they were overly jittery. They brushed themselves off and continued their trek towards the quiet village. It took three hours to finally arrive at El Corral and the soldiers were fortunate to find a cluster of mesquite trees where they could hide. They heard dogs barking nearby and the village looked eerie as a fog began to roll in from the large lake. They would now have to rely on sound and their instincts since they couldn't see three feet in front of them.

The young Captain in charge of the soldiers, Wilfredo Sánchez, told his men to keep a watchful eye. He is a tall, lanky man in his early thirties with a cocky demeanor and brimming with confidence. Tonight, both of those attributes are absent and he is unsure of the actions he must take as he is now operating in the blind. He graduated at the top of his class at the prestigious Heroico Colegio Militar en Tlalpan, in Mexico City. He has high aspirations of becoming a General and has meticulously planned his career to reach this objective. He married his childhood sweetheart and has twin infant daughters that he adores.

"Fuck," he thought, "Why did I have to get this shit duty just when my career is beginning to go places?" He mumbles, "God must be trying to fuck me." Ordering his men to check their FX-05 assault rifles, he also ensured that he had a bullet chambered in the event he had to use it. Captain Sánchez knew the weapon well and liked the three fire selections that it had, single shot, a three-shot burst, and fully automatic. It had a tremendous capability as it could fire 750 rounds per minute. Each soldier carried six 30-round detachable box magazines. They were more than ready for a large-scale military battle. The Captain ordered his men to have their weapons on full automatic. He was not taking any chances and did not intend to take any prisoners tonight.

Comandante Castillo, of the Mexican Federal Judicial Police, arrived in the area three hours before the soldiers with thirty of his men who were armed with AK-47 assault rifles and each man also carried either a .38 or .45 semi-automatic handgun. They, too, were wandering around in the dark trying to find the specific area where the traffickers would be operating. Comandante Castillo, with his men, had been involved in these types of operations before. He was a survivor, as were many of his men, of numerous confrontations with drug traffickers in the past. He was calm and relaxed as he moved his men down the shoreline of Lake Pastoría. In Mexico, the federal police don't use uniforms and most of the men dress in jeans and casual shirts, so it is difficult to distinguish them from an ordinary citizen. Some of the federal police wear Stetson cowboy hats. Their long weapons were at the ready as they slowly walked down the wet, rocky shore of the large lake. Suddenly, one of them accidently squeezed the trigger and fired off a round, which hit the man in front of him in the leg.

The wounded man screamed, "Pinche Puto," and fell on the ground in agony. He was bleeding profusely from a major artery and screeched in pain. He quickly went into shock and was dead in less than a minute.

The soldiers, who were within thirty meters of the federal judicial police, heard the discharge from the federal police AK-47 and assumed they were under attack from the traffickers and begin to fire simultaneously in the direction of the gunshot. It was total bedlam, as the federal police, in response to the barrage of bullets, also began blasting away. The repetitive explosions, from opposing sides, filled the night with a deluge of indiscriminate lead projectiles. They ripped through the soft tissue, muscles and shattered the bones of their victims sending them to an early grave. Some were wounded and their screams could be heard above the thunderous gunfire. After several minutes, the shooting stopped and a soldier yelled, "Ejercito Nacional." One of three surviving federal police officers shouted, "Policia Federal." It was too late; the air was filled with the rancid smell of gunpowder and pools of glistening blood were splattered throughout the area of the horrific firefight. Captain Sánchez lay on his stomach, dead of multiple gunshot wounds to the head and torso. Comandante Castillo would never see another sunrise again. He caught a bullet that caused his head to explode like a ripe watermelon. It was a massacre of monstrous consequences. A total of twenty-seven federal police and twenty soldiers were brutally killed.

Less than twenty-four hours later, the Mexican government issued a press release to all the national media outlets reporting that members of the valiant federal police and national army lost their lives in the service of their country fighting the powerful drug cartels. They reported that a large confrontation with a large force of traffickers resulted in the killing of the Federales and soldiers. The last thing they wanted was for the general public to know they accidently slaughtered each other. The government was fully aware that the federal police and the military didn't trust one another. Tragically, they seldom ever coordinated or de-conflicted operations that would have prevented the two security forces from engaging in a shootout with one another during tactical operations in the field. Even continuous mandates from the Mexican President couldn't get them to work with one another. Now, with this disaster, the possibility of collaborative efforts was even further down the toilet.

Both Mariano and Antonio disappeared into the rugged mountainous terrain of Oaxaca with more money than they ever dreamed of having in their lifetime. They would never be found or heard of again. Lisa was elated that Mariano and Antonio followed her plan flawlessly. When she heard the news of the violent massacre, a smile appeared on her face because she knew the truth of what actually happened. She planned the whole thing. At a young age, Lisa had been given a book called "The Art of War", which was an ancient Chinese treatise dating from the fifth century written by Sun Tzu, the famous military strategist. Lisa had applied some of his military tactics to facilitate the movement of cocaine through Oaxaca. Adroitly, she used Tzu's principle that "all warfare is based on deception; when we are near, we must make the enemy believe we are far away; when far away, we must make him believe we are near." Lisa also used another of his strategies, "If you know the enemy and know yourself, you need not fear the result of a hundred battles." Her voracious reading and capacity for planning and strategy made her a formidable adversary to her enemies and government security forces.

At the same time that the army and federal police were killing each other hundreds of miles away, a twin-engine Beechcraft 350 was landing at Juancho's ranch in Lopez Matias. It was loaded with five hundred kilos of pure cocaine. As the plane approached the ranch, the pilots communicated with one of Juancho's men via HF radio. Lights, along a stretch of pasture, were turned on illuminating the strip. The plane made one pass and then began to reduce airspeed and descended rapidly. As it touched down, a large cattle truck made its way onto the makeshift strip. Reaching the plane, several thuggish looking men jumped from the truck and began to offload the large bales of cocaine from the fuselage of the plane. Others started refueling the plane from several fifty-five-gallon barrels filled with aviation fuel. The aircraft had a fictitious tail number painted on it in the event it was seized. The fictitious tail number would make tracing its ownership and origin very difficult. Within eight minutes after landing, the plane accelerated its engines and ascended back into the dark, ominous sky like a giant bird of prey. By the time the shooting between the army and federal police ended, the half-ton of cocaine was already headed north to the U.S. border in a large truck covered by several tons of melons and chili peppers.

CHAPTER 4

The Killing

Through Lisa's leadership, she and Juancho made tens of millions of dollars from the cocaine trade. But even so, they remained mid-level traffickers and somewhat independent operators. They had not yet become a full-fledged cartel making them a force to be reckoned with by the government and other traffickers. With money came enormous power and they soon became more powerful than the governor of Sinaloa. Actually, they were paying him several millions of dollars every year for protection. Roberto Duarte was a conservative politician who belonged to the Partido Revolucionario Institucional (PRI), the dominant and most corrupt political party in Mexico. He had an oversized head with thinning black hair, small shoulders and was about forty pounds overweight. Duarte had little education, but he had been a loyal political hack for many years and was literally given the governorship of Sinaloa because he could be trusted to funnel bribe money up the PRI chain of command. He had several bagmen who acted as couriers that took millions of dollars in cash to Mexico City every month. They used Duarte's personal Lear Jet to transport the dirty money.

Lisa built schools, churches, and gave money to the people in need. Her pet project, however, was establishing libraries in the isolated villages of Sinaloa that were quickly stocked with hundreds of thousands of books. She also hired the best teachers to educate the children and paid them well for their efforts.

As soon as he was eligible, she sent her brother, Armando, to Georgetown University law school in Washington, D.C. Armando was an excellent student, but Lisa made sure he was accepted through a generous, million-dollar contribution to the university. She was fully aware that it was the tenth most selective law school in the U.S. and a little insurance never hurt anyone. He wanted to be an attorney, but was only interested in attending one of the most prestigious universities in the United States. Lisa paid slightly less than eighty thousand dollars for each academic year, which covered tuition, fees, and living expenses. To her it was chump change.

Anita was not interested in going to college. In her early twenties, she decided to live in Miami for a few years to study Santeria. Lisa purchased a beautiful condo for her in the Latin

Quarter and a bright red Mercedes Benz convertible so she could move around the city. Shortly after she arrived, Anita began an intensive weeklong initiation process to become a high priestess of Santeria that involved four phases. Before undergoing the four phases, however, her designated Padrino performed a cleansing ritual with special herbs and water. He rubbed them into her scalp in a specific pattern of movements. It was known as the "blessing of the head." Now she was ready for the first ritual known as the "acquisition of the beaded necklaces" called elekes. The *elekes* necklace was bathed in a mixture of herbs, sacrificial animal blood, and other potent oils. When the red and white necklace was given to Anita, she bent over a bathtub to have her head washed. She was told that the elekes would serve as her sacred banner and protect her as well. She was cautioned never to wear the necklace during her menstruation period, nor during sex, or when bathing. In the second ritual known as the "medio asiento," Anita went through a consultation with an established Santero, where her entire past, present, and future were carefully reviewed. The Santero then decided, which path of Elegua, she would take. *Elequa*, being the deity representing the beginning and end of life, and the opening and closing of paths in life, was considered a very powerful Orisha (spirit). Based on his findings, the Santero selected materials in order to construct the image of Elegua, a sculpture to keep evil spirits away from Anita's home. Anita was told that only a man could perform this phase of the ritual since the Orishas took some of the Santero's masculine spirit during the process. She was now ready for the third phase known as "receiving the warriors." During the ritual, she was given objects representing the warriors, an iron bow and arrow, a silver chalice with the base in the shape of a rooster. This symbolized a formal relationship with warrior spirits who would protect Anita on her journey. Anita's last step was called" "asiento" meaning ascending to the throne. It was the most important and secretive ritual where she was born again in a spiritual way. It was a long process of purification and divination. She was told that it was now a new life for her of deeper growth within the faith. Anita was now a full-fledged Santera Priestess.

Lisa was pleased that she could help her siblings. She was on top of the world and now a very wealthy woman, who could buy anything and anyone she wanted. One day, she told Juancho that she was going to Culiacan for a few days of shopping. He didn't object and told her to take her time. Lisa kissed him and said, "Te amo, mi amor!" She grabbed a large stack of one hundred dollar bills from a large steel safe located underneath a marble tile in the bedroom. After thinking twice, she grabbed another one, each consisting of ten thousand dollars. She wanted more clothes and jewelry. Buying things made her feel good, even if she never used them. It was therapeutic and it was better than paying a psychiatrist. She decided to take her driver and two bodyguards. They all piled into a black Toyota Land Cruiser with oversized tires and gold-plated rims. The windows were overly tinted so the passengers couldn't be seen from the outside. The grey leather seats were extra comfortable and spacious. Lisa sat on the front passenger seat and immediately turned on the stereo to the pulsating beat of Los Tiburones del Norte, a Norteño band. She swayed gently back and forth as though she was dancing. She loved corridos, which were about oppression, history, daily life for peasants, and other socially relevant topics. She turned the volume up and the men with her felt like their eardrums were going to explode, but they dared not complain.

They drove through the plush, rolling green valleys with gentle flowing streams and stopped frequently for campesinos who were slowly crossing the road with crops from the field or small herds of cows and goats. After three and a half hours, they reached the outskirts of Culiacan, the state capital of Sinaloa. They drove by the beautiful Culiacan River formed by the confluence of the Tamazula and Humaya Rivers. Passing by the botanical garden, Lisa admired the brightly colored flowers and large palm trees. As a child, she loved the smell of the rainbow-colored flowers that grew in abundance in her home state.

Traffic was thick as they entered the center of Culiacan. No one respected the traffic lights or stop signs and it all boiled down to who had the most "cojones" going through intersections. Lisa's driver made a sharp right turn onto Calle Obregon and a short time later pulled into the five-star Hotel San Marcos. The white building, with palm trees in front, had five horizontal rows of tinted windows on the top floors. Lisa jumped out of the Land Cruiser and stretched her legs as a bellboy quickly approached with a gold colored cart.

He smiled, "Bienvenidos al Hotel San Marcos!"

He handled the suitcases carefully in case they contained anything fragile. Besides, he wanted a good tip and from the way Lisa was dressed, she exuded enormous wealth. He followed Lisa and her bodyguards through the lobby, which had beautiful white marble floors and gray and red sofas. Lisa loved the huge oil painting of a nude couple hanging on the wall, but more so the eight-foot bronze sculpture of a naked, voluptuous woman seductively holding her hand behind her head. She made a mental note to have one made for her house. Lisa checked in her small entourage using her credit card and handed out a thousand dollars to each of her bodyguards so they could have spending money. She cautioned them not to drink since she wanted them to be alert at all times.

"I do not need drunks to protect me. You need to be in full control of your senses at all times, understand?"

In unison, they responded, "Sí, señora! Entendemos."

The bellboy followed Lisa to her room and placed her suitcase on a wooden luggage rack close to the spacious closet. Reaching into her brown Louis Vuitton purse, Lisa pulled out a one hundred-dollar bill and handed it to him. The bellboy almost had an orgasm.

"Gracias señora!" You are very generous. If you need anything at all, please let me know. My name is Fernando."

As he walked out of the room, he leaped with joy as he entered the elevator.

After unpacking and placing all her super expensive cosmetics and perfumes in the restroom, Lisa decided to call Governor Duarte. She used her personal phone to call him on a dedicated cell phone that he used only for her calls. No one else had the number! He was very cautious and knew that he could very well be under surveillance by the federal police or Mexico's intelligence service, known as the Center for National Security Investigations (CISEN). Duarte, through time, had become more and more paranoid and thought his phones were being tapped. His wife, Maria, was fed up with his late-night scurrying around the house checking for monitoring devices and peeking out the windows until the early morning hours. Maria was an attractive, tall blond, born in Mexico City who married the governor strictly because of his political position. She thought he was a pig and she was happiest when he was away from home on business. Many times, she thought of poisoning him and taking his money and opening an exclusive women's clothing store in San Miguel Allende. She had become more receptive to the idea through time, but the thought of being sent to a shithole

Mexican prison prevented her from carrying out her biggest desire.

Duarte was on his way to the office surrounded by four bodyguards, who were personally selected by him from the ranks of the state police. His phone rang loudly and he knew it was Lisa. His spirits lifted rapidly. He answered on the second ring, "Hi, I'm on my way to the office. Let me call you when I get there."

Lisa didn't say anything. She instinctively knew that he was with someone and didn't want to talk or do anything in front of his security escort. He didn't even trust his family members or his wife. Duarte had the "hots" for Lisa since the first time he laid eyes on her. He sold his soul to her for money, but deep down he would rather have her as a lover than take large monetary bribes. Lisa disliked Duarte, but understood that any criminal enterprise needed corrupt officials in order to survive. Protection was absolutely critical and required skill in corrupting people. It also required lots of money. She had both!

Twenty minutes passed and Lisa's phone rang. It was Duarte. "How dare him keep me waiting, the bastard," she mumbled to herself. She purposely let the phone ring several times to make him sweat. She finally answered.

"Governor, what the hell took you so long? Don't you know I have things to do?"

Duarte responded with a laugh, "Mi amor, I'm sorry, but

I was on urgent business and surrounded by my employees. You know I can't talk about our personal business in front of them."

Annoyed, Lisa told him, "We need to meet while I am here to discuss some issues regarding our business, if you know what I mean?"

Duarte again laughed, "I will be delighted to see you. What if we meet in about an hour on the deserted dirt road next to the large water tank on the southern outskirts of the city? We need to meet alone."

Lisa agreed and took a quick shower and put on a pair of blue jeans that were so tight, they looked like they were spray painted on her. She selected a black silk blouse, but decided not to wear a bra. It was too hot and humid. Lisa took the elevator to the lobby and saw her driver and one of her bodyguards sitting in a sofa checking out the women coming into the hotel. She grinned, "Pinches perros!" Men are all the same and only think of one thing. You are so fucking predicable."

"Dame las llaves," Lisa told the driver. "I won't need you to come with me. I will be back in about two hours. Keep your cell phones on and go do something productive instead of drooling over women like dogs in heat."

Lisa took the keys and a minute later was on the congested highway out of Culiacan. Fifty-five minutes later, she made a left turn onto a rustic road and traveled about five miles over rocks and large potholes. She noticed Duarte's black Mercedes Benz a few hundred yards ahead. He was standing next to it. Lisa thought to herself, "My God, he is as big as his fucking car." She slowly pulled up behind Duarte's car and grabbed her large purse from the passenger seat. Getting out of the car, she stepped on a rock and almost fell after losing her balance, but caught herself at the last moment. She was now in a much fouler mood and stared at the Governor who was leaning on his car with a smirk on his face.

"Hola, mi amor! I hope you didn't hurt yourself?"

Annoyed, Lisa responded, "I am fine, no thanks to you. Couldn't you find a better place to meet instead of this fucked up place? Listen carefully; we are going to be bringing in three loads of cocaine to our bodegas near Culiacan until we can move them to the U.S. You need to ensure that the municipal or state police under your command don't interfere. Understand?"

He replied, "Of course, have I ever failed you before?" As he said that, Duarte got closer to Lisa, who quickly pushed him away. Emboldened, the Governor aggressively pulled Lisa by the arm towards him and tried to kiss her.

Lisa yelled, "You fucking pig, have you lost your mind? Get your filthy hands off of me."

At being referred to as a "fucking pig", Duarte was now furious and got behind her, wrapping his left arm around her small waist. With his powerful right hand he began to pull her pants and underwear down. He was now completely blinded with raw animalistic lust. They tumbled to the ground violently and Duarte was grunting in both pain and pleasure. Lisa struggled wildly against his grip and somehow was able to reach into her purse and pull out her pistol of choice, a Walther PPK .380 semi-automatic. She put the short barrel of her PPK against his chest and squeezed the trigger three times. The blasts were muffled between their bodies. Duarte groaned loudly and rolled off Lisa. He was still alive and his watery eyes stared at her. One of the bullets severed his aorta and dark red blood gushed from the wound. He was going into shock and had less than a minute left on earth.

She looked at him with revulsion, "Pinche perro!" She glared at him for a few seconds and then put the gun in his mouth and pulled the trigger once more. The pistol recoiled in her hand and the explosion echoed through the small valley. Duarte's neck stiffened and his mouth and eyes remained open in testament to the horror of his final seconds. Lisa had warm, sticky blood on her blouse. Luckily, she had some bottled water in her Land Cruiser. She took her blouse off and washed the blood off. Next, she took Duarte's cell phones from his pockets and smashed them with a nearby rock. She buried the fragments about ten meters away and covered them with desert brush. Her heart was racing and she tried to remain calm. She knew that she couldn't leave any evidence or traces connecting her to the crime scene.

Lisa finally drove off and dismantled the PPK throwing the various pieces in streams and small lakes on the way back to the hotel. She rushed into the lobby in her soaking wet blouse as a group of tourists was crowding the front desk trying to check in. No one paid attention to her. Lisa went to her room and called her bodyguards and told them they were leaving in fifteen minutes. Lisa felt badly about killing Duarte, but she also had a strange sense of pleasure playing the role of God. She had now for the first time tasted the beastial pleasure of the kill. Little did she realize that the violence for her was not yet over. It was only beginning. With suitcases in hand, Lisa and her security escort quickly left the hotel and began driving home. The bodyguards knew something was wrong, but remained silent. Lisa also stayed quiet. She was also furious that her shopping trip had to be canceled and her return home was much earlier than anticipated. Her disposition became worse with each passing minute. After what seemed like days, Lisa arrived home and gave instructions to her bodyguards.

"Muchachos, you can go home. I will not need you until tomorrow morning."

When Lisa entered the house, she heard laughing and giggling coming from upstairs. She quietly climbed the carpeted stairs and peered into her bedroom. She was aghast to see Juancho in bed with two young girls who couldn't be more than sixteen years old. Her legs buckled, but she recovered quickly. She went into the next room and retrieved a fully loaded Browning .9mm from a shoebox on top of one of the closets. Juancho's horrific betrayal had taken away Lisa's capacity to think logically and rationally. She charged into the bedroom with tears in her eyes. Juancho was surprised, but rapidly recovered with an arrogant smirk on his face.

"Mi amor! I didn't expect you back so soon. I was just having a little fun, nothing more."

Staring into his eyes, Lisa screamed, "I trusted you and thought our love was special, but now I see that you are nothing more than a treacherous bastard like most men. Go fuck yourself."

Lisa ordered the girls to dress and get out of the house. Terrified, they grabbed their clothes in their arms and ran naked out of the room. Lisa then pointed the weapon at Juancho and fired three shots. Two of the hollow point projectiles hit him in the chest and blood spurted out turning the white bed sheets into a crimson color. The third bullet slammed into his forehead with the force of a sledgehammer and blew his brains out through the back of his head. He slumped over the side of the bed head first and dangled like a discarded ragdoll. The loud gunshots were mostly swallowed by the cavernous house, but could still be heard by the three men providing security to the house. They ran into the room seconds later with AK-47's at the ready and screamed, "What the fuck happened?"

She yelled, "Someone shot him and fled out the back." When they turned their back to her, Lisa fired three more rounds and the three men yelled in pain and seconds later fell to the floor lifeless. Lisa stared at Juancho for a moment, a tear ran down her cheek, and then quickly grabbed bundles of money and jewelry out of the wall safe and jumped into the Land Cruiser and drove away in a cloud of dust. She looked back at her beautiful village in the rearview mirror knowing that she may never see it again. A multitude of emotions engulfed her; sadness, fear, and anger. In the end, she felt pleasure in taking revenge on those who betrayed her. It was a lesson that later served Lisa well in her career as a drug trafficker. Empathy and forgiveness was for the weak and certainly not for someone in a business where treachery was part of the culture. In this type of enterprise, one must make examples of disloyal people. Fear was a valuable tool in maintaining order within a criminal organization. Lisa also realized that she couldn't trust anyone. She was becoming hardened and more cunning with time.

Lisa decided to flee to Juarez, Chihuahua, located on the other side of the border from the bustling border city of El Paso, Texas. She had a girlfriend, Victoria, whom she had known for years who lived there. Victoria also grew up in Sinaloa and would travel with her father selling brooms, mops, disinfectants and other items for household use. One of the stops was always the village where Lisa lived and through time they became good friends and kept in touch by telephone. Victoria was a tall, beautiful brunette with almond shaped hazel eyes. She looked more Middle Eastern than she did Mexican. Victoria owned and operated a high end French pastry shop, which Lisa on occasion used to launder drug money.

When Lisa arrived in Juarez, she called Victoria. "Hola muñeca, cómo estás? Lisa explained that she had just arrived in town. Victoria was excited to see her old friend and gave her the address to her new house located near the center of the bustling city. Lisa quickly drove through the busy streets dodging skinny street dogs and distracted pedestrians who were oblivious to oncoming traffic. She finally pulled up to a large, white stucco house surrounded by a pristine white, wrought iron fence. The yard was well kept and had a sprinkling of rose bushes and the red flowers were in full bloom. Lisa took out her suitcase and walked briskly to the front door, which had a butterfly design on the stained glass. She rang the doorbell and Victoria, within seconds, opened the door with a broad smile.

"It is so good to see you again, bienvenida!"

Lisa and Victoria hugged each other and were genuinely happy to see each other. Lisa stayed with her friend for several weeks and kept a low profile. She seldom ventured out of the house, but soon started to get anxious about her self-imposed confinement. One late Friday afternoon, Victoria came home early and told Lisa they were invited to a private party at a ranch on the southern outskirts of Juarez. Lisa was elated and couldn't wait to mingle with other people. She rushed to her bedroom to get ready and selected a provocative red silk dress to wear. A hot, bubble bath relaxed her. Soon, her thoughts drifted to memories of Juancho and the life they could have had together. All of it destroyed because of Juancho's inability to keep it in his pants. Oh well, time to move on to bigger and better things, she reflected.

In less than two hours, both women were on the road headed to the party and were eager to engage in some festivities. They were dressed to the nines and their clothes highlighted their sexuality. Their good looks could revive a dead man and they knew it. On the way, they made small talk and finally approached a hand-painted sign on the side of the road that said, "Fiesta Aqui" in bright red letters. They make a sharp right turn on a dusty dirt road that was quite bumpy and full of rocks and potholes. A kilometer down the road, they reached a security checkpoint manned by six men brandishing AK-47's. Victoria slammed on the brake when one of the men gestured for them to stop. A nasty looking man with a scar running down his left cheek approached their car and greeted them. "Buenas tardes!" He then instructed Victoria to park in front of the house and mentioned that more security would be nearby.

The women noticed at least fifty expensive cars parked in

front of a very large two-story house made of dark red brick with tall palm trees in front. The grounds were perfectly manicured and the bushes were trimmed artistically into the shapes of different animals. They also noticed a white wooden corral with at least a dozen expensive, gorgeous-looking horses to the side. As they walked to the house they observed dozens of armed men patrolling the perimeter on foot communicating with one another using hand held radios. Two guards at the door smiled at them and opened the door to a large, boisterous crowd and the sound of a live mariachi band. Everyone had a drink in hand and Lisa immediately recognized the glasses as Irish Waterford crystal based on their brilliance under the glaring lights. Victoria and Lisa were immediately given glasses of red wine. There were immense tables filled with different meats, fruits, salads, desserts, and platters with kilos of expensive beluga caviar.

Lisa whispered to Victoria, "This is a first-class party with no expense spared."

In a short period of time, the loud party gained momentum and everyone was talking over one another, but it was of little concern to anyone since the alcohol was flowing like the Rio Grande River. After about an hour, Lisa spotted a handsome man with dark hair and a captivating smile who was dressed impeccably, in a dark suit, white shirt and a beautiful red silk tie coming down the stairs. From national media reporting she recognized him as Albino Romero, the undisputed leader of the Cartel of the North. He was one of the most feared and powerful drug lords in the country, if not the entire world. In comparison, she and Juancho were nothing more than adolescents selling simple aspirin. Like two strong magnets, he approached Lisa and extended his hand, which was covered with large rings, studded with canary yellow diamonds. Lisa also noticed that a large gold esclava adorned his right wrist.

He spoke first, "Yo soy Albino. It is pleasure to meet you." Lisa blushed and could barely get the words out of her mouth, "My name is Lisa Rochin. Nice to meet you."

During the entire night, Albino and Lisa didn't leave each other's side. He finally pulled her into a dark study in the back of the house and kissed her passionately. They wrapped around each other with wild abandon and insane, hot passion for one another. They tore each other's clothes off and made love on the carpet. Their lovemaking was fiery and it was over with in less than a couple of minutes. Lisa ended up spending the night with Albino. They became inseparable and she became his confidant and she quickly began to help run his vast drug empire. She was happy and willing to do anything for him. But like most drug lords, Albino was a hunted man. Life was good for a couple of years until Albino's untimely death after he was captured in Colombia.

Lisa was devastated when Albino died, but she was now completely addicted to the money, power, and the control she had over other people. She would never leave the drug trade and return to a life of poverty. Never!

CHAPTER 5

The Colombians

The majestic blue skies were splattered with puffy white clouds and the bluish-green Caribbean waters splashed quietly against the sides of the old sixty-foot fishing boat with large nets hanging from the sides. The boat was on the southern tip of Haiti, which was part of the Greater Antilles Archipelago. It had been anchored in international waters for several hours. The crew sat patiently eating over ripened, mushy bananas and drinking bottled water. They were hardened men and had been sea dogs all their lives. The salt water and hot sun made the skin on their bodies look more like worn leather than human flesh. They wore nothing but tattered, baggy pants and old deck shoes. They were the new pirates of the Caribbean.

Finally, they heard the roar of powerful engines in the

distance and saw a large, sleek go-fast boat approaching from the west. Four black men bounced up and down as the speedboat plowed through the choppy water. They slowed the engines and pulled alongside the fishing boat. One of the black men wearing a bright red and blue Hawaiian shirt spoke Spanish.

"Buenos dias, mi amigos," he yelled. "As you can see we brought plenty of fuel and even some of the best food Haiti has to offer."

The Colombian captain of the fishing boat snarled, "Putos we have been waiting for a while. You should have been here waiting for us!"

"We were delayed because there were police swarming all over the marina and we had to wait until they left," the black man responded.

The crew of the fishing boat pulled out three large wooden planks and laid them across the sides of the two boats. The black men began rolling metal barrels full of fuel, over the well-placed and secure planks, onto the fishing boat. It only took a few minutes. Next, they passed plastic bags of cooked fish and containers of steamed rice. It smelled appetizing to the famished crew of Colombian smugglers.

The wooden planks were quickly pulled back into the fishing vessel and the engines were revved up. One of the Colombians yelled, "We will see you on the return trip. Make sure that you don't keep us waiting. We can always find someone else to refuel us. Keep that in mind!"

"Okay, okay, we won't let you down. Safe trip."

The fishing boat continued its journey northward through the Windward Passage between Cuba and the island of Hispaniola (Haiti and the Dominican Republic). The passage was fifty miles wide and easy to navigate. Unfortunately, twenty miles north of the passage a U.S. Naval warship picked it up on its radar systems and notified a U.S. Coast Guard cutter loitering in the area. The cutter, named Rio Arriba, went into full operational mode and the crew scrambled to their posts picking up gear and weapons on the way. Within four hours, the fishing boat was in sight traveling at about fifteen knots per hour. The Colombians didn't notice the cutter approach since they were gorging themselves with the food the Haitians had given them. Worse, they were washing it down with bottles of rum and were three sheets to the wind. They were startled and jumped to their feet when they heard the blast of a deafening horn.

"This is the U.S. Coast Guard! Please stop your engines and prepare to receive a boarding party."

One of the Colombians yelled, "Hijos de puta! We are not going to stop. Increase our speed. Now!"

A gunner on the cutter took aim and let loose a barrage from a mounted .50 caliber machinegun. The bullets raced along the water towards the fishing boat until they reached the engines and completely obliterated them. Scared out of their wits the Colombians quickly surrendered. They put their hands high in the air and waited. A boarding crew from the Rio Arriba took them into custody and a search of the boat turned up twenty tons of high-grade cocaine packaged in kilo bricks that were well placed in hundreds of burlap bags. The cocaine had several different logos on the packages, to include a scorpion, an eagle, and the Colombian flag. Based on the different logos it indicated that the boat was acting as a transporter for various cartels. It was the largest seizure in decades. The load was worth at least three billion-dollars.

When word of the seizure reached the leaders of the most powerful drug cartels in Colombia, they were dismayed and enraged at incurring such a big loss. Within days, they convened a meeting at a finca south of Medellin. Pedro Serrano, leader of the Cartel of the Eastern Plains, took center stage. He was a powerfully built man with long stringy hair and an oversized nose.

Serrano animatedly commented, "Muchachos, we have to quickly change the route for our cocaine away from the Caribbean. We are losing too many loads to the pinche gringo Coast Guard and the DEA. The last load of twenty tons should be a lesson that we cannot become complacent. I have studied the situation carefully and have come to the conclusion that we must work with the Mexicans and use their country as our new route. Besides they already have existing pipelines into the U.S. for their heroin and marijuana. What do you think?"

Jairo Velasquez, a small thin man with white hair, was the next to speak. He was the ruthless head of the Buenaventura Cartel. He slowly looked at everyone in the room, "It is true that we need to quickly shift our fortunes elsewhere and I agree that Mexico is the place to go. It has a two thousand-mile border with the U.S. that can easily be penetrated, but if we work with the Mexicans they will want the lion's share of our product. This is not acceptable! I suggest we set up a base of operations in a strategic location in Mexico and work independently without the Mexican cartels being involved. It is risky, but that is the nature of our business."

A consensus was finally reached that Mexico would be their next primary route for funneling their deadly tonnage of cocaine into the U.S. market. They would send a team to Mexico to establish a base of operations, preferably one close to the border. They selected Roberto Castillo, a highly intelligent middle-aged man who had been involved in the drug trade since the age of fourteen. He was stocky and had enough hair for two men. Castillo was the perfect man for the job since he knew all facets of the drug trade, but what separated him from all the rest was his uncanny ability to corrupt even those with great integrity. Castillo selected another two individuals to travel to Mexico with him. They were friends and would follow orders to the letter.

Before leaving, Castillo took out a large map and began looking for strategic locations that they could use. After several hours of studying the map, he was attracted to a small town in the Mexican state of Tamaulipas called La Pesca. It was a fishing village located on the Gulf of Mexico at the mouth of the Rio Soto La Marina and it was not far from the U.S. border. Castillo was elated.

Three days later, Castillo and his two men boarded an Avianca flight bound for Mexico City. Once they landed, they had a little over three hours to make their connecting Aero Mexico flight to Ciudad Victoria, which was the capital of Tamaulipas. It was raining and dark clouds loomed in the sky when Castillo and his men arrived at the General Pedro José Mendez International Airport on the outskirts of Ciudad Victoria. After getting their bags, they rented a blue four-wheel Toyota Land Cruiser and drove to the Hotel Paradise Inn. They checked in and paid cash, in advance, for a week. They went to their rooms to leave their bags and then met at the hotel restaurant. They ate a hearty meal of steak and lobster, and chased that down with several ice-cold Tecate beers.

Castillo wiped his mouth with a red linen napkin and commented, "Muchachos, let's get a good night's rest and we will leave here at eight in the morning for this place called La Pesca. It is only about an hour's drive from here. I want to get a feel for the place and see if it is what we will need for our business."

The next morning, the men got on the road and passed the Museo de Historia Natural with its modern architecture and its white exterior walls. They were all impressed with the Catedral with its Corinthian style columns. Traffic was light and they soon were on the road to La Pesca at a high rate of speed. When they entered the town, they were immediately struck at the poverty. The buildings were old, in disrepair and poorly constructed. The people walking along the road wore old and raggedy clothes. Only a few businesses were sprinkled along the two-lane main street. The few restaurants that were still open for business in La Pesca resembled each other, nothing more than a dilapidated shack with white plastic chairs and tables. Many dogs maneuvered between the tables begging for scraps. Castillo, however, was impressed because there was not a lot of infrastructure or government presence. He did, however, discover that there was a small naval base nearby. In conversations with some of the villagers, he was told that the marines at the base seldom ventured out because of increasing gun battles with drug traffickers and assorted criminals.

As they moved away from the village in the Toyota Land Cruiser, they came upon a long, paved runway about half a mile from the road. It was in an isolated area and the strip was about twelve hundred meters long. They pulled over and parked alongside the road. "I must have the luck of the Irish," mumbled Castillo, as he saw an old man, probably a villager, with an old mule walk by them.

Castillo asked, "Buenas, what is this runway used for and who does it belong to?"

The old toothless man wearing huaraches answered, "Es de la Marina. The navy, once in a great while, uses it to land one of their planes. It is such a waste of money for the government to have it here. By the way, that small yellow building next to it is where five marines live. They take care of the field and are bored with nothing to do all day."

The next day, Castillo and his friends returned to the area of the airstrip. They waited in the heat and sweltering humidity in a field of tall grass and a small grove of citrus trees. It was almost noon when they noticed a gray/brown truck driving from the airstrip to the road. They ran quickly to their Land Cruiser and followed the truck at a safe distance. The truck pulled off the road in the middle of La Pesca at a restaurant called Los Mariscos. Four uniformed men jumped from the military truck and sat at a table.

"Horale, this is our chance," said Castillo. "It is now or never. Park across the street and let's walk over like we belong here."

They sat at a table next to the marines and ordered some beer. They didn't order any food because of the swarm of flies swarming over it. It would not be a good time to get

Montezuma's revenge. Castillo waved an old woman over and told her to send beer to the marines. A minute later, she appeared at the marine's table with four beers on a rusty metal tray. The marines seemed surprised. She nodded over to Castillo and his men, indicating that they had paid for them.

The lieutenant, a short, dark man with big ears smiled and spoke up, "Muchas gracias! I am lieutenant Lunar. Are you caballeros from around this area?"

"No, we are here on business. Do you mind if we join you? I have something that may interest you," answered Castillo.

The two tables were moved against each other, joining the two tables to make one, and more beer was ordered. They made small talk as they drank and once the marines were slightly intoxicated, Castillo made his move.

He opened up the conversation, addressing the lieutenant, "I am curious, how much do you make for putting your lives on the line? It can't be enough, especially with all the killing and violence taking place all around you."

The lieutenant replied, "It is very true. We get paid shit while our politicians make millions of dollars every year. We can barely support our wives. It is a fucked-up situation."

Castillo smirked, "What if I told you that you could become rich beyond your imagination by doing nothing?"

A look of shock formed on the lieutenant's face. Then he regained his composure, "What bullshit are you talking about? Is this a joke that you are about to make?"

Castillo took hold of his arm, "No! All we want is to use the airstrip that you guard every day. I am willing to pay you fifty thousand dollars each and every time we use it. All you have to do is turn a blind eye and let us know when it will be clear of any military planes. What do you say?"

"Chingado," whispered the lieutenant. "Are you bringing in drugs?"

Castillo also whispered, "It is best that you remain ignorant! I am offering you more money than you will make in a million lifetimes. Think of your families. Do you want to live in poverty for the rest of your lives?"

Lunar looked at his men's faces and the three of them nodded their heads. They knew that another opportunity like this may never come again. They had nothing to lose as far as they were concerned. All of them shook hands and ordered another round of drinks to toast to their future. Castillo got the lieutenant's phone number and after paying the bill left with his men. They drove through the wind swept trash swirling on the road.

A day later, Castillo and his men returned to Bogota and met with the cartel leaders. He gave them a detailed briefing on the meeting with the marine detachment who guarded a seldom-used airstrip, which was capable of handling any type of aircraft. The capos listened intently and smiled. The bribes they would have to pay would be nothing but chump change. Two weeks later, a blue and white Aero Commander 500B made its approach for landing at the marine airstrip. The loud hum of the engines lowered significantly as it reduced its speed. It hit the runway smoothly and taxied to the far end where it couldn't be seen by prying eyes. Waiting was a large truck with fuel and an electric gas pump. The plane executed a quick turn facing the opposite direction and was now ready to depart once the two tons of cocaine were off-loaded and it was refueled. Four men with AK-47's moved quickly and loaded the cocaine onto their truck and fueled the plane from fifty-five-gallon drums. The entire operation took less than eight minutes. The Aero Commander's engines roared and it moved faster and faster down the strip until it was in the sky on its way back to Colombia. A tarp was placed over the duffel bags full of pure cocaine and the truck drove away rapidly. Lieutenant Lunar and his men had already been paid and they smiled and waved as the truck went by.

Forty-eight hours later, on a very dark night, a pair of truck lights illuminated the southern bank of the Rio Grande River near Matamoros. The lights were then flashed on and off three times. The same signal came from the U.S. side of the river next to Brownsville, Texas. Several Colombians inflated two large rubber rafts and put them in the slow moving water, where the river was very shallow and the current was not very strong. Duffel bags full of cocaine were put on the rafts and the men with water up to their knees waded slowly across the river, guiding the rafts to their destination. They made several trips until the entire two tons of cocaine were safely crossed into the U.S. The loaded cargo truck drove through the dark streets of Brownsville headed to a warehouse in Chicago. It had cost the Colombian cartels three thousand dollars to produce each kilo of cocaine and now that it was in the U.S. the price had increased to thirty thousand or more per kilo. Within a month, the Colombians had moved over thirty tons of cocaine through La Pesca. They had not lost a single load and were making hundreds of millions of dollars with little risk.

One day, the cartel leaders met at a high-rise apartment in the downtown area of Medellin. They poured glasses of Moet and Chandon, Dom Perignon Charles and Diana champagne at five thousand dollars a bottle. One of the capos raised his glass and said, "Coronamos otra vez! Compañeros, we are doing better than expected and our profits have skyrocketed. We need to take advantage of the situation and move even more product through Mexico. We cannot waste time."

Another one of the cartel leaders chimed in, "That is right! We never know when that window will close and it is now wide open to us. Let's do it."

They all agreed and sent orders to their lab operators to step up production immediately. It was full speed ahead. The labs began converting coca paste flown from Peru and Bolivia into cocaine hydrochloride by the ton. At the same time, the number of planes landing at La Pesca turned the airfield into a microcosm of Chicago's O'Hare International Airport.

It was a rainy day in Mexico City and Villa was nursing a bad cold. He had gone to the embassy health unit earlier in the day to see the doctor. He was given over-the-counter medicine and told to drink lots of liquid. Villa made a mental note to pick-up a bottle of tequila on the way home. It wouldn't cure the cold, but it would sure make him feel much better. Seconds later, his secretary Ursula peeked in and told him someone on the phone wanted to speak with him, but didn't want to give his name. Villa took the call as he popped a couple more pills into his mouth.

A man with a raspy voice said, "Hola, I will remain anonymous since I value my life and don't want to die prematurely. I live in La Pesca and the airstrip located there, which belongs to the Mexican Navy, is being used to transport drugs. I live a short distance from it and planes are landing there day and night. They are private planes, not military."

Villa asked, "Why do you think its drugs?"

"Just before the planes land, a truck transporting large barrels shows up and parks at the farthest end of the strip. It is worth your while to check it out."

Villa responded, "Ok. I believe that you are telling me the truth. I will definitely look in to it. Thank you for the information."

As soon as he hung up the phone, Villa dialed Ventura's

cell number and got him on the first ring. He told him of the conversation with the anonymous source and was of the opinion that they should at least do a preliminary investigation. It could lead to something. Villa made arrangements to meet with him in the morning for breakfast. He was going home to get some rest and take more medicine to try to shake his cold.

The next morning, Villa dragged himself out of bed after spending the night with numbing cold chills. He still felt weak, but drank large gulps of orange juice from a large plastic container. The sugar content would carry him for at least a few hours. He took a long, hot shower and put on a dark blue suit and a red tie. He was getting dizzy as he drove to a restaurant in the Zona Rosa. His cold was getting worse. Ventura was already waiting at a sidewalk table.

Ventura looked at Villa, "Dios mio, you look like death warmed over. I have seen cadavers in better shape."

"Tell me about it. I feel like someone ran over me and then backed up and did it again. But such is life. We have to take the ups and the downs."

In half an hour, Villa and Ventura had hashed out a plan taking into account all the operational variables. The first step would be to send a team of nine men to conduct surveillance on the airstrip. They would work in teams of three and each team would work an eight-hour shift. Each team would work out of separate hotels in Ciudad Victoria. If they detected unusual activity, Ventura and Villa would travel there with more men.

Villa was not hungry and only ate a small bowl of yogurt, which he could not taste. Ventura had steak and eggs with a side dish of pancakes.

Villa laughed, "If I ate as much as you, I would weigh over four hundred pounds. You consume more food than a small army."

After breakfast, they gave each other an "abrazo" and went their separate ways. Villa drove to a nearby pharmacy and bought some powerful antibiotics. In Mexico you could buy most drugs over the counter and did not need a prescription like in the U.S.

Villa got a call from Ventura after five days. "Miguel, my men report that they have observed almost daily landings at the airstrip and the planes are definitely not military aircraft. The planes land and quickly take off again. A lot of suspicious activity is taking place and they have seen marines lighting up the airfield with lanterns so planes can even land at night. We need to go there as soon as possible. I will get one of our large planes to take us to Ciudad Victoria. It will not raise suspicions since we go there on a regular basis now that the gubernatorial elections are coming up."

"Ok. I will be ready to leave tomorrow morning. I will meet you at the airport at 9 am. Does that work?"

"Of course. That is perfect," replied Ventura. "I will take

some of my best men. By the way, bring some of your night vision scopes since you know we cannot afford any."

Villa laughed, "I will bring several. It's the least I can do. See you tomorrow."

The following morning, Villa left his house in Bosques de Jardines and quickly got on Avenida Reforma where traffic was always heavy. He saw the mustard colored sky, which meant that the smog was thicker than usual. Weaving, and speeding up when possible, Villa finally navigated his way to the airport. Ventura and his men were waiting. They boarded the blue and white colored, twin engine King Air 350. The two pilots switched on the engines and the propellers began to turn rapidly. Once cleared by the control tower the aircraft began to move slowly onto the runway. Minutes later they were airborne and headed due north. Villa still didn't feel well, so he slept most of the trip. Several hours later, he was awakened by the sound of the landing gear being lowered for landing. The plane dropped rapidly and hit the runway hard, bouncing a few times until it stabilized on the asphalt.

Four black sedans were waiting. They were federal judicial police assigned to Ciudad Victoria. Ventura knew them well and trusted them. That night, they all checked into separate hotels, as planned. During dinner, Villa and Ventura laid out the final plan and added contingencies in the event things didn't go as planned. The following day, they would have to hike at least five miles to arrive at the northern end of the strip, which was furthest from the building housing the marine garrison.

It was a windy morning and the humidity was unbearable. After breakfast, the local Federales brought fresh jalapenos, and meals-ready-to-eat (MRI's) given to Mexico's security forces by the U.S. government. Villa didn't like them and always said that even starving dogs wouldn't touch them. Ventura and Villa would take ten men and make the trek to the airstrip. The rest would be near La Pesca and would make an assault through the front entrance of the airstrip where the marines were quartered. Before deploying they did a communications check to ensure that the hand-held radios worked. Villa then passed out bottles of mosquito repellent to all the men. There was nothing worse than being eaten alive by pesky, mosquitos that were in abundance in the area. All of the men wore black tactical clothes and carried either AK-47's or AR-15's.

The men drove north and then took an isolated, rural dirt road. They were dropped off in a large field of tall grass. Villa was not feeling well, but marched along towards their objective. They would stop and rest about every half hour. Fortunately, there were no houses within eyesight. By mid-afternoon, they stood on a small hill and saw the long airfield. At a distance they could also see the small house where the group of marines lived. It seemed quiet and no movement was detected outside. Villa noticed that small, sloping hills and tall weeds flanked both sides of the airfield. He sent two men to watch the house and two men to the middle of the field as a rear guard to prevent the escape of anyone once the action started. He knew most of the operation would be at the end of the field where he was. Most of the men would be deployed there.

The first night was quiet and Villa was glad he had brought the mosquito repellent since the blood-sucking pests swarmed around them in thick clouds. They slept in the weeds and the next morning they woke up stiff and tired. They opened some tins of sausage and some and ate it with bread. It tasted better than normal since they were famished. Some had the MRI's and Villa thought to himself, "God bless them." In the late morning, the radio buzzed slightly and Ventura's men reported that a couple of marines had come out of the house to smoke cigarettes, but then quickly went back inside. The hours went by ever so slowly and sitting in the tick-infested grass was excruciating.

As sunset approached, the men figured they were going to have to spend another long miserable night in the weeds. Less than half an hour later, they saw a large cattle truck drive onto the airstrip and head to the far end where Ventura, Villa, and several Federales were hidden. The truck stopped on the side of the strip and four men unloaded several metal barrels and lined them up in a straight row. The men, dressed in cowboy boots and worn blue jeans, could be heard talking to one another as they leaned on the barrels. Villa could tell by their accents and the words they used that they were not Mexican, but Colombians. All of them had .9mm handguns tucked in their waistbands. Minutes later they returned to the truck and pulled out several strobe lights placing them on both sides of the airstrip. Then they congregated by the truck and waited.

As darkness enveloped La Pesca, the hum of aircraft engines could be heard at a distance. The sound got louder and louder until the lights of two aircraft could be seen directly above. Minutes later two Aero Commanders touched down and they rolled down the strip towards the waiting truck. The pilots did not leave the aircraft and kept the engines going. As the planes were being fueled dozens of bales were being offloaded and placed on the bed of the truck.

"Ahora muchachos," whispered Villa into the radio.

"Policia Federal," yelled Ventura. "Put your hands in the air."

All hell fucking broke loose and the Colombians began firing and running in different directions. The planes pushed forward with the doors still open and they began moving rapidly down the runway. Villa and the Federales opened up with their long weapons and sprayed tracers into the night. The tracers looked like giant fireflies moving across the airstrip. When the planes were about thirty-five yards down the strip, they suddenly veered off the runway and tilted sideways and then pitched forward hitting a sandy hill with their propellers. What the trafficker pilots didn't know was that the Federales had salted the runway with caltrops after they had landed. The caltrops, better known as road spikes, are small spiky objects like those used in the game of jacks. They always have one sharp point sticking up. They had punctured the tires of the aircraft making it impossible to get airborne.

The Colombians on the field continued firing and the loud blasts filled the night air. One of the traffickers took a round to the face and his head splattered like a ripe tomato. The other three that were still standing, were peppered with hot lead projectiles that ripped through tissue and bone shredding everything in their path. All four were dead in less than thirty seconds. At the other end of the field, the marines charged out of their house with AR-15's, but were riddled with bullets before they knew what hit them. The pilots were pulled out of their planes and forcibly thrown on the asphalt and handcuffed. They offered no resistance and were traumatized for several hours. The total seizure came to three tons of cocaine. The Mexican government would eventually repair the two aircraft taken from the traffickers and put them into service. A press release issued by the Mexican Secretary of the Navy reported the seizure and lamented that several marines had died valiantly in the operation. The government did everything in its power to preserve the integrity and honor of its military, even if they had to lie.

A week later the Colombian cartel leaders sadly agreed that they now had no choice but to work with the Mexican traffickers based on the huge loss they had incurred at La Pesca. They would have to pay more than they wanted, but at least they would have the broad political protection they needed to operate.

When they returned to Mexico City, Villa invited Ventura for dinner. They had a great bottle of wine and two huge steaks. They agreed that life had to have its little pleasures once in a while.

CHAPTER 6

The Take Over

It was late spring and a soft wind swept across the mountainous village of Badiraguato, Sinaloa, the birthplace of the majority of Mexico's most notorious and violent drug lords. The choking poverty remained a constant reminder that the central government had disenfranchised the forgotten poor here. Many of those who became successful drug traffickers never returned to the area. The distant, but painful memory of when they were indigent and hungry was too traumatic for them. At an isolated area, surrounded by trees with large, bulging buttress roots with warty, yellow green fruit hanging from the branches, sixty armed men brandishing AK-47's and handguns provided security at an opulent ranch. Security was configured in concentric rings, much like the circles on a bull's-eye, making it difficult to penetrate. The security force to communicate with each other regarding any suspicious activity or the approach of government forces used expensive HF hand-held radios.

Inside the spacious house there were almost thirty hardened and evil looking men dressed in western shirts, denim jeans, and expensive cowboy hats. They were all packing .9mm or .45 caliber semi-automatic pistols that visibly stuck out of their waistbands. The banter was loud and vulgar. There were occasional outbursts of laughter, especially when someone told a joke of how some of their victims begged for mercy before they were shot dead or burned alive. Killing had become a ritual for these psychopaths who cared little for human life and their only God was power and greed. The men were all high-ranking plaza bosses of the Cartel of the North. Just as they were beginning to get drunk on tequila and expensive scotch, Lisa walked into the room with an air of arrogance and supreme confidence. She was wearing skintight jeans and brown eel skin cowboy boots. Her silk blouse was unbuttoned halfway to her waist. She also carried a Colt .45 with gold grips bearing the image of the Virgin Mary. It was tucked behind her large, round solid gold belt buckle. The men became quiet and drooled at Lisa's sexuality.

Lisa strolled into the middle of the room and addressed the men, "Muchachos, I called for this meeting to discuss the future of our organization, especially now with the death of Albino in Colombia. It was his desire that in the event of his demise that I would assume the leadership role. I am the only one who knows the sources of supply for cocaine in Colombia, the politicians that we pay for protection, and also all the routes used to smuggle our product into the U.S."

One of the men, Victor Arteaga, a thin, short man with a jagged red scar running down his left cheek spoke, "Si, this is true, but this is a man's business and it has always been this way. In all of history, a woman has never been in charge of a cartel! We will be the laughing stock of our enemies, not to mention that they will view it as a weakness and want to take over the territory under our control. You are being delusional."

Lisa angrily responded, "Weakness and delusional? I was the one Albino relied on because he knew I could be trusted to get things done. I have also killed more cabrones than any of you! I am not weak and you all know that."

Arteaga yelled, "Pinche Puta! Only over my dead body will I let you take over the cartel."

Lisa stared angrily at him for a couple of seconds and with great speed pulled out her pistol and shot him in the face three times. The loud explosions startled everyone, who immediately ducked for cover. They looked up to see Arteaga's face, which was now a wet mass of bloody flesh. Lisa yelled, "Ok, you stupid son of a bitch! Now you have your wish! Does anyone else have a problem? If you do, we can settle the matter with plomo right now! She glared at everyone holding the smoking gun at her side ready to pull the trigger again if needed.

One of the plaza bosses at the back of the room yelled, "Que viva Lisa!" Everyone loudly repeated the words with complete respect and clapped as they came to their feet. One by one, they walked up to Lisa and shook her hand pledging their undying support. One of them took off his twenty-carat diamond pinky ring and gave it to her as a token of his loyalty. Shots of expensive tequila were poured and everyone drank in honor of the new and undisputed leader of the Cartel of the North. The reign of its top leader, Romero, had ended violently and the emergence of the new leader, Rochin, had begun in violence. This transition of power was fitting since, like any criminal organization, its survival was interwoven with the methodical slaughter of those who posed a threat.

Lisa smiled and declared, "I will make you all rich beyond your wildest dreams. We will pump more drugs into gringolandia, but also expand our market share into other countries. But first, we will consolidate our power and ensure that we are the most powerful cartel in Mexico. This means that we have to destroy the cartels that are our enemies and make alliances with others who can help us grow. Understand?"

Almost in unison all the men said, "Of course! We are in agreement."

As Lisa began to consolidate her power she decided it

was time to have her siblings, Armando and Anita, join her in expanding the power and control of the Cartel of the North. She called them on the telephone and told them it was important for them to return to their home state of Sinaloa and she would send them whatever money they needed for the move. They were more than pleased to help their sister who had done so much for them. Lisa was happy because she would now have family around her that she could trust to watch her back and provide sound counsel.

A few weeks earlier, changes had also been occurring with the rival Blood Alliance Cartel, whose leader, José Atenco, had been killed by Lisa using an improvised explosive device planted on the road. In the aftermath, the cartel fractured into two cartels as rivals fought for control. Mario Martinez, one of its powerful lieutenants, took over the larger portion of the cartel and kept its name. Martinez was a short, thin man with thick coarse hair who had become a criminal at the age of fifteen. He was born in Mexico City and was abandoned by his parents at the age of fourteen. His parents were addicted to heroin and lived on the streets. They begged for money on street corners, which they used to buy small amounts of heroin for their personal use. Mario, in order to survive his harsh life, began burglarizing homes and one day he stole a .9mm pistol in one of the homes he had broken into in the exclusive Bosques de Las Lomas neighborhood. The weapon provided him with new criminal opportunities and he quickly graduated to armed robberies. He had just turned sixteen when he was walking near Avenida Reforma near the Chapultepec Castle when he noticed a tall man dressed in a black three-piece suit coming towards him. Mario looked around and didn't see other people in the immediate area. This is a great opportunity that has fallen into my lap, he thought. When the man was about eight feet away, Mario pulled out his pistol and pointed it at the man's chest. He shouted, "Give me all your money and jewelry or I will kill you!" Mario pulled the hammer back, but became nervous and applied too much pressure to the trigger and a loud boom startled him, as the gun went off unexpectedly. He saw the man clutch his chest with both hands as he looked at Mario with shock, for a split second, before he fell head first onto the concrete sidewalk. A pool of blood began to form as the man desperately tried to suck air into his lungs. He was dead in seconds as the bullet had severed the aorta. Mario was shocked since he had never seen a man die so violently before, especially by his own hand. He turned and ran as he threw the pistol into the nearby bushes. Less than half a mile away local uniformed police officers who were patrolling on foot took him into custody.

Mario was charged with murder and attempted robbery. A judge sentenced him to fifteen years to be served at Almaloya, Mexico's most violent and secure prison. During his imprisonment, he met Alfonso Calderon, who was a plaza boss of the Blood Alliance Cartel and was serving time for the torture/murder of ten individuals in Hermosillo, Sonora. Calderon thought the ten individuals were sicarios from the Cartel of the North, but they were actually innocent civilians. Alfonso was given forty years and he doubted that he would ever be a free man again. Alfonso took Mario under his wing and prevented predatory inmates from raping or harming him. He shared the food that was delivered to him each day. The prison food was so bad that not even the hungry cats that roamed the prison yard would touch it. The days passed slowly for Mario, but eventually he was released. He went to say goodbye to Alfonso and thank him for taking care of him. Alfonso wrote a telephone number and gave it to him. He told Mario, "Call this number and ask for Chano. He is like my brother and will give you a job where you can make some real money."

"Gracias, Alfonso. I will call him right away and I am willing to do anything. I need money to live and I have no education to get a regular job. Thank you, again!"

True to his word, Mario called Chano who was initially suspicious of him, but the recommendation of Alfonso was all that mattered. Chano met with him and explained to him that he would be working as a sicario for the Blood Alliance Cartel, the most powerful one in Mexico. Mario was excited, but unsure that he would be able to execute people in cold blood.

Within a week, he was given his first assignment. He was provided a photo of a journalist who worked for La Reforma newspaper and told he needed to kill him quickly. He was writing daily articles exposing the cartel and its leaders and a "green light" had been passed down to eliminate him. The next morning, Mario was given a .38 caliber revolver equipped with a professionally made silencer. He was then driven in a new Nissan sedan past a modest home south of Mexico City so he could become familiar with the journalist's house and its location. The house was painted brown and had colorful bushes with purple flowers in the front yard. He also noticed that all the windows and the front door were secured with wrought iron. This meant the killing would have to be done outside, which was risky. Later in the day, Mario was dropped off near the house and slowly walked the two blocks to get there. After checking for the presence of neighbors, he quickly ducked into the bushes, surrounding the house, and hid. After two hours of waiting, he heard a vehicle pull into the driveway. A car door slammed and Mario peered from behind the bushes. He immediately recognized the journalist from the photo and as he began to approach, Mario jumped from behind the bushes and stumbled on a water hose, but regained his balance quickly. He lifted his pistol and fired twice hitting his target in the chest and face, killing him instantly. The journalist fell hard onto the concrete driveway. Suddenly, the front door opened. An attractive woman with bright red hair appeared and screamed as she caught a glimpse of her husband, whose white shirt was covered in blood. Mario panicked and shot her in the throat. She fell to her knees, and then face first near her husband. Mario walked away rapidly and was picked up six blocks away by an accomplice. His heart was still pounding, but the adrenaline rush that came with these killings was intoxicating. After proving himself, by killing over a hundred enemies of the cartel, Mario was rewarded by being put in charge of cartel operations in the southern state of Guerrero. As the heroin capital of Mexico, the state of Guerrero was highly lucrative for Mario and he made millions for the cartel.

Jaime Santana, Mario's longtime rival, met with supporters in the Blood Alliance Cartel at a hotel suite in Puerto Vallarta, where he made his case against remaining with the cartel. He gave a fiery speech saying, "We have all done well and earned a lot of money but things change and sometimes not for the best. We are all aware that Mario, will in all likelihood, take over the cartel since he was Atenco's chosen heir. But make no mistake, he is a greedy person and we will be nothing more than his pawns. Now is the time to make a move and break away and start our own cartel."

The men in the room all nodded in agreement. One of them spoke up and said, "Jaime, you know that we will now have to engage in a war with not only the Cartel of the North, but also with many of our friends in the Blood Alliance Cartel.

It will lead to violence, which will cause the government to go after us more aggressively than normal."

Jaime responded, "We can't be afraid of our destiny. We will kill todos los putos that don't join us and take over all drug operations in the country. I plan on becoming a parallel government in Mexico. Everyone will fear us. Who is with me?"

Everyone agreed to support Jaime, partly because of greed and more so out of fear. Jaime decided to call the organization that he would lead, the Invincible Jalisco Cartel. Jaime was a former state judicial police officer from the state of Sinaloa. He eventually rose to become the head of security for the governor of the state. This opened two important doors for him. As a police officer, he came in contact with many drug lords, many of whom paid him for protection and as a result he developed close connections in the drug trade. Secondly, working directly for the governor allowed him to meet several high-level politicians who could provide him with protection when he transitioned from police officer to drug trafficker.

As a police officer, Jaime was making $6,000.00 pesos a month, which was not only an insult, but slave wages, and not enough to put food on the table for his family. One day, Jaime got out of bed and as he showered he made the decision to join the Blood Alliance Cartel. For a couple of years, they had tried to recruit him, but he was afraid of landing up in prison. He wanted a better life and after seeing the wealth displayed by traffickers and corrupt officials, he decided that it was better to live one good year than ten bad ones. The cartel soon relied on him to protect their activities by bribing key officials in the government, police, military, and even judges. He became known as a man who would get things done. He was also a ruthless man and didn't hesitate in killing anyone who stood in his way.

On many occasions, Jaime and Mario clashed, as both were ambitious and driven. Each knew that the time would come when the more cunning one, as they both climbed the ladder of power within the cartel, would eliminate the weaker one. Their rivalry led to treachery and they would try to undermine each other on a regular basis. Their hatred for one another grew, year-by-year, until they couldn't work together. The cartel leadership kept them apart and moved them to different states to diffuse the situation. The viciousness between them was starting to impact cartel operations and destroy internal cohesiveness. The eventual separation between both factions would not end amicably and the two hostile forces would create more violence in the country, which had literally been converted into a giant cemetery.

CHAPTER 7

Undercover in Honduras

The die had been cast and the leadership of the Blood Alliance Cartel and the Cartel of the North had changed dramatically. Now instead of two major organizations, there were now three. Jaime named his criminal network, the Invincible Jalisco Cartel and established his organization's command and control in Guadalajara, Mexico's second largest city. It was a strategic location for the new cartel since it was the money laundering capital of the country. Banks were a dime a dozen and were more than willing to clean the money of criminals, for a fee of course.

Months later, a national election took place that brought a National Action Party candidate to the Presidency. It was a historic moment in Mexico with Imelda Cecilia Maestas becoming the first female President of the Republic. No one, including seasoned political analysts, had thought she stood a chance in hell of winning, especially in a country where machismo reigned supreme. Her famed beauty and intelligence were well known throughout the land and she was highly revered. She was from the northern state of Sonora and her campaign was based on getting rid of corruption from all levels of government, improving health care, education, judicial reform, and attacking the drug cartels that she adamantly believed were a threat to the national security of Mexico. She was a pragmatic woman who truly cared about the welfare of the country and not using a political office to seek wealth like all the other politicians. She had never married and dedicated her life to one of public service. Imelda came from a middle-class family and her father had been a highly respected marine General. Her mother was an accomplished corporate attorney.

Imelda had served as the Governor of Sonora for eight years and the cartels had offered her millions of dollars to allow their drugs to transit the state and move unhindered across the border into the U.S. She had thrown them out of her office and later they had tried to kill her, but had failed.

One scorching summer day, during the peak high temperatures of the Sonoran Desert, Imelda by happenstance had been looking out the front window when she saw a late-model white sedan park on the two-lane road about thirty yards from her house. She saw two young men in their late twenties leave the car and start walking towards her house. To her horror, they held large pistols in their hands. She maintained her composure and ran to the nearby bedroom closet and pulled out a 12-gauge shotgun loaded with lead slugs. The slugs were more than twice the size of a regular bullet and were extremely lethal. She took the safety off and waited. Her heart beat rapidly, but she steadied herself. Within seconds the door came crashing in and the first man charged into the house. Imelda pulled the trigger and a reverberating boom filled the air. The slug tore into the assassin's chest leaving a gaping hole. He fell, lifeless, to the floor. The second man was right behind him and knew it was too late to turn and run. The last thing he saw was Imelda pointing the large barrel at his face. She fired again and blew his head off, completely off. Fortunately, her father had taught her marksmanship with various weapons at an early age. If not for that, Imelda would now be a victim and not the victor. The scene was a bloody, gory mess that looked like a scene from a horror movie. Imelda felt terrible remorse, but found solace in that it was self-defense. She used her cell phone to call the police, who immediately launched an investigation. But their ineptness, and the fact that Mexico didn't have a national fingerprint database, prevented the identification of the assassins, and therefore also those who had hired them. Within twenty-four hours, Imelda moved out of her home and moved to an apartment in a gated community. She also had the state police provide full-time security. She knew that complacency had almost ended her life, never again.

Meanwhile, DEA agent Miguel Villa was working on backlogged paperwork in his office when he received a telephone call from headquarters in Washington, D.C. He was told that a high-level informant had been recruited who could make an undercover introduction to the leader of the violent MS-13 gang in Honduras. Villa had been picked for the undercover assignment because of his vast experience in working undercover missions, his fluency in Spanish, and his nerves of steel.

Villa was very familiar with the MS-13, which had proliferated in El Salvador, Guatemala, and Honduras, the so-called northern triangle of Central America. The ill-conceived plan by the U.S. in the late 1980's and early 1990's of deporting MS-13 members to Central America had backfired with horrific consequences. The gang members quickly recruited others from the poverty-stricken streets and the overcrowded jails. Within a few years they became a major security threat to the region. Their war with other gangs, such as the Barrio 18, had displaced tens of thousands of people trying to escape from the murderous violence. Waves of immigrants from the northern triangle were flooding Mexico and the U.S., seeking safety. It was a catastrophic situation.

Two days later, Villa with a suitcase in hand arrived at the Mexico City International Airport. The airport was bustling with people tripping over one another. The shop owners aggressively attempted to corral tourists in an effort to strong-arm them into buying their cheap trinkets. Villa checked in his bag, but still had over an hour before his flight left. He decided to grab a hamburger at one of the little eateries in the airport. He took a bite and pushed the plate away. The meat tasted like dog food and the bun was hard and stale. He thought to himself, I should know better than to order American food in Mexico. It was never any good.

The flight was uneventful and Villa slept most of the way. He only woke up once when the airplane hit a rough patch of turbulence. Earlier, the elderly flight attendant, who had a nametag on her chest with the name Mable on it, had brought him a large glass of red wine. Like a potent tranquilizer, it put Villa out for the remainder of the trip. Villa had been in Honduras several times and considered the Toncontin International Airport one of the most dangerous places to land in the world. A night landing on the moving deck of an aircraft carrier was much safer. The Toncontin Airport was far more gut wrenching because of its unusual surrounding mountainous terrain and short runway. But what the hell, life was full of dangers and Villa was not one to let it get in the way of his mission.

The plane shuttered as its tires hit the runway with a jolt. It abruptly woke up Villa from his catnap. Within minutes, the aircraft arrived at the gate. Villa jumped from his seat and made his way out to the main terminal. As he visually scanned the area, he saw Brad Sosney, the head of the DEA office in Honduras. Brad approached Villa with a broad smile and gave him a hug. Villa liked him because he was an outstanding agent and worked hard to carry out his responsibilities. Brad was the rough and tumble type who loved a good brawl. He participated in ultimate fighting events, which were brutal fights to say the least, but he loved the sport. He had a muscular build and wore the scars from his numerous fights proudly.

Brad said, "Miguel, I hope you had a good flight. It is great to see you again. It has been quite some time since our paths have crossed!"

"It has been, but it is good to be here," replied Villa. "I hope the family is doing well."

Brad replied, "They are all doing well and thank you for asking. The informant we are going to use against the MS-13 gang is at the office waiting to meet you. He has been a member for fifteen years and became disillusioned with the group a few months ago because one of the leaders got his younger sister pregnant. Later, he dumped her for another woman and left her to fend for herself and the child. He is out for revenge and doesn't care how he gets it."

Villa smiled, "Treachery is the fabric that makes up the very character of all criminals. It is in their DNA and all we have to do is exploit it."

Before going to the U.S. Embassy where the DEA offices were located, Brad took Villa to the Hotel Plaza San Martin. The hotel was pristine white with gold trim and a dark blue awning in front. Brad parked in front and told Villa he would wait for him while he checked in. Villa hustled into the lobby and was impressed with its cleanliness and the sparkling light and dark tiles on the floor. After signing in, leaving a copy of his credit card and obtaining a room key, Villa took a small, quaint elevator to the third floor. The room was cozy and the white comforter on the bed made it inviting, but Villa had a lot to do and rest was not part of the equation. He heaved his suitcase on top of the bed and quickly left the room. He startled Brad, who had dozed off, as he opened the car door.

Brad yelled, "What the fuck!"

Villa laughed, "Relax, it's me! You need to get some sleep tonight so you don't have to do it during the day." Villa then slapped him on the head playfully.

The ride to the embassy located on Avenida La Paz was quick. As they arrived at the embassy, Villa admired the large, square structure housing the U.S. diplomatic mission, which,included a multitude of U.S. agencies, to include the DEA. Several men in dark blue pants and light-colored shirts approached the car once it had entered the front gate. They were the men who provided security to the embassy. Using a large mirror with a long extension, they scanned the undercarriage of the car for bombs. They also had Brad open the trunk of his car for their inspection. All was good and the guards lifted the second security gate and allowed Brad to drive through. After parking in back of the embassy, Brad and Villa showed their credentials to a young marine dressed in a camouflage uniform. He closely scrutinized the credentials, especially Villa's and looked him up and down suspiciously. Finally, he handed their credentials back and pushed a button opening the heavy bulletproof door. Both men walked briskly through the door towards a large elevator on the right. After a minute the doors opened and both men slid in quietly. The elevator moved slowly up to the third floor where the DEA was situated. It was a small office consisting of six agents and a secretary. They were tasked with the huge responsibility of trying to stop the movement of cocaine from Colombia through Honduras. Once it arrived safely in Honduras, it was quickly smuggled into Mexico and then to the U.S., its final destination.

Villa was soon introduced to Juan Salinas who was quietly seated in an interview room. Salinas stood up from his chair and shook hands with Villa. Salinas was dark skinned and extremely thin, which made his clothes seem ten sizes too large. He had tattoos throughout his arms and face with the typical MS-13 insignias. Villa didn't waste any time and immediately got down to business. He knew that revenge was the motive behind Salinas's cooperation and he played it to the hilt. He didn't want Salinas to have a change of heart as they moved forward.

Villa told Salinas, "I know what happened with your sister and that was a terrible thing. You have to ask yourself about the loyalty of those you call your brothers in the MS-13. No brother would have fucked you by getting your sister pregnant and then dumping her like she was nothing more than trash."

With a deep frown, Salinas said, "Claro! It is very true and that is why I'm here. I no longer consider myself a member of the gang and will now help you bring all of them down. Pinches putos!"

Villa asked him, "I understand that you can introduce me to the head of the gang here in Honduras."

"Si, that is true. His name is Santos Rodriguez. He took control of the MS-13 by killing five of his rivals. He then slowly killed off all the others that he thought were his enemies. He is a psychopathic killer and doesn't know the meaning of remorse or compassion."

After completing the debriefing of Salinas, Villa came up with a cover story that Salinas would use in making the undercover introduction to Rodriquez. It had to be airtight. No mistakes from here on out!

Villa told Salinas, "You will tell Rodriguez that I'm a drug trafficker from Mexico and that my name is Miguel Sanchez. You will mention that I am interested in buying large quantities of cocaine on a regular basis if the price is right. If he asks, you tell him I'm into the heroin business, but want to diversify and get into cocaine distribution as well. Keep the information simple and don't go into a lot of detail. Got it?"

"Muy bien, I understand. I will meet with Rodriguez tomorrow and will let you know how it goes. Ok?"

Villa made one last remark, "Just play on his greed!"

Salinas smirked and stood up. He extended his hand and shook Villa's hand as if to say, "We are in this together." Villa knew that being the predator or prey could change as quickly as the tropical winds.

The following day, Brad received a telephone call from Salinas who advised him that an introduction had been arranged with Rodriguez. The gang leader was eager to meet the potential new client. The meeting would take place at a restaurant called La Cacerola located on 1642 Calle Copan at 3pm. Salinas would arrive an hour early at the restaurant to meet with Villa and go over any details before the arrival of Rodriguez. It was a go!

Brad met with Villa and made arrangements for surveillance during the negotiations with Rodriguez. It was decided that it was too risky to follow Rodriguez after the meeting and therefore Brad and some of his agents would only be in the area to provide security to Villa. At exactly 2pm, Villa entered the restaurant, which radiated a cozy ambience. It had bright yellow walls and small round wooden tables and leather cushioned chairs scattered throughout the dining area, He found Salinas sitting in an isolated corner towards the back, glancing nervously at the front door. Villa shook hands with him and pulled out one of the wooden chairs positioning himself to face the door. Villa never sat with his back to the door. It was too damn dangerous!

Salinas said, "Rodriguez is very interested in meeting with you. He is seeing big dollar signs, but make no mistake, he is more treacherous than a fucking rattlesnake. Es un bandido!"

Villa responded, "I understand! You told him the cover story I gave you, right?"

"Of course! He asked me a lot of questions, but I told him he should ask you."

Rodriguez arrived thirty minutes late with three other men wearing khakis and white t-shirts. They all had gang tattoos on their arms. Rodriguez approached Villa and introduced himself as Santos. The men with him looked at Villa warily and slowly moved away and took another table on the other side of the room.

Villa quickly sized up the top leader of the gang as a ruthless psychopath by his coldness and lack of empathy by the way he spoke. Rodriguez was tall, dark skinned, and had short cropped hair. He was covered with tattoos on his face, arms and neck. The MS-13 symbol was prominently displayed on his right forearm with a serpent wrapped around it. Villa thought he looked like a poster child for a cheap tattoo parlor.

Villa had studied his criminal record and found out that he had served twelve years in a prison for the cold-blooded murders of two men who had stolen five kilos of cocaine from him. He had strung them up by their feet, poured gasoline over them and set them on fire. It was reported that Rodriguez laughed crazily as their screams of pain filled the air. He was incarcerated in a prison called La Granja outside of La Ceiba and while there had led a massacre of sixty-nine rival gang members. As a result, the Honduran government had divided prisoners into three groups, MS-13 (active gang members), Pesetas (former gang members), and Paisas (those who had never been in gangs before their incarceration). Rodriguez had miraculously escaped being charged with the killings. No one dared testify against him. It would have been an instant death sentence.

Rodriguez smirked at Villa and stared intensely into his eyes. "I understand you are interested in buying some of my white powder."

Villa returned the stare and didn't blink, "I am, if the price is right. I am looking to buy a ton of coke every month. I need a reliable source and good quality merchandise. Understand! If you can't do it then we will both walk away and not have any issues with one another."

Rodriguez laughed loudly and slapped Villa on the back. "Estas loco! A ton is nothing for me. I sell tons every month. It will not be a problem as long as you have the money. But if you fuck me, I will cut your head off and hang it on a light pole, where everyone can see my artistic talents."

Villa quickly responded, "And if you fuck me, I will cut your balls off and feed them to the street dogs. How much per kilo?"

Rodriquez chuckled and then whispered to Villa, "I will let you have each one for fifteen thousand and you can be sure that it is a hundred percent pure. You will not have any problem getting rid of it."

Villa with a serious, almost menacing look on his face responded to Rodriguez's offer, in a strong voice, "You are not talking to a fool. Your price is fucking bullshit. You are paying about five thousand dollars depending on your supplier. I know you have to make a profit, but so do I. I will give you eight thousand for each kilo. I have to take the risk of getting it through the border into Mexico and all the way to the U.S."

Rodriguez chuckled, "I just wanted to see if you would bite because then I would know that you were a drug agent. We have a deal. I will start making arrangements and you better have the money. It will only take me a few days to have it delivered here."

Rodriguez and Villa shook hands in a firm grip, as if testing each other, to see who was stronger. Villa told Rodriguez that he would be in touch soon and then waited until Rodriguez left, followed by his goon squad. After a few minutes, Villa left the restaurant after peering outside to see if he was being watched. He stepped outside and flagged down a beat up old taxicab. He jumped in the back seat and had the cabbie drive in circles until he was sure no one was following him. After twenty minutes, he had the cab driver drop him off three blocks from the hotel. Villa was tired and it was only the adrenaline rush that was keeping him going.

In the succeeding days several conversations took place between Rodriguez and Villa. Villa kept pressing Rodriguez for a definitive date as to when he would deliver the cocaine. On one cloudy, dreary day, Villa and Rodriguez sat outside of the Restaurant Dorado in the central Morazan Plaza, sipping margaritas made with cheap tequila. Villa could see the well-preserved Spanish colonial architecture of the surrounding area and appreciated the Cathedral of Saint Michael the Archangel that dominated the entire landscape. He thought to himself, "Too bad, I have to be here with this scumbag. I could really enjoy this with anyone else, including the devil." Villa could no longer keep his impatience within him. He turned abruptly to Rodriguez and asked forcefully, "When can I expect you to deliver the cocaine? We have been talking for a week and nothing has been resolved!"

Rodriguez grinned revealing several gold-capped teeth. He whispered, "All in good time, my friend. You have to stop being so impatient and enjoy life, otherwise you will die from a heart attack or worse a bullet to the head." He burst out laughing and Villa had half a mind to grab him by his scrawny throat and choke him out.

Rodriguez, with a fourth-grade education, had become one of the richest men in Honduras by trafficking cocaine. In the past few days, he had been encountering problems with his source of supply based in Cali, Colombia. The Colombian National Police had been conducting large anti-drug operations in the area and everything was at a standstill until they left. He knew it was only a temporary setback and he was stalling Villa until he received a call from his source that everything was back on track. Rodriguez was suspicious of Villa simply because he didn't know him well. He had been introduced to him by an acquaintance that he trusted. Regardless, Rodriguez had a motto, "Trust, but verify." He continually questioned Villa and then would ask the same questions at a later time to see if his answers matched. They always did and Villa's calm and deliberate demeanor impressed him. Rodriguez noticed that nothing rattled Villa. After their initial meeting Rodriguez was suspicious of Villa, however Rodriguez was greedy and decided to move forward and deliver the ton of cocaine to Villa. He also knew that everything was stacked in his favor. It was his area and he had a virtual army of gang members.

After finishing their fourth margarita, Villa told Rodriquez to call him when he was ready to do the deal. Villa also told him, "I will not wait more than three more days since I have other business to attend to. I have been here wasting fucking time with you."

"Ok, ok, man! Have some fucking patience. I am just as frustrated as you. Don't worry it will happen. In the end, we will both make millions of dollars. You will be very happy with the quality of the product and I know that you will be my client for a long time."

Villa stood up and almost knocked the table over. "Esta bien! I am going to my hotel. You know my number. Call me when you hear something. I am quickly tiring of this shit."

Rodriquez frowned, "Don't worry man! I will call you soon. Do you want me to get you a girl? We have hundreds that work for us as prostitutes. I can send you as many as you want and I won't even charge you."

Villa got a murderous look on his face and said, "I am not into prostitutes. You are a fucking lowlife for using young girls as sex slaves. In our prisons in the U.S., you would be killed in less than a day for that type of crime. We don't tolerate that crap."

Villa quickly flagged a taxi, which looked like it had seen better days. He told the skinny driver, in tattered clothes, to drive him to the Humaya Inn. Earlier in the day, he had switched hotels. He believed that staying in the same hotel could compromise his safety. The taxi driver zipped through traffic as though they were standing still. He cursed and honked his horn at everyone he passed. He almost ran over a couple that were crossing the street and at the last second stepped on the brakes. Villa pitched forward and almost went head first into the front windshield. The cab didn't have seatbelts and Villa noticed that it also lacked air bags. Safety was not a priority in this country.

A few minutes later, they arrived at the hotel and Villa paid the cabby in Lempiras, the currency used in Honduras. He felt sorry for the kid and gave him a large tip, which was extravagant by Honduran standards. Villa stood in front of the small, brown colored hotel and was amazed at how much it resembled the pueblo architecture of his home state of New Mexico. It had been at least a year since he had visited his hometown of Española. He missed the cool, crisp air and the beautiful Sangre de Cristo Mountains. Villa was a proud son of New Mexico where he had been born and raised with traditional values. He made a mental note to make every effort to visit there soon. He knew that it would be difficult to get away. In his profession one couldn't just breakaway from ongoing operations. But yet, he would try!

Villa entered the small hotel lobby that was eerily quiet and didn't have the normal hustle and bustle of most hotels. Once in his room, he walked to the window and used his cell phone to call Brad.

"Brad, just to let you know that I just met with Rodriguez and we are still in a holding pattern. He is such a smug son-of-a-bitch and it will be fucking great to put him behind bars. It is a good thing we decided not to have anyone do surveillance of the meeting. I know he had some of his idiots checking out the area."

Brad replied, "Not a problem! We will wait to hear from you. I have a vetted unit from the Honduran National Police on standby. I have not given them a lot of details, but they know something may be going down."

"Great! It is always good to use discretion in cases like this one. I will be in touch," said Villa.

Villa liked the concept of vetted units, which were groups of host country police at the national level that were trained for five weeks at the DEA Academy situated at the Marine Corps. Base Quantico. They were trained on surveillance, investigations, informant recruitment and handling of same, interview and interrogation techniques, drug identification, evidence handling, arrest tactics, and other relevant courses. Prior to the training, each officer went through a background investigation, drug analysis, and polygraph examination. The vetted units allowed the DEA to pass sensitive information to them and minimize its compromise. As far as Villa was concerned the big issue with the Sensitive Investigative Units (SIU's), as they were called, was that the upper chain of command was not vetted. As a result, he was still cautious with the units.

Early the next day, Villa received a call on his cell from Rodriguez. Villa was not in a good mood. He had not been able to sleep because of the cheap liquor he had drank the previous day. Villa said, "What the fuck do you want so early in the morning? It better be good."

Rodriguez laughed, "I have some good news. The merchandise will be here in three days. Let's meet at the same place as yesterday so we can discuss."

In a sarcastic tone, Villa replied, "Fuck no! I am not going to that shithole. I didn't sleep at all last night because of the moonshine they serve there. Name another place."

Rodriguez was equally sarcastic, "It is not my fault if you can't hold your fucking booze. Okay, let's meet at the El Torito that is located on Calle Ruben Dario. It is one of the best steak restaurants in Tegucigalpa. I will see you at noon."

Villa arrived at the trendy restaurant with heavy wooden tables and chairs with blue leather cushions. The walls were a light shade of red and it was dimly lit. At the center of each table was a white linen napkin and Melinda's hot sauce produced in Belize. Villa sat and waited for Rodriguez. Meantime, he ordered a local beer, Salva Vida, to quench his dry throat. Villa was not a beer drinker, but once in a great while he indulged, especially if it was ice cold.

Ten minutes later, Rodriguez walked in with a swagger wearing a white tank top with his gang tattoos in full display. He came in with two other goons who could have been his twins and they too were covered with the same ugly tattoos.

Rodriguez said, "Horale! These are some of my men who wanted to meet you."

Villa responded, "Do you really feel a need to call attention to yourself with all the MS-13 tattoos?"

All three men laughed and Rodriguez proclaimed, "You forget that we control this country and everyone fears us. No one dares fuck with us otherwise we will kill them like dogs." Rodriguez and his men ordered the same beer that Villa was drinking. Everyone raised their bottles and touched them with a loud clinking sound and said, "Salud."

Rodriguez leaned over to Villa and said, "The cocaine will be here in three days and it will be coming from Barranquilla on the Colombian north coast. It is being shipped on a go-fast boat and we will meet it about two kilometers from the town of Tela near a stretch of isolated beach. You will come with us so you can see how we do things here."

Villa grinned broadly, "Good news and I look forward to seeing how professional you are. Are you doing the offload during the day or night? How many men will you use for the operation?"

Rodriguez proclaimed, "We only do the operations at night. It is less risk, and why do you want to know how many men we will use?"

Villa again smiled, "Cabron, if I am going to be out there with you I want to know that there is going to be enough security, understand?"

"Bien! I am going to have about fifteen of my best men out there to provide security and a couple of trucks to move the cocaine to a stash location. Once you give us the money, it is all yours," commented Rodriguez.

Villa's mind quickly began to envision everything that would be involved in the planning of a successful operation involving the seizure of the cocaine and the arrests of the gang members. Suddenly, Rodriguez interrupted his thoughts.

Rodriguez mumbled, "Vamos! I want to show you something. It is only a few blocks away, we can walk there."

They walked along the uneven, cracked concrete sidewalk for seven blocks and then went down an alley full of trash and empty beer bottles. Finally, they came to a large isolated field covered by weeds. In the middle of the field were about thirty individuals with buzz cuts. Many were not wearing shirts. They all had the same tattoos as Rodriguez. It looked like an international tattoo convention.

"We are initiating two new members into the Mara Salvatrucha or the MS-13, as we are usually called," said Rodriguez. "Our initiation ritual is called a "beat down" where they will be punched and kicked by several of us for sixteen seconds. It will show us that they have the balls necessary to do our bidding."

One of the inductee's, a skinny kid of about fifteen years, got into the middle of the gang members and six larger men immediately surrounded him. They moved in like ravenous animals moving directly towards a piece of meat and they started kicking, punching, and even biting him. He screamed in pain, but held out until the sixteen seconds were over. As soon as the beating stopped, they lifted him off the ground and yelled, "Welcome to the Mara Salvatrucha." The second teenager, with missing teeth, had coarse black hair. He smiled as they pounced on him. He fought like a madman and actually knocked out two of his attackers. He screeched and cussed like he was possessed and gave more than he received.

Rodriguez laughed, "Cojones, muchos cojones! That is exactly who I want in our ranks someone who is not afraid despite being outnumbered."

Someone brought out several coolers of ice-cold beer and Villa had one and then told Rodriguez that he was leaving to plan the logistics for getting the cocaine into Mexico and then into the U.S. Rodriguez only mentioned that Villa better have the money once he was given possession of the cocaine, otherwise there would be hell to pay. Villa just frowned at him and turned and walked away. He walked a few blocks and caught a cab back to the hotel. It had been a long day.

Later in the evening, Villa, on his cell phone, called Brad's cell phone. It turned out that Brad was still working at the office. Villa could tell the fatigue in his voice, but he knew that dedicated agents always burned both sides of the candle and didn't go home until the job was done. Villa was also tired, but asked Brad to meet him several blocks away at a hole-in-the-wall diner that was quiet. After brushing his hair and changing clothes, Villa left the hotel through a back door and walked through forbidding and dark alleys to avoid being followed. He could hear dogs barking nearby and a half moon was shrouded in black clouds. He jumped a fence and ripped his pants near the ankle on a protruding piece of wire. He cursed, but kept moving rapidly. Suddenly, he stopped and could hear someone's footsteps behind him. He quickly crouched and hid under a large bush and pulled out his Beretta 92F semi-automatic pistol that was concealed in his waistband under his loose-fitting shirt. The tap, tap of shoe heels against the pavement got louder. Villa peered out from the bush and saw it was a street beggar who was probably looking for a place to crash for the night. Villa continued through the eerie alleyways avoiding the empty liquor bottles scattered everywhere.

Finally, he reached the small café and, before entering it, quickly scanned the outside surrounding area to see if he saw anyone, but it was deserted. He darted into the café and found Brad sitting at a corner table. The only other patron was an old lady with white hair, dressed in tattered clothes.

Villa smiled, "Nothing better than a five-star eatery! Thanks for coming."

Brad laughed, "Hell, yes! Eating at these great places is one of the perks of DEA foreign assignments, right?"

Villa's tone then got serious, "Listen, everything is

getting geared up. According to Rodriguez, the coke will be transported on a go-fast boat coming from Colombia. An MS-13 off-load crew will wait for it about two kilometers from the Atlantic coastal village of Tela. You should also know they will have about fifteen gang members involved in the operation. Also, Rodriguez expects me to go with them. I know it is dangerous, but they will suspect something is wrong if I don't go. Besides, our operation will go much better if I am on the ground."

Brad responded, "You are either a brave son-of-a-bitch or crazy as hell! You know that even a small error will cause your death. Okay, what plan do you have in mind?"

Villa laid out the plan in detail, "I will need a miniature personnel tracker that will allow you to track me and also give you timely geo-coordinates on the exact offload location. We need to preposition a group of your guys in the immediate area so they can communicate with you via HF radio and also respond on the ground when the time is right. We will also require some air support in the form of helicopters to transport assault teams, but also have heavy weapons to provide air support once our people are on the ground. Is there cell phone coverage in the area of Tela?"

Brad took mental notes and said, "Sounds like you have covered all the bases. I will coordinate all this, first thing in the morning with my guys and brief them on our plan. For helicopter support, I will call the U.S. military's Joint Task

Force Bravo located at Soto Cano Air Base. It is a Honduran military base that is also used by our government. I can get at least two Blackhawk helicopters and they are each equipped with two 7,62 mm machineguns, which is plenty of firepower. I can also have them prepositioned close to Tela for a quick response. I don't want to see your ass get blown away by these violent gang bangers. Fortunately, there is cell phone coverage throughout Honduras."

Villa added, "The signal for you to move in with the Honduran police will be when I call you on the cell phone. I will have your number preset and will just push the button to dial your cell phone. I can do that without taking the phone out of my pocket. The secondary signal, just in case, will be when I take off a baseball cap that I will be wearing. Your men will have to get close and should have some night vision goggles. It will probably be pitch dark out there."

"I am concerned that you will be right in the middle of these scumbags if it escalates into a firefight," said Brad. "The Honduran police will just open up and spray the area and will not be concerned about you being there. You could end up being another DEA casualty."

Villa laughed, "It is a risk that we are used to taking. What the hell, we can't live forever, right?"

Both of them laughed and settled down to enjoy a few shots of tequila. They talked about war stories and remembered old friends and family. The bond between Brad and Villa was strong and made rock solid by common shared danger. Villa and Brad shook hands and departed silently into the dark shadows. Villa took the same route back to his hotel. Once in his room, he took a long hot shower, then went to bed.

The next afternoon Brad called and told Villa that two Blackhawk helicopters would be deploying the following morning to an isolated area next to the Aguan River about five kilometers from Tela. The helicopters would be transporting seventeen Honduran National Police officers and five DEA agents. They would be on standby until the day of the operation. Six DEA agents, brought in from Mexico City, would be on the ground near Tela and once they had solid coordinates they would surreptitiously approach the area to assist in the operation. They would be equipped with Sight mark SM15070 Ghost Hunter night vision goggles. Importantly the goggles had a high-powered infrared illuminator, which provided a bright, clear image. Brad also mentioned that he would have one of his female agents drop off two miniature satellite trackers within the hour. Two, just in case one malfunctioned. Brad stated that he had borrowed them from the CIA that also had an office at the U.S. Embassy in Tegucigalpa. The devices could track a target within five feet anywhere in the world. They would certainly do the trick. The CIA's budget allowed for the research and development of sophisticated technology. Federal law enforcement agencies that did more dangerous work against terrorism, to include drug trafficking were not provided the same funding or resources. They did it on sheer tenacity, determination, and pure guts.

An hour and a half later there was a soft knock on Villa's door. He grabbed his Beretta from the nightstand and walked quietly across the room and looked out the peephole of the door. He saw a young attractive woman about thirty years old standing outside. Villa opened the door.

The woman introduced herself, "Hi, I'm Maria. Brad sent me to bring you the tracking devices. He wanted me to come, since I am not well known here. I just transferred here two weeks ago from New York."

Villa smiled, "Thanks for coming. I hope you are enjoying Honduras thus far. It has a lot of challenges, but I am sure that you are up to the task."

She handed Villa a small plastic bag with two small personnel trackers the size of a dime. They would work perfectly since Villa could hide them in his clothes, cell phone, or even in his shoes. There was something to be said about micro technology. Villa's geo-coordinates could now be tracked by satellite on a real time basis, which was critical to the operation. It would boil down to technology, planning, coordination, communication, perfect timing and execution. If any of these factors went awry, things would get very ugly, especially for Villa who would be in the midst of some very treacherous and murderous men.

Maria sat on a wooden chair while Villa examined the

trackers. She smiled each time Villa looked at her. Villa could sense a connection, an intense one. He was sure that she felt it as well. As they talked, he studied her beautiful facial features with high cheekbones and voluptuous lips. He loved her shimmering blond hair that greatly complemented her ice blue eyes. Her smile could make an iceberg melt. Forget about global warming!

After about fifteen minutes, Maria said she had to go. Villa sensed that she was reluctant to leave, but didn't do anything to impede it. His instinct was to take her in his arms and kiss her, but he was cautious about relationships. Working undercover demanded strict concentration. Thoughts that caused detractions were dangerous.

Maria said, "It is really great to meet you. I could stay here and chat with you all evening. Hope everything goes well with your operation."

"Thank you," said Villa. "Will you be involved in it?"

She smiled again, "Of course, I would not miss it for the world. I want to hit the ground running here and this would provide me with that opportunity." Maria left as quietly as she had come. Villa closed the door behind her and secured the safety chain. He sat on the bed and played and replayed the operation in his mind and came up with different contingencies in the event things didn't go as planned. Villa was a meticulous strategist and he was not one to leave loose threads dangling in the wind. He lived and survived by his wit. He had been involved in many undercover operations, in which his back up had failed to show up or they had not seen the bust signal, leaving Villa in great danger. Villa was quick on his feet and became very proficient in coming up with solutions on the fly.

Just before bed, Villa got into the shower and was grateful for the strong water pressure. It was not long after, that he started to doze off when he heard a faint knock on the door. He threw the covers off and walked to the door and looked through the peephole. Wow! It was Maria. He quickly opened the door and in a rush Maria embraced Villa kissing him with wild abandon. Villa responded and tore off her clothes. They fell onto the bed. They made incredibly passionate love for hours. Completely spent, they lay next to each other.

"That was amazing," said Maria. "I wanted you the moment we met. I expected you to make the first move, but all is well that ends well."

Villa responded, "I felt the same way, but my discretion overcame my desire. You are a beautiful woman and I am surprised you are not married."

"Like you, I am married to the job," said Maria. "Unfortunately, it is the nature of the beast. You, however, exude masculinity and sexuality. I know I am taking a big bite of the fruit of the poisonous tree. But you are definitely worth it."

Villa blushed, "Thanks, I hope we can spend some time after the operation is over. If everything goes well, of course!"

Maria laughed, "You are a strategic thinker and I know you have planned it well."

Very early the next morning, Maria jumped out of bed and took a quick shower. She dressed and slid her feet into her fashionable red shoes with four-inch heels. They made her legs look longer and much sexier. Villa took everything in and wished they could spend the entire day together. But he knew that much had to be done in preparation for the following day. Maria needed to get ready to deploy with some of the other agents and time was of the essence. Before leaving, Maria hugged Villa and gave him a passionate kiss that made him dizzy.

Villa spent the entire day mulling over the operation over and over again. He checked his Beretta and made sure a round was chambered and the magazine had a full capacity of fifteen hollow point bullets. He also planned to have an extra magazine in his pocket, which gave him a total of thirty-one rounds. In a moment of humor, he thought that if he could not hit anyone with that number of rounds, he would just throw the gun at them. Just then, he remembered to set aside his portable phone charger to take with him. He could stick that in his pocket to ensure that his phone would not go dead at a critical time. Next to the charger, Villa placed his Denver Bronco's orange and black cap.

During the early evening, Villas went down to the hotel restaurant and ordered a traditional Honduran dish, which they called baleadas. It consisted of a flour tortilla with a generous filling of cheese, avocado, beans, scrambled egg, and ground beef. Villa liked it since it was similar to a burrito in his home state of New Mexico. After wolfing it down with an ice-cold coke he went back to his room. As he was starting to relax, his cell phone rang with the theme of the Godfather. It was Rodriguez.

"I have good news," he said. "My friends down south just confirmed that they will be here tomorrow at about seven in the evening. We will have to leave Tegucigalpa at noon to get there on time. It will take us slightly less than five hours to get to where we will meet with them. Make sure the money is in order. We are not transporting the merchandise any further than Tegucigalpa. Understand?"

"I get the picture," replied Villa. "I have told you several times the money is safe at a friend's house and is being guarded by my people. And don't get any funny ideas of trying to kidnap me for the money. They are under strict orders not to give you the money under any circumstances until we take custody of the product, got it? Holding me for ransom only means that you will have to kill me and the money will never get into your greedy hands."

"Why would you even think that we would do such a fucked-up thing," countered Rodriguez. "We don't play that way. We make more money having reliable and regular customers. Kidnapping is for petty criminals. The MS-13 gave up that bullshit business long ago. We ended up matando most of the people because no one wanted to pay for them."

"Where do you want me to meet you tomorrow?" asked Villa.

Rodriguez replied, "Do you know where the Basilica de Suyapa is located? We will pick you up there at noon tomorrow. Don't be late!"

"Everyone knows where it is," replied Villa. "I will be waiting for you there."

Villa had been to the Basilica several times to see the most revered religious image in Honduras, the Virgin of Suyapa. It was an 18-century statue of the Virgin Mary and each year thousands of people from all over Central America made pilgrimages to visit the statue on February 3, her name day. Although Villa was not religious, he believed that a little divine intervention was what he would need to survive what was about to happen. Once again, he began to strategize and have a plan for everything that might go wrong. He was all about expecting the unexpected and he was a firm believer of Murphy's Law, if anything could go wrong it would. After his usual psychological preparation, Villa called Brad and told him that they were on for tomorrow and gave him all the details provided by Rodriguez. Villa and Brad agreed that it would be too risky to try to follow them. It would be too easy to detect the surveillance. They would allow satellite tracking to work its magic. Brad mentioned that the helicopters were in place and some of his men were in the area of Tela and would quickly get to the operational site once Villa gave the bust signal.

Villa decided to go to bed early, he knew tomorrow would be a long day. He had been through these scenarios hundreds of times. The long trip to Tela meant that the MS-13 would have plenty of time to ask questions and test Villa. To Villa it was like being on the witness stand for days, during a trial, and being cross-examined by some of the best criminal attorneys in the country. It was grueling and psychologically tiring. He had to be on the top of his game and mistakes were certainly not an option. Regardless, Villa loved undercover work and the adrenaline rush that he felt when he was in extreme danger. It was truly exhilarating to him!

In the morning, Villa took a hot shower and checked and double-checked that he had everything he needed. When he was satisfied, he went downstairs and had scrambled eggs, thin sliced bacon, potatoes, and white toast with heavy butter. Before leaving, he went to the glass counter where the cash register was at and saw a box full of Milky Way candy bars. He purchased four of them paying four times what they cost in the U.S. He knew they were probably old and hard, but what the hell nothing was perfect. They would provide a good energy source and they were one of his favorites. It was all that mattered! Once outside, he flagged down an old taxi that was passing by. He jumped in the back seat that was full of grease and quickly stained his yellow and blue flowered Tommy Bahamas shirt.

"Fuck, this is a brand-new shirt and one of my favorites," he yelled.

The old wrinkled man shrugged his shoulders as to say, "What would you have me do?" The shirt probably cost more than the poor man's pay for a week. Villa felt bad after making the comment. He knew the old man probably didn't even own the cab and was making almost nothing for his day's work. They had traveled about half a mile when they came up to a stop sign. The old man stopped abruptly and three men in white cotton tank tops wearing the typical MS-13 gang tattoos approached the cab. They were all armed with semi-automatic pistols that looked like Browning 9mm's. Pointing them at the old man and Villa, they demanded money.

The leader growled, "Give me all your money and jewelry or I will fucking kill you! I have half a mind to kill you anyway."

Villa smiled, "Pendejos!" I am on my way to meet with your leader Santos Rodriguez and he is not going to be happy that you delayed me and more so that you tried to rob me."

"Santos," said the leader in total shock. His face dropped, "This is a big mistake, please forgive us! We will let you go on your way."

They walked away with their heads down and disappeared down an alley filled with garbage.

The cab driver sighed, "Gracias! Being a cab driver in Tegucigalpa is very dangerous. In the last two years a hundred and fifty drivers and thirty-two passengers have been killed here. The MS-13 wants us to pay a war tax that is most of the money we make. I am now looking for another job before these animals kill me."

Villa was solemn for the rest of the trip as he concentrated on making his best performance ever as an undercover agent. It had to be flawless. No errors! Nervousness was erased from his mind. He literally rewired his brain to become a drug trafficker. He expunged from his mind any memory of being a DEA agent. The transformation was complete and he was now ready.

Twenty minutes later the cab pulled up to the Gothic Basilica with its large stained windows. The white structure shot up into the blue sky and gleamed brightly under the rays of the sun. It was one of Villa's favorite churches and he was not a religious person.

Villa asked, "How much do I owe you? I have to say it was an exciting trip."

"I shouldn't charge you for making sure those fucking thugs didn't rob me," responded the cab driver. "Unfortunately, I need the money. It will be one hundred and seventeen lempiras."

This was the equivalent of five dollars. Villa felt sorry for the old man and slipped him a crisp, new fifty-dollar bill. Christmas had rolled around very early for the cab driver. Tears welled in his eyes and he thanked Villa profusely. Before getting out of the cab, Villa watched him fold the bill and then tuck it into his shoe. He was not taking any chances of being robbed of his small fortune. Villa smiled at him and left the cab.

The day was hot, but Villa was used to it. Over his career he had been assigned to many countries and areas with hot tropical climates. Because of this, he had developed a penchant for Hawaiian shirts. They kept him cooler than any other type of shirts. He loved their colorful designs. Villa didn't have to wait long before a black, Mercedes Benz AMG S63 sedan pulled up. The front passenger window opened and it was Rodriguez.

"Come on, we don't have all fucking day," he exclaimed. "I have sent most of my men ahead to get ready and make sure there aren't any soldiers or police in the area. We pay them to stay away, but sometimes they can be assholes."

Aggravated, Villa growled, "Fuck you! I have been waiting. It is you who just arrived. By the way, where did you steal the hundred thousand dollar car? You stick out like fucking vultures at a display of canaries."

Rodriguez howled with laughter and his gold teeth glowed eerily in the sun. Villa knew he was a classic psychopath, but then again, what trafficker wasn't. Villa jumped into the back seat and the car sped off in the blink of an eye. He could tell it was going to be a fun day. His adrenaline was already beginning to flow rapidly through his system. Now the ultimate chess game of life and death would be played out on some desolate beach along the Caribbean coast. Villa knew that he would be right in the middle of a murderous gang when the helicopters approached. The loud choppy sound made by the rotating blades would be heard from a distance. He knew the MS-13 gang members would immediately turn their attention to him once they heard the sound. He would be on his own for at least five minutes and have to survive the longest and most intense seconds of his life. Villa thought to himself, "What the fuck, I have been in worse situations before! What other job is more exciting?" Villa was just not psychologically wired to do humdrum work. He would rather die from a bullet than suffer painful boredom.

Rodriguez interrupted Villa's concentration, "Tell me how you plan on getting the cocaine into the U.S. Maybe we can go into business together, what do you think? We can make more money, if we pool our resources, sources of supply, routes, and the politicians we have in our pockets."

"Maybe we can, but I will have to see how this thing of ours goes today," replied Villa. "I have two tunnels that I built four years ago across the U.S./Mexico border. They cost me a little over a million dollars each and they paid for themselves with the first load I crossed."

Rodriguez bragged, "We get all the cocaine we want from the largest paramilitary group operating in Colombia, which is headed by Don Bernardo. He is godfather to my oldest daughter."

Does he always transport cocaine to you by boat?", asked Villa. "It is very risky to ship it by go-fast boat instead of by air."

Rodriguez laughed, "Sometimes it is shipped by twin engine airplanes, sometimes submarines, and other times on commercial trucks through the Pan American highway. It is transported using many methods. It keeps law enforcement off balance."

The conversation went back and forth between Villa and Rodriguez, continuing their verbal cat and mouse game. The two other men in the car remained silent and just listened to the banter. Villa noticed that the one sitting next him had about ten tattooed teardrops running down from each of his eyes. Each one represented a murder he had committed. Rodriguez obviously had brought some of his most ruthless killers with him. They would not hesitate to pull the trigger. In fact, they callously loved snuffing out lives.

The trip took them through poor, small villages and the two-lane roads were in horrible disrepair with large gaping potholes that dotted the entire highway. After hours, they arrived at the town of Tela. The downtown area had a paved main road, but all the side streets were made of dirt. Villa noticed the main street was a bustling business district with small grocery stores, clothing shops, restaurants, Internet cafes, hotels and banks. The power lines hung from poles like black strands of spaghetti. Old men sitting on blue colored benches stared at the luxury car as it moved slowly through the busy streets. All the other cars were old, dented and had seen better days.

As they left the town behind, Rodriguez mentioned that they were a few kilometers from the place where they would wait for the load of cocaine. It was not long after that the driver pulled off onto a barely visible trail full of brush and weeds. It was a bumpy ride and the driver kept swerving to avoid rocks and holes. Villa thought it was such a waste of an expensive car to drive through such fucked up roads. About four kilometers later they came to an isolated beach where Rodriguez's men were milling around. There were about fifteen and all of them were carrying AK-47's or AR-15's. Several brown and black Toyota Land Cruisers were parked nearby. Villa also noticed a large farm truck next to them. Obviously, the truck would be used to transport the cocaine.

Rodriguez jumped out of the car, "Muchachos, is everything ready?"

A small, skinny boy of about seventeen years of age dressed in khaki pants and a torn orange shirt approached.

He answered, "Si jefe! We are ready and we have security in place all around us. We are also in contact with the boat using the HF frequencies the Colombians gave us. The boat should arrive in about an hour."

Rodriguez and the other two individuals with him opened the trunk of the Mercedes Benz and pulled out three AK-47's and a military rocket propelled grenade launcher with a large red grenade attached to it. Villa knew that the MS-13 and Mexican cartels had access to a vast array of military weapons left over from the many civil wars in Central America.

Villa stood among the well-armed gang members and watched the sun begin to set. He watched the brown sand beneath his feet and heard the continuous roar and crashing of the undulating surf. The smell of the salty breeze felt good. He looked to his left and saw a small grove of palm trees nearby. He knew that there was nothing more to do but wait for the boat to arrive. Villa was in the middle of a nest of rattlesnakes that were unpredictable and extremely menacing. He reached into his pants pocket and made sure his cell phone was still with him. He leaned against the Benz and waited. As the sun began to set in the west the MS-13 group talked loudly in Spanish and smoked cigarettes. Villa looked at them and thought it looked like a movie set of a futuristic rebel army that survived a nuclear holocaust, much like cockroaches.

After what seemed like an eternity someone yelled that the

boat was approaching. Villa looked and saw a large go-fast boat coming fast over the water. The hum of the powerful engines could soon be heard. As the boat got closer to the shore the engines were throttled back. He saw two dark-skinned men on the sleek, blue colored boat. Rodriguez yelled at some of his men to begin off-loading the cocaine. They formed a line and the men begin to pass the bales containing about thirty kilos to each other.

Villa calmly waited for most of the cocaine to be brought to shore. He didn't want to give the bust signal prematurely and have the boat speed away into the darkness. Villa watched as he saw a virtual mountain of cocaine piled up on the beach. It was time, he removed his cap and reached into his pocket and push the call button. He had preset it to call Brad's number. The operation would now reach critical mass! Rodriguez kept barking orders and the two boatmen now began to load twenty-five gallon plastic barrels of gasoline for their return trip to Colombia. The MS-13 had brought the fuel in the farm truck. Villa's adrenaline was now at its maximum level. He was in heaven!

No more than four minutes later, the sound of chop-chop-chop could be heard. The helicopters were rapidly approaching. The gang members dropped everything and brought their assault rifles to the ready. The helicopters made a low pass with their searchlights illuminating the ground. In seconds, all hell broke loose as the helicopters made their approach. The rattle of gunfire coming from the MS-13 was ear splitting. The gunners in the helicopters returned fire with the heavy machineguns. The repetitive sound of boom-boom-boom filled the night air. Villa ducked for cover behind the engine block of the Benz. He saw Rodriguez begin to point his rocket-propelled grenade at the semi-stationary helicopters. In an instant, Villa pulled out his pistol and fired two shots at Rodriguez from thirty feet away. One bullet went through his right shoulder causing him to drop the lethal weapon. The second projectile struck him in the right knee and he pitched forward into the sand screaming in pain. Villa's intent was to disable Rodriguez and not to kill him. He was more valuable alive and could provide valuable information on the MS-13 and their criminal activities. The hail of bullets now coming from the approaching ground forces and helicopters shredded the ranks of the MS-13.

A handful of survivors tossed their weapons onto the ground and put their hands in the air. The men on the boat were not going to surrender and they began shooting with AR-15's. Big mistake! One of the helicopters turned its heavy guns on the boat and in seconds turned it into a million toothpicks. Some of the hot projectiles hit the gas containers and it went up in a brilliant fireball. The cries of the dying and wounded replaced the deafening gunfire. Rodriguez lay on the ground writhing in pain.

One of the helicopters landed nearby while the other

remained in the air providing cover to those on the ground. Brad and Maria along with other DEA agents and Honduran National Police jumped out of the helicopter on the beach and approached Villa.

Brad smiled, "Great job! I thought you might have gotten hit in the crossfire. Our guys on the ground arrested several gang members who were providing security around the area. The National Police will take custody of the cocaine and we will join them when they interview Rodriguez and his cronies. You can ride back with us in the chopper."

Maria smiled and kissed Villa on the cheek. She was happy that he was still alive and kicking. Villa was elated to see her and wished he could be more passionate with her, but knew they had to be discrete. On the flight back to Tegucigalpa Villa relaxed and slowly the massive infusion of adrenaline began to ebb. He knew that depression would set in if he didn't engage in another dangerous mission soon. He was addicted to the rush of adrenaline. The only cure was putting his life on the line as soon as possible.

Upon arriving back very late, Villa and Maria met at the hotel lounge and had several drinks. They held hands and kissed each other. The animalistic passion they felt for one another was totally consuming. They were in a romantic mood when they went to Villa's room. They made hot passionate love for hours. Maria eventually fell asleep in Villa's arms and both slipped into a comfortable dream world where they escaped from the carnage and horror they had lived through that day.

They next few days were spent interrogating the MS-13 defendants. Rodriguez who was still in the hospital being treated for his wounds began to sing like a canary. He knew that the Honduran police would love to torture him and it was only a question of time before he spilled his guts anyway. Rodriguez gave a detailed confession on the politicians they had bribed and the Colombian paramilitaries who acted as their source for cocaine. He disclosed drug routes; money laundering schemes, and identified other MS-13 leaders in Guatemala and El Salvador. He gave information on several storage areas that led to the seizure of thousands of military grade weapons, including concussion and white phosphorous grenades. The information he provided also resulted in the seizure of hundreds of millions of dollars in properties, hotels, shopping malls, dairies, houses, cars, and bank accounts belonging to the gang. The DEA and Honduran National Police, based on the wealth of information provided by the incarcerated gang members, arrested over two hundred other gang bangers. The information also led to numerous wiretaps on both cell and hardline telephones being used by the organization. The data that was gleaned was far more important than the ton of cocaine that was seized.

The Honduran government had a small ceremony in which they presented Villa and the other DEA agents with their medal of honor for meritorious acts of bravery. The function was held at their training academy and everyone had a great time interacting with the Honduran police. Afterwards, Villa joined Brad and his agents for drinks at a rustic cantina with loud music blaring loudly from an old jukebox. They could barely hear each other talk, but they all had an enjoyable time blowing off steam. The operation against the MS-13 had been a huge success, but Villa knew that unless the DEA continued pursuing them with a vengeance they would mend their wounds and grow again like a malignant cancer. Villa and Brad came up with an idea to create a database that would be used strictly to create files on MS-13 gang members. It would allow the DEA to quickly identify them and track them, especially if they came to the U.S. They agreed to jointly write up a proposal so they could get funding then later coordinate the effort with the three northern triangle countries.

The next morning, Villa stopped by the U.S. Embassy to say goodbye to Brad and the other agents before heading to the airport to catch a flight back to Mexico City. His last farewell was to Maria. He walked into her office and closed the door. He kissed her passionately and they agreed to keep in touch. Villa knew that their relationship would not progress, since both were married to the job. He held her very tight, then let go and slowly walked out the door.

CHAPTER 8

Cartel Restructuring

Lisa took her role as the new leader of the Cartel of the North very serious knowing that it would be the most difficult undertaking of her life. She understood that the turbulent winds of treachery were both internal and external. Keeping a pulse on it was important, but her main responsibility, as she saw it, was growing the organization and making it more profitable and structurally sound. Lisa didn't believe in maintaining a status quo; that was for people with no vision and incapable leaders. She now wanted to take the cartel to new heights. It had to be efficient and generate massive profits that fueled survivability and power. Lisa's first priority was to restructure the cartel, but she would have to do it gradually.

Her first order of business was to create a governing council consisting of five of her most trusted regional bosses.

She also wrote rules and operational guidelines that defined the conduct and function of the council. Lisa would be the chairperson and the council would meet at least once a month or more often, if needed. During the initial meeting, the cartel leaders discussed the need to develop new sources for cocaine in Colombia. The FARC was in disarray and strong rumors indicated that the government had forced them to the negotiation table to discuss a potential peace accord. They also spoke of creating a new business model for the cartel, which would carve out new criminal enterprises other than just drug trafficking. Lisa decided that the cartel would now expand into extortion, kidnapping, and the theft of petroleum. The gas pipelines from the state owned Petroleos Mexicanos, better known by its acronym PEMEX, ran through areas controlled by the cartel and they could make millions by tapping into them. Besides, the company was highly corrupt and unscrupulous politicians had ripped off billions. Lisa's rationale was that it was better if they profited from the petroleum rather than the puto politicians who professed integrity, but in reality were the true criminals.

Lisa commented, "We are going to become a global enterprise and make more money than most countries in the world. It will require much effort from everyone. Planning and strategic investment will be the key to our future."

Several days later, Lisa took Avianca flight 399 into Barranquilla, Colombia. Accompanying her was Gonzalo

Garcia who was now her second in command. Garcia was a former member of Mexico's Special Forces known as the Grupo Aeromovil de Fuerzas Especiales, the Special Forces Airmobile Group. He had reached the rank of Captain before being recruited by the Cartel of the North. He loved the military, but money was a far greater love for him. The motto of the Special Forces was "Todo por Mexico", but for Garcia it was now "Todo para mi." He was tall, good looking, and had olive green eyes. He was ruthless, but more importantly was extremely competent and loyal to Lisa. He watched her back and protected her. She had made him a member of the cartel's council.

Upon landing at the Ernesto Cortissoz International Airport, Lisa and Gonzalo confidently walked up to one of the Immigration officers checking passports. Both of them had false documents under assumed names. A corrupt official from the Secretaria de Relaciones Exteriores had provided the tourist passports for a few thousand dollars. The Colombian Immigration officer quickly stamped both passports with an entry stamp and waved them through. As they walked towards the exit of the airport a short stocky man with long black hair approached them.

He smiled, "Lisa?", to which Lisa nodded. Once he was satisfied that she was Lisa, he continued, "My name is Avaristo. I work for Otto. He sent me to pick you up. My car is right outside. Please let me help you with your bags. I hope your trip was enjoyable. Welcome to Barranquilla."

Lisa handed her bags to him and stated, "Muchas gracias. Thank you for coming. How is Otto?"

Avaristo replied, "He is well and looking forward to meeting you. It will take us less than an hour to get to where he is at."

Lisa, through some friends, had made contact with Otto who was one of the biggest cocaine traffickers in Colombia. He was of Lebanese descent and had a long bloody history working for armed groups in the country. Initially, he was a member of the guerilla organization known as the Popular Liberation Army. Later, he switched sides and became the head of the Urabenos, Colombia's most powerful paramilitary network. He was responsible for many atrocities and massacres. He was not a man to be trifled with. The U.S. had branded him a drug trafficker and a terrorist. A reward of ten million dollars was being offered for his capture. To date, there had been no takers.

The conversation was minimal as the driver drove close to the blue waters of the Caribbean Sea. The roads were old and pockmarked making it an unpleasant ride. Eventually, they approached a large, rural ranch home referred to as a finca in Colombia. Lisa immediately noticed about thirty men with assorted long weapons surrounding the area. Before being escorted into the house, both Lisa and Gonzalo were thoroughly searched by two large men. Once inside, they noticed opulent furnishings to include bronze sculptures by Fernando Botero, one of Colombia's most famous artists. They were given a glass of aguardiente and a few minutes later Otto came into the room. He was dark-skinned and had short cropped salt and pepper hair. He wore blue jeans and a flowered, tropical shirt.

Upon seeing them, Otto stated, "Bienvenidos, welcome to my humble home. It is a pleasure to meet you Lisa. I have heard many great things about you."

Lisa replied, "Gracias, it is also good to meet you. With me is my second in command, Gonzalo Garcia. I hope we can see our way to developing a solid business relationship that will be beneficial to both of us."

"Tell me, what quantities of my product are you looking to purchase? I know they have to be large, but want to hear specifics from you," Otto commented.

To that, Lisa replied, "Claro, they will be big amounts. I will purchase anywhere from seven to ten tons each month provided you can handle it."

Otto broke out into laughter, "You insult me, mi amor! Of course, I can supply you with whatever you want. I buy tons of coca paste from Peru and Bolivia every week and then covert it into hydrochloride in my labs in southern Colombia. I should also mention that the majority of the coca cultivations in Colombia are under my control. In other words, the three source countries in South America supply me. Does that answer your question?"

Lisa remarked, "That is great news because it means that I don't have to seek other sources to ensure a reliable and steady supply for cocaine. What will you charge me per kilo? Keep in mind that we are talking very large amounts, right?"

Otto looked at her for a moment and a frown formed on his face. He replied in a guttural voice, "I will give you a great bargain and will let you have each kilo for seven thousand dollars each. The quality is guaranteed and you will not find any better cocaine anywhere. Do we have a deal?"

Negotiations between drug traffickers were tough, but Lisa was no push over. She smiled and sat back on her chair. Looking at Otto squarely in the eyes, "Do you take me for a pendeja? You must think that you are dealing with a young schoolgirl! I have been around this business for a while and your price offends me. You must be fucking insane!"

Otto, like most traffickers, was greedy and wanted to get the highest price possible for his product. He smirked, "Okay, okay. Only because it is you, I will give you each kilo for three thousand dollars, but you will have to handle the transportation from Colombia to Mexico. We will provide airstrips and also staging areas along our coast if you choose to use boats for transportation. Additionally, we will take care of security and political protection on this end. Once the loads are in your hands they are your responsibility."

Lisa grinned, "That is much better. We have a deal and from now on it will be Gonzalo who will act on my behalf to coordinate the purchase of the cocaine and the logistical details."

Otto was also content with the agreement, stating, "That is fine. Before you leave, I will give you the radio frequencies that we use and the cell number to one of my men that will deal with Gonzalo. Obviously, we use code words and a list will also be given to you and once they are changed you will be notified. Well, let's have a little toast to our partnership."

Aguardiente was poured and shot glasses lifted into the air. They were brought together and the deal was now solidified and Otto uttered, "Salud! To money, love, and time to enjoy them!"

There were no formal contracts between drug traffickers and everything was done with a handshake. But all parties involved knew that to fuck the other by stealing drugs or money was a death sentence. There was no forgiveness because to do so was a sign of weakness and would encourage others to also take advantage.

After a few hours of discussions on how coordination and payments were to be made, the meeting began to wind down. Lisa, at the end, was able to get a concession from Otto in which she would only have to pay half the money up front for any quantity of cocaine and get the rest on consignment.

"Adios Otto, it was a pleasure to meet you and we should

all be happy that we have a deal in place! I will be in touch very soon," said Lisa.

"Of course, the pleasure was all mine and have a safe trip back home," replied Otto.

The following day, Lisa and Gonzalo returned to Mexico with great satisfaction that they had been able to make a connection with Otto. Lisa was pleased that she would only have to pay three thousand dollars for each kilo of cocaine. Once her organization crossed it into the U.S. it would sell for a hell of a lot more, depending on the geographical area.

Within months, Lisa's plan was moving forward. Her plaza bosses throughout the states of Chihuahua, Sonora, Baja California Norte, Tamaulipas, Coahuila, Durango, and Zacatecas were extorting money from lowly hotdog vendors to large unions, and global corporations. Millions of dollars began to pour in and Lisa knew they could now expand recruitment, purchase more weapons, and corrupt more officials. The plaza bosses were also now stealing hundreds of thousands of barrels of petroleum from the virtually unprotected oil pipelines in the country. Lisa did her homework and knew that Mexico had slightly over thirty-seven thousand kilometers of pipeline making it highly vulnerable. This criminal activity brought enormous profits. The Cartel of the North began to also corner the market on kidnappings by concentrating on super wealthy families that could be squeezed for millions of dollars.

Lisa's strategic plan for her cartel was highly ambitious, but things were starting to fall in place.

Next, she established training sites in different geographic areas in Mexico where her army of sicarios and new recruits could be trained in combat shooting, surveillance, concealment, torture, killing targets from a moving vehicle, and evasive maneuvers. The training sites had obstacle courses, firing ranges, and other areas that could be used to practice assassinations. She also built makeshift structures for the sicarios to learn tactical entries. She purchased hundreds of motorcycles for her sicarios. The motorcycles would facilitate the killings of designated targets because of their great mobility. They could weave through traffic and travel through areas that cars couldn't navigate, come up on their target, make a quick hit and disappear in seconds.

Now that her business was in its growth and expansion stage, Lisa fully incorporated her brother, Armando, into the business. By this time, he was one of the most capable attorney's in Mexico. He quickly bought two trucking businesses, which transported produce such as melons, tomatoes, and assorted vegetables to the U.S. These trucks would also be used to transport drugs mixed in with its legitimate cargo. To ensure that the trucking businesses appeared reputable, Armando put them under the name of a friend of his, who didn't have a criminal record.

Armando also established multiple accounts in several

international banks in Mexico. Apartment complexes, shopping centers, jewelry stores, dairies, homes, and properties were also purchased to launder the millions of dollars that the Cartel of the North was making each day. Apart from investing in legitimate businesses, Armando created shell companies, which took in dirty money for alleged goods or services, but actually didn't provide them. Armando and his accountants created the appearance of legitimate sales transactions for the shell companies through the creation of fake invoices and made periodic deposits into bank accounts established in the names of the shell businesses. Armando had the accountants create income statements, balance sheets and other financial statements for the businesses to further legitimize their shell businesses should anyone ever want to investigate them. He also adroitly used offshore accounts in Panama and the Cayman Islands, which had very strict bank secrecy laws. They allowed for anonymous banking. He conducted hundreds of bank transfers to and from these offshore banks. Armando came up with another scheme and had some of his people buy diamonds in the Los Angeles jewelry market and then smuggled them into Mexico in toothpaste tubes. They were then sold for cash once the Colgate was washed off. Armando's value to the Cartel of the North was invaluable and soon he had a small army of competent accountants and finance specialists working for him.

Lisa's other sibling, Anita, who was now a revered Santeria priestess, also had a role in the cartel. Most of its members, especially the sicarios, were highly religious and superstitious despite their violent dispositions. Anita set up shrines where the sicarios could go and pray before a statue of the Santa Muerte, the skeletal female deity. Santa Muerte was the personification of death, but was also associated with devine protection. The sicarios would light a candle in her honor, prior to carrying out an assassination. Anita would, on occasion, bless a handful of bullets so that they would find the intended target. Others would have her sacrifice a rooster to protect a drug load being sent to the U.S. Although, Lisa was not a believer she knew that her people were and if it fortified their resolve, it was well worth it. Besides, she completely trusted Armando and Anita. Being surrounded by family gave Lisa great comfort.

One day, Lisa met with Gonzalo to discuss strategy on how to corner more of the U.S. market. Lisa remarked, "We need to come up with a plan to expand into many more cities in the U.S. for our heroin, methamphetamine, cocaine, and marijuana. I think it is time for you to focus on all the major urban areas. We have many people from Mexico living in poverty in the U.S. that we can recruit to distribute our drugs. They know the cities in which they live in very well and all we have to do is get the drugs into their hands. The ones that are more entrepreneurial can handle multiple cities or states depending on their contacts."

Gonzalo replied, "Lisa, I agree with your concept completely. As a matter of fact, many of the people that work for us have family members living in Los Angeles, Phoenix, Tucson, Denver, Albuquerque, Houston, Dallas, Detroit, Miami, Chicago, New York City, and other large cities. But, it is imperative that we only get people who are smart and street savvy, because with pendejos, we are asking for major problems."

"Claro, Gonzalo! I will leave this project in your hands. Please plot it out on a map by next week and we can finalize it," Lisa said.

All of the cartels in Mexico and other countries had a pyramidal organizational structure with defined vertical authority. Lisa was of the opinion that this type of organization was susceptible to attack and exploitation by the police. She began to change the Cartel of the North by creating a more dynamic, robust and resilient horizontal structure. This type of structure would allow the authority for decision-making to flow horizontally across various components rather than moving downward in a formal chain of command. Knowing that her cartel was rapidly expanding globally, Lisa wanted to structure it like a subsidiary based company. Lisa felt that with this type of an expansion, she could better leverage resources and alliances to expand the financial and geographic scope of her criminal empire substantially.

Lisa was much smarter than any corporate CEO and definitely much tougher and much more cunning. She was well underway to supersizing the Cartel of the North.

CHAPTER 9

The Affair

Every year, the DEA in Mexico would have a management conference with all of the supervisors based in Mexico City and the bosses from the satellite offices scattered throughout the country. This year it was being held at the Fiesta Americana Hotel in the downtown area of Guadalajara, Jalisco the second largest city in Mexico. The conference was a very important forum to discuss investigations, operational and administrative policies, intelligence collection, security, and coordination with domestic offices. After the first day, Villa and some of his friends went out to dinner at the Santo Coyote Restaurant. Villa ordered the molcajete mixto, which consisted of chicken, beef and shrimp cooked with tomatoes, cilantro, onions, jalapeno peppers, and sliced cactus leaves called nopales. It was served in a bowl of basalt stone, which was called molcajete. It was one of his favorite dishes, especially with warm corn tortillas.

As they prepared to leave, Villa's cell phone rang and he stepped away from the table that was full of loud conversation. A man's voice greeted him, "Hola, Mr. Villa, this is Arturo Nieto and I am the executive assistant to President Imelda Maestas. She wishes to speak with you. Can you please stay on the line while I connect you?"

Seconds later an alluring voice came on, "Señor Villa, this is President Maestas. How are you?"

"President Maestas, what an honor. I am fine and thank you for asking. To what do I owe this great pleasure?"

"I have heard much about you and know that you are a man who can be trusted. My country, as you are well aware, is under siege from the drug cartels that are destabilizing my government by corrupting public officials and sending shock waves of violence into the very hearts of our citizens. Not even journalists are safe anymore. I would like to meet with you as soon as possible to discuss a potential solution."

Villa replied, "Of course, I am currently in Guadalajara at a conference, but I can fly back to Mexico City and meet with you early tomorrow afternoon. Is that convenient for you Madam President?"

President Maestas replied, "Claro, I look forward to meeting you in person tomorrow. Please have a safe trip back."

That night, Villa took a flight to Mexico City and was

excited to meet President Maestas. The next day in a brownish haze of pollution, Villa zigzagged at a snail's pace through relentless bumper-to-bumper traffic on Avenida Reforma. An old brown sedan whose driver was not paying attention came within inches of sideswiping Villa's car. Using his quick reflexes, Villa turned the car to the left, avoiding an accident that would have taken half a day for the local police to respond to and investigate. Almost an hour later he reached Bosque de Chapultepec with sprawling trimmed shrubs and manicured lawns. Scattered throughout the area were over a thousand ahuehuete trees that were considered the "lungs" of Mexico City because of the clean oxygen they produced.

As Villa approached Los Pinos, he was stopped by security and asked for identification. He whipped out his DEA credentials and the guards proceeded to do a thorough search of the car. Finally, one of them called ahead on a handheld radio. Through much static, Villa heard the words, "Que pase."

With a broad smile revealing several gleaming, silver-capped front teeth, the guard waved Villa through. Driving slowly, Villa came to the looming, white mansion with a large red, white and green Mexican flag in front, surrounded at the base of the flagpole by a low lying circular hedge. One of the Presidential guards approached, "Bienvenido a Los Pinos! I will take your car and park it for you."

Another guard approached and escorted Villa inside where

he had to present identification and sign a visitor's log. He was given a badge and then had to walk through a metal detector. Anticipating this, Villa had left his weapon in the trunk of his car. He walked down the Hall of Presidents, which had oil paintings of every president in the history of Mexico. A beautiful portrait of Guadalupe Victoria, the first President of the United Mexican States, caught his eye. Victoria was captured on canvas in his colorful red and black tunic, white pants, and knee high, black military boots, and a gleaming sword hanging on his left side.

Villa was asked to wait at an informal living room with two large white couches and a square glass coffee table. A short, dark haired woman entered and brought some tea and a tray of sugar cookies. A minute later, President Maestas quietly entered the room with two members of her staff that looked like twins. They were bald, heavy-set men and wore conservative dark suits with striped ties. Villa was taken aback by the natural beauty and grace of the President. She had dark hair and eyes. Her smile was captivating and she illuminated the room. She held out her hand, "Señor Villa, I am President Maestas and thank you so much for coming, es un placer."

"Es un honor, gracias por invitarme," answered Villa. I am here at your service and hope that I can be of help."

The President, wearing a beautiful red dress with black shoes, sat facing Villa and when she crossed her legs it sent cascading hot flashes into every pore of his body. With a serious look on her face she commented, "I asked you here because I need your help and would like your recommendations as to how I should address the drug problem in my country. It has become a national security threat and the violence is getting worse by the day. As you know, we have drugs going north to the U.S. and weapons flowing south into Mexico, which are being used here to commit wholesale slaughter."

Villa was pensive and said, "With all due respect, President Maestas, it is a complex problem and it is driven by the insatiable desire of my country to consume illegal drugs. We need to do a better job reducing the demand and that will require a community effort by families, religious institutions, and schools to educate our young. We have lost too many generations to this problem. With regards to Mexico, you need to eliminate corruption at all levels and the impunity that comes with it. You will also need to restructure the state and municipal police forces throughout the country. They are all corrupt and in the pockets of the drug cartels. The judiciary needs to be strengthened since they are extremely weak. I am sure that you are aware that only about three percent of criminal prosecutions are successful and rarely does anyone go to jail. Switching from your accusatorial justice system to an adversarial one like we have in the U.S. will help in many ways. Your system has become cumbersome and inefficient, and it lacks transparency."

President Maestas smiled, "All that you say is very true.

I have started to move forward to eliminate corruption, but it is no easy task since it is so ingrained in our culture. I have also introduced legislation to switch to an adversarial court system that somewhat mirrors the system in the U.S. Once it is passed, however, it will take years to educate all of our judges and prosecutors, build courthouses and necessary infrastructure. I can see your point in that this is a very complicated problem."

Villa replied, "Regardless, I am here to work with your government and the U.S. Embassy is also providing a lot of resources. We are continuing to exchange information with your security forces, and those exchanges have had some significant results."

"Thank you! It makes me feel better," stated President Maestas. She continued, "By the way, I would like to continue our discussion. Sometimes, I sneak out of Los Pinos and go incognito to get away from this job if only for an hour. Perhaps we can meet again. I will let you know."

Villa grinned, "Sure, we can have dinner at my place since you would be recognized at any restaurant. Besides the State Department people would not appreciate me interacting with you."

"I understand. We will keep it to ourselves," replied President Maestas.

Villa provided her with his address and his personal cell number. They agreed that on any calls between them she would identify herself as Leticia and Villa would use the name of Victor. Shortly thereafter, Villa shook hands with the President and one of the guards walked him to his car. He was smitten with President Maestas. She was highly cultured, educated, and ultra-sexy. Her smile melted him. He knew that he shouldn't see her, but sometimes even hardened DEA agents succumbed to the beauty and charm of the opposite sex.

Lisa was working harder than ever and one day one of her plaza bosses came to see her. Ricardo, one of her most trusted leaders, arrived at the safe house she was hiding. Ricardo had previously been a top official with the Policia Federal de Caminos, which was the U.S. version of the State Police, but in Mexico it was a federal agency. He was tall and walked with a swagger. He was missing his right ear that had been severed during an accident several years before. He told Lisa, "Buenos dias, Jefa! I have some good news. One of my men has a friend who is working for the Invincible Jalisco Cartel under that perro Jaime Santana. He passed information that the cartel just imported a ton of cocaine from Colombia through the seaport of Manzanillo, Colima. As you know it is one of the busiest ports in the country and Santana now controls it."

Lisa had a puzzled look, "Why is he giving us this information?"

Ricardo answered, "He is angry with another cartel member who is having an affair with his wife. Apparently, he told Santana, but he did nothing to resolve it. Also, he is looking to get paid for helping us steal the cocaine. If we agree to pay him two hundred thousand dollars, he will let us know when they start to move it to the U.S. border. What do you think, Jefa?"

Lisa with a grin, "I think that something unexpected and great has just fallen into our lap, but we must be careful it is not a trap. Those hijos de puta are treacherous snakes, so let's proceed with caution."

Later that night a thunderstorm sent jagged lightning bolts streaking across the dark night. Lisa was startled and woke up in a cold sweat. She was startled a second time when her cell phone rang. It was Ricardo on the other line. He whispered a coded message, "The party is on for tomorrow. The birthday girl will be leaving the area of Guadalajara and plans to travel to Nogales. I will be there in a couple of hours so we can plan all of the festivities. Fucking weather is miserable. See you soon!"

Lisa was now fully alert, "Gracias, Ricardo! I will have Gonzalo here as well so we can all meet to plan a great surprise party. Be careful."

Actually, Lisa convened the entire council of the Cartel of the North. All had arrived in Juarez by mid-afternoon despite the weather. Ricardo provided a briefing based on all the information he had obtained from his contact. The ton of cocaine would be transported in a large truck and would be mixed in with a load of avocados in large wooden crates. The truck bearing Jalisco license plates JDD-45-42 would only have one driver in order to avoid suspicion. Two black Toyota RAV4's loaded with sicarios would follow it and provide security all the way to the border. A third Toyota would travel two to three miles in front of the load truck to check for roadblocks. If they detected any, they would alert the load truck by radio, which would be more than enough time for it to turn around and avoid the checkpoint. All of them were armed to the teeth with handguns and AK-47's.

Using a large map of Mexico, Lisa and her council plotted the route the rival cartel would have to take. The only viable road was highway 15 that stretched from the southern part of Sonora all the way up to the border city of Nogales. All the other roads were so fucked up they would not dare risk such a big cargo of cocaine by using them. Additionally, the Mexican military was now conducting widespread surveillance on all unimproved roads used by drug traffickers. The plan by Lisa and her council was hatched quickly and they would leave later that afternoon in order to be in place early. Lisa wanted a piece of the action. By putting herself out there, she kept her psychological edge in dealing with dangerous operations. It was important to keep her instincts highly sharpened.

In the early morning hours, in the cover of darkness, Lisa and her men arrived at an isolated stretch of highway

15 between the cities of Navajoa and Ciudad Oregon. She pushed the button on her radio, "Hugo, me escuchas?"

A long pause and then, "Si, mi jefa! I can hear you. What are your orders?"

Lisa again, "I want you to take two cars further south near the Sinaloa border to let us know when the truck passes. This will give us plenty of time to get ready, understand? Once it goes by, I want you to fall in behind them, but don't follow them to closely. Stay alert and don't let that truck get by without you seeing it, entiendes?"

Hugo was now sweating, "Si jefa, don't worry we will not miss it. I will have a car right next to the highway with the hood up like it is having engine problems." Hugo was now thinking about what his fucking escape plan was going to be in the event he missed the truck. He knew it would be an automatic death sentence and a brutal one at that.

Now it was a waiting game. Lisa sat in her car with some of her men hoping that they would not have to wait long since the sun was now starting to scorch the Sonoran Desert. She started the car and turned on the air conditioning. The heavy cologne that a couple of her sicarios had marinated themselves in wafted through the air and it was beginning to nauseate her.

An hour went by and Lisa's radio hissed loudly, "Jefa, me copia? Do you copy? This is Hugo. The truck followed by two cars just passed us and we are about thirty miles from your position. They should be there in about twenty minutes. They are not traveling very fast and there are not many other cars on the road."

Lisa answered, "Te copio, Hugo! Very good and we are waiting to spring the trap. Get in behind them because you will be our rear guard to ensure no one escapes."

"Claro, Jefa! We are now a mile or so behind them," said Hugo.

The area was flat and Lisa had chosen her operational terrain with great care. They would be able to see the truck and the escorts from a distance. The lead car checking for military and police roadblocks would be allowed to pass since they were insignificant. Minutes later, they saw the lumbering truck coming down the road. Lisa clicked on her radio, "Listos muchachos! Get ready here they come. You all know what you have to do. I want no fucking mistakes."

As the truck approached, a large tractor-trailer rig coming in the opposite direction veered onto the path of the truck effectively blocking it on the narrow two-lane highway. Then all hell broke loose, as automatic weapons exploded loudly sending fiery hot armor piercing projectiles through the two cars that were following the load truck. The bullets peppered the cars with hundreds of bullets making them appear like metal Swiss Cheese. In less than half a minute all of occupants were shredded into bits and pieces of gory, crimson flesh. The driver of the truck was pulled out and shot in the head at point blank range with an AK-47. His last words were, "Por favor no me maten!" Cars approaching the scene panicked and quickly turned around and bolted. Two of Lisa's men jumped into the truck carrying the ton of coke and drove away followed by Lisa's men. Before departing the area, Lisa pulled a white bed sheet, with large, painted words on it, from the trunk of her car and put it close to one of the burning cars, anchoring it with large rocks. It was a narco message, which read, "Putos of the Invincible Jalisco Cartel obviously you are not so invincible. Pinche cabrones."

Lisa calmly walked back to her car and got into the front passenger seat. She shook hands with all three homicidal maniacs in the car with her. She grinned, "Muy bien, muchachos, muy bien! The dogs of the Invincible Jalisco Cartel will regret the day they fucked with Lisa Rochin. I will destroy them and the other cabrones from the Blood Alliance Cartel."

Lisa knew that she had an exceptional talent for both tactical and strategic planning. It was an instinct that came natural to her. She studied situations and was able to quickly develop military style plans that focused on surprise; security; concentration of force; economy of effort; flexibility; and coordination. As a result, she was a force to be reckoned with and was becoming more cunning with time.

Her planning of the operation had been impeccable and now she would be hundreds of millions of dollars richer, once she crossed the ton of cocaine into the U.S. It would be a piece of cake and she had not even lost a single member of her cartel. As she headed north, she was already planning and plotting. Her mind was consumed with these thoughts.

Villa was sitting at home late one Friday when his cell phone rang. He picked it up and put it to his ear. He heard a soft voice say, "Victor, this is Leticia. I hope that I am not interrupting you?"

Villa responded, "Oh hi, I'm so glad to hear from you, Leticia. Hope you haven't been too busy lately? When can I see you?"

She responded, "Actually, I've been very busy. I called because I can get away for a few hours and would like to see you."

Villa's heart was beating like a war drum, but he kept his composure. He replied, "Of course! Why don't you come to my house, is that ok? You recall I gave you the address."

She replied, "Ah, yes, I remember that you live in the ritzy part of Mexico City. Very nice! I will be there in about half an hour."

Feelings of passion, danger, and even love were now short-circuiting his entire system. But for Villa it was a great feeling. He would have to play it cool and not be overly assertive as was his nature. Minutes seemed like hours, but to kill a little time, he went in search of a bottle of wine in his kitchen cabinets. He found a good Chilean red wine and two dusty wine glasses and after washing them cleaned them with a dishtowel. He waited nervously. Finally, the doorbell rang and Villa bounded up the stairs like a star athlete. There, standing in front of him was the President of Mexico in a tight beige skirt, slightly about the knee, which gave Villa shivers. A black, silky blouse, which she was wearing, made her even more desirable. She gave him a hug and a peck on the cheek. It almost vaporized Villa and his emotions raced wildly. He escorted her downstairs to his living room and popped the cork to his bottle of cabernet. As he nervously poured the vino, she crossed her legs lifting her skirt much higher.

Imelda lifted her glass and toasted, "A nuestra amistad, salud!" The glasses clinked together and they looked at each other passionately as they both took a drink. They relaxed on the couch, sitting next to each other. They talked incessantly about their backgrounds, families, and aspirations. The President's hand glided gently to his forearm and both simultaneously leaned into one another and kissed with intense passion. Neither could tear their lips from each other and their embrace only fueled the desire. When Villa couldn't stand it any longer he took her hand and led her to his bedroom. They undressed like the world would end within a few seconds. Both felt the most incredible ecstasy and intensity.

As they lay in bed completely exhausted, Imelda said in a soft whisper, "Miguel, I wanted you from the first time I saw you and was hoping this would happen. You are incredible and I want to see you again."

Miguel replied, "I felt the same way and want to see you again as well. We must be careful though because if we are discovered it will create an international scandal. You are a very special woman in so many ways."

An hour later, Imelda made her exit and Villa watched as she drove away down the steep winding road. He was completely smitten with her.

CHAPTER 10

Cartel Violence

The plaza bosses of the Invincible Jalisco Cartel were gathered at an isolated house twenty miles west of Guadalajara. Their leader, Jaime Santana, hadn't yet arrived as he was stuck in heavy traffic. While the cartel bosses waited, several women served platters of grilled steaks and fresh lobsters taken from the Pacific Ocean waters. Fried potatoes, frijoles charros, and rice served as side dishes. Drinks consisted of the most expensive brands of tequila, scotch, and vodka. They settled in to wait as they enjoyed the food and beverages. The chatter was loud and boisterous. All were well armed and they felt secure since the house was surrounded by some of their best men. They could let their guard down and relax.

Twenty minutes later, Santana made his grand entrance surrounded by eight bodyguards armed with AK-47's. His

Pretorian guard had been personally selected by him and stood out from all his sicarios in that they were extremely efficient killers and followed orders blindly.

"Amigos, thank you all for coming," he said. "As you know, we are a new organization and as a result we are not known by too many people. Fear and intimidation are what define both the weak and powerful cartels. Unfortunately, we are still not as strong as we will be. It is time for us to send a clear message to everyone that we are men with fucking cojones and we fear no one."

"What do you mean, Jefe?", asked Teofilo. "We have all killed in the past and were part of the Blood Alliance Cartel, one of the most feared organizations in Mexico."

Santana quickly replied, "Teofilo, that is true, but we are now a completely new cartel and have to do something for the people and government to fear us. We will be able to operate with impunity, but only if they are intimidated by us. It is all about respect, understand?"

"Claro, entiendo," replied Teofilo, who was now in a somber mood.

"This is what we are going to do. Five days from now, we are going to block all of the roads in and out of Guadalajara with tanker trucks that we will set on fire. Teofilo, you will take enough men and steal as many as we need from the city's public works storage area the night before. Jairo, you will have all of our men ready to deal with the military and police when they arrive understand?"

Jairo just nodded his head in agreement. He was a capable and intelligent leader who carried out assignments with deadly efficiency.

Santana continued, "By barricading and paralyzing the second largest city in Mexico our reputation will be established. Let's get moving on this."

Days later, as the sun was beginning to peek out over the horizon, several large tanker trucks rolled out and simultaneously blocked all the main roads leading in and out of Guadalajara. They were accompanied by carloads of sicarios armed to the teeth with all kinds of military grade weapons. As frustrated commuters began to honk their horns, the sicarios fired salvos of gunfire into the air. People panicked and jumped out of their cars, fleeing to safety behind trees and buildings. The men driving the trucks stuck gasoline-soaked rags into their fuel tanks and ignited them. Immediately, they burst on fire and black smoke lifted into the blue sky.

An army Cougar EC725 helicopter carrying twenty-nine soldiers, having been alerted, now approached the city from an easterly direction. The French-made troop transport aircraft began to descend near one of the fiery tankers not having a clue of what the hell was going on. They erroneously misread the situation thinking it was local protesters trying to bring attention to some bullshit social cause. They believed the problem would be taken care of in short order and they would return to their base in less than an hour. Santa Muerte, however, was watching and waiting anxiously.

Suddenly, a man wearing a cowboy hat and python boots stepped out from behind a car with a long evil looking tube and pointed it at the helicopter. It was a rocket propelled grenade launcher. He pulled the trigger causing a large grenade to explode out of the tube. It spiraled into the air like a football and smashed into the belly of the helicopter. A direct hit! The explosion could be heard for miles and the rotary aircraft plummeted from the sky with such force it made a crater five meters long and three meters wide. It was completely shattered into small pieces and its remains were scattered throughout the immediate area. Bloody body parts covering the ground made for a gruesome scene. It resembled one of the rings of hell depicted in Dante's Inferno. Similar chaotic and bloody scenes ravaged the other major roadways into and out of the city of Guadalajara. Santana had accomplished his mission, letting all the people of Mexico know that the Invincible Jalisco Cartel was a criminal enterprise to be reckoned with. Announcements via radio and television followed, where messages were read from Santana that the violence and mayhem were courtesy of his cartel!

For days after the gruesome and spectacular pandemonium, Santana's men scattered and went into hiding until things cooled down. They had made a horrific statement and the entire nation was in shock. But the Invincible Jalisco Cartel was not done with its week of terror. Three days later, a call came into the Jalisco State Police headquarters. The caller told Lieutenant Beltran that he had important information regarding the brazen cartel attack that temporarily crippled Guadalajara and downed the army helicopter.

The man with the raspy voice identified himself as Antonio Garcia. He stated, "Quiero reportar that the Invincible Jalisco Cartel is planning another similar attack in the city of Zapopan. I can't tell you anymore, but it will happen in four hours."

"Why Zapopan?", asked Beltran. A loud click and the phone went dead. Beltran decided to act on the information. He had been trying to get promoted for a number of years and had been passed over for snot-nosed kids who had college educations or families that had palanca, political influence. This was his chance to do something heroic and be noticed by his superiors. A great fucking opportunity was just over the horizon for him or at least he thought. He smiled and two of his gold teeth reflected the spinning fan on the ceiling. He had plenty of time to react since Zapopan was only about ten kilometers from Guadalajara.

An hour later, four black Chevrolet sedans in a convoy were speeding along Calzada Lazaro Cardenas, Carretera Guadalajara towards Zapopan. They zipped past other cars and slow-moving trucks. A total of twenty well-armed men in the cars looked at the surrounding countryside and hoped the information Lieutenant Beltran had received was just a prank. The amount of money they were paid each month was not worth being sent to the Promised Land prematurely. One of the men, Jacobo, was sitting in the backseat of one of the cars and was being philosophical.

He burst out, "Me vale madre! What if this turns out to be true? There is no way we can survive an attack by a major cartel. Our fucking government doesn't care if we get killed and I guarantee they wouldn't even give our families a pension."

Mario sitting in the front seat replied, "Es cierto! Jacobo is right, but what can we do now, except pray that nothing happens to us and we can be home in time for supper. Que Dios nos bendiga!"

Two kilometers from Zapopan, the lead state police car noticed two large, steel gray colored vans parked on each side of the freeway. They were identical. As the police convoy was about a hundred meters away, the rear doors of the vans suddenly opened. Two M60 machineguns opened up with a continuous roar of thunderous discharge of bullets. Each machinegun fired a staggering six hundred projectiles per minute. The first two police cars were completely torn apart. The second two cars stopped and the remaining police officers, including Beltran leaped out and took cover behind them. They quickly returned fire, but didn't dare stick their heads out to aim. They cautiously lifted their weapons slightly above the hoods of the cars and fired aimlessly into the air. They hit nothing but trees and bushes on the other side of the road. The high velocity bullets continued to rain down on the outgunned police officers shattering the windshields and flattening the tires of their cars.

Beltran screamed, "Get on the radio and ask for reinforcements! Rapido, a la chingada!"

Fuck you, thought Jacobo. It would be suicide to even try to get into the cars that were being sprayed with lead. Besides the fucking radios had been blown to pieces. They continued to hide behind the car engines that were thus far stopping the onslaught of bullets.

Minutes later, three rocket propelled grenades were launched simultaneously with a loud roar towards the four disabled sedans. The rocket motors ignited after ten meters increasing their velocity to almost three hundred meters per second. The high explosive anti-tank warheads slammed into the police cars and literally disintegrated them. A fiery mushroom shot into the air. All twenty police officers were now dead, some burned beyond recognition. Investigators later identified Beltran's body. Horrified, they projectile-vomited for over a minute. He had been decapitated by a large piece of shrapnel. His eyes and mouth were wide open. His tongue was hanging from the side of his face in a grim reminder of violence in its most monstrous form.

The Invincible Jalisco Cartel, less than eight hours later, posted a video of themselves on social media holding assault rifles high in the air and wearing black masks so they couldn't be identified by local authorities. Santana read a prepared statement, "People of Mexico, we are the Invincible Jalisco Cartel and our primary goal is to protect and help the poor people of our country. We will fight against injustice and oppression, even against the government that continues to operate with impunity. The Blood Alliance Cartel and the Cartel of the North are enemies of the people. Through extortion and violence, they have created a reign of terror. We are the saviors of the disenfranchised and take our role very seriously. *ARRIBA EL CARTEL INVINCIBLE DE JALISCO.*"

The video was also sent to various Mexican television networks. As with terrorist networks like ISIS, the cartel had learned the value of social media. Santana was a quick study and learned that these forums were cheap, accessible, and provided rapid and broad dissemination of information. Even more important, they provided unfettered communication without the filter or selectivity of mainstream media. Social media was a critical tool that would be used by Santana and his cartel to spread their message, recruit members, and collect intelligence. It was a savvy move. With brazen attacks, their rivals in the drug trade and the government began to take the Invincible Jalisco Cartel much more seriously.

In an isolated ranch near Esquinapa, Sinaloa, Mario Castillo, the head of the Blood Alliance Cartel, sat surrounded by a small army of sicarios waiting for a special guest to arrive. Finally, three large, camouflaged military trucks and a jeep arrived kicking up choking clouds of dust. General Ricardo Martinez, the head of Mexico's ninth military zone, stepped down from the jeep, which flew the Mexican flag. Hanging from his hip, he had a Colt .45 handgun in a black leather holster. He had been born and raised in Sinaloa and at the age of eighteen had joined the army. After a long career and making critical contacts along the way, he was finally promoted to General. Martinez was tall and handsome. He had light brown hair and green eyes. His greatest strengths were his confidence and ability as a field commander.

But, he had a dark side. He was totally corrupted and had made millions of dollars by protecting drug traffickers. He was about to meet Castillo for the first time. Martinez knew that if he played his cards right, the doors would open wide for greater financial opportunities. Martinez left his men outside and walked to the front door that was guarded by two mean looking men brandishing AK-47's. He slapped away the dust from his uniform before making his entrance. As he walked in, Castillo stood up and shook his hand and introduced himself.

"Mi General, es un placer," commented Castillo. "Thank

you for coming. I'm sure that we will come to some agreement that will be very lucrative to both of us."

General Martinez shook his hand and said, "It is a pleasure to meet you. I have heard about you and appreciate the opportunity to finally meet with you."

One of Castillo's men brought a silver tray with several bottles of expensive assorted liquors. The General poured himself a glass of vodka on ice and Castillo chose a shot of potent yellowish tequila.

"Salud, to a long and fruitful relationship," Castillo uttered. Both men lifted their glasses and downed the bitter liquid.

Castillo quickly got down to business, "General Martinez, I wanted to meet with you to discuss an arrangement so your interests don't come into conflict with mine. You know what my business consists of and I am willing to pay you for two things, protection and intelligence."

The General replied, "That will not be a problem if the price is right, but exactly what type of intelligence are you wanting?"

Castillo smiled, "I want intelligence as to the movements of all security forces in *Sinaloa*, especially when we are moving drugs into and out of the country. Secondly, I know that the military does a lot of telephone intercepts without going through the courts. You are aware that our enemies, the Cartel of the North and the Invincible Jalisco Cartel are at war with us. I want you to help me locate their leaders so I can kill them. You are friends with all the other zone commanders. This gives you access to a lot of information, right?"

"Claro! That will not be a problem," replied Martinez. "What you want me to do will cost you ten million dollars a year. Keep in mind that I will have to pay some of my men and funnel some of the money all the way up to the Secretary of Defense. But this should be pocket change to you."

Castillo laughed and took another shot of tequila. He reached across the table and shook the General's hand, stating, "We have a deal and I look forward to working with you," he said.

Before Martinez left, Castillo provided him with an encrypted Blackberry cell phone that would only be used to conduct cartel business. Martinez, quite pleased, jumped into the back of his dust covered jeep and drove slowly away followed by the three trucks full of green uniformed soldiers.

Not more than a week had passed when Martinez called Castillo and gave him some good news. He told him that they had been intercepting a telephone belonging to a family member of a drug trafficker for over a month. He reported, "We were able to identify several telephones that the family member was calling, which led to more and more telephones being identified, which we intercepted. We were finally able to collect information from one of them about Lisa Rochin, the head of the Cartel of the North. Apparently, she is going to have a meeting with her plaza bosses tomorrow afternoon. The meeting is going to take place in Santa Ana, Sonora. It is in the northern part of the state, as you know."

"Are you sure?", asked Castillo excitedly. "Do you know exactly where the meeting will take place? Ay caramba, this is really good news!"

The General continued, "They talked about a little farmhouse, ten kilometers south of the city. Apparently, there are dozens of mango trees in front and you should not have a problem finding it."

Castillo thanked Martinez, "Muchas gracias. I will let you know how it turns out. If you hear anything else please call me right away."

Castillo wasted no time and called one of his men, Geronimo, to meet with him. He briefed him on the information he had received from the General. He also instructed him to take thirty of their best men and should leave right away. Geronimo was from Tamaulipas and had been in the Mexican marines for over twenty years. He was well versed in military operations and had conducted hundreds of missions all over Mexico. Geronimo was also a psychopathic killer who enjoyed torturing people. During his career in the military, he had executed hundreds of people; most of them were innocent of any crimes. Dozens of complaints had flooded the Mexican Human Rights Commission, but when passed onto the Secretary of Defense they had been completely ignored and covered up.

Geronimo personally handpicked thirty of the most gruesome killers and loaded them into six Land Rovers and began their northward journey to the state of Sonora. Near Ciudad Obregon, Sonora they ran into a military checkpoint. Traffic was backed up as soldiers searched the cars. Geronimo watched as one man jumped out of his car and began yelling obscenities and wildly waving his arms. A soldier slammed his rifle butt on the side of his head and blood spurted into the air in a fine mist. The man fell hard onto the asphalt. Two soldiers then grabbed him from the ankles and dragged him behind some bushes and left him there. A soldier approached and looked in Geronimo's car and immediately saw a vast array of weapons. With a mean look in in his eye, the soldier was about to alert his companions when Geronimo lifted a stack of ten thousand dollars and stuck it in his hands. A smile came across the soldier's face and he motioned for Geronimo and his convoy to pass. The soldier yelled to the other soldiers, "They are police. Que pasen!"

Over two hours later, the convoy of gunmen split up as they approached the small town of Santa Ana. Geronimo, on the way in, identified the farmhouse where Lisa Rochin would be having her meeting. A long wall made of large rocks formed a boundary next to the two-lane highway. A narrow dirt road led to a house about two hundred meters away. The building was nothing to look it. It was a single-story abode, made of adobe and the roof was covered in red Spanish tile. Geronimo made a mental note that the mango trees would provide excellent cover and allow for them to gain the advantage of surprise. Lisa Rochin, the famous Narco Queen, was now taking her last breaths on earth. Geronimo was supremely confident of his ability to kill and he thought little of women and their abilities. What the fuck does Rochin know about this violent business, and worse, what can she possibly know about running a large cartel, he thought. He decided that if she were captured alive they would torture her for days. They would slit her throat and hang her where everyone could see her corpse. Geronimo was beginning to get delusional and was not focusing on the operation itself.

As the sun was setting on the horizon, one of Geronimo's men called him on the radio and told him that at least thirty cars were at the house. He also reported that there was no visible security, at least in front.

Geronimo laughed, "Pinche Pendeja! She is even dumber than I thought. Muchachos, this is going to be easier than I anticipated."

Darkness began to envelope the area as Geronimo and his small army of assassins arrived. They parked a safe distance from the house and quickly jumped out of their cars with their fully loaded AK-47's. As they approached the dirt road, Geronimo gave the order to spread out. They walked at a brisk pace in a long line. At thirty meters from the house several massive explosions occurred almost simultaneously. Then, there was complete silence as gray smoke hung like an eerie fog among the branches of the trees.

A month earlier Lisa had purchased a hundred Claymore mines from a Central American arms dealer. They were surplus equipment from stockpiles the U.S. had provided the Contras in their struggle against the Sandinistas in Nicaragua. She had her men place the directional anti-personnel mines around the house hours before Geronimo and his crew arrived in Santa Ana. When trip wires detonated the mines, each one shot seven hundred steel balls into the air at an extremely high velocity. Geronimo and his men, for a split second, heard the loud blasts before a shower of steel pulverized them into small pieces.

Several hours' later, local police and forensic investigators arrived at the scene. They found two mines that hadn't been detonated and were able to neutralize them. They were not, however, able to identify any of the remains since very little survived. The clothes and potential identifications in their wallets were completely vaporized. Even recognition through medical legal means, to include dental work or past surgeries would prove impossible. The investigators, using rakes and shovels, began filling green trash bags with the pieces of human flesh. They were only able to fill two bags. That was all that remained of Geronimo and thirty of his killers.

It was two days later that Castillo learned of the fate of his men. He went into a violent tirade and kicked and turned over furniture in his blind rage. Pulling out his Colt .45 handgun, he began shooting at the large screen television and then wildly at the roof. One of his men grabbed him in a bear hug until he quieted down.

"Pinche puta! Lisa Rochin must have more fucking lives than a cat," yelled Castillo. "In one operation, where we had the upper hand, we lose all of our best sicarios? Fuck me! That doesn't even make sense."

Castillo was not really upset about his men being killed. Although they were some of the best sicarios, he felt that they were expendable and could easily be replaced. The reason he was livid was because a woman had, symbolically, put him on his knees in front of his men. Not a good start for a fledging drug lord.

Lisa, hearing the horrific detonations, quickly fled from the area with all of her men. She surveyed the ghoulish scene in front of the house and thought that it looked like a scene from the bowels of hell. She made a mental note that she definitely needed to get her hands on more Claymore mines. They were worth every penny. Now to more pressing matters. She was the target of the assault and she had to quickly identify the person responsible. To do nothing was to invite another attack. Her mind was twirling like a top.

A month later, Castillo received a call from General

Martinez. The General requested to meet with Castillo and mentioned that he couldn't discuss the matter on the telephone. Castillo agreed and told him to come to the same place where they had met before. Castillo was hoping that Martinez had more information on Rochin so he could eliminate her presence on this earth forever. This would restore his standing with the cartel he now commanded. He knew that if he was not feared, it was only a matter of time before someone made a move to replace him. It was now about honor and big cojones.

With storm clouds in the sky and a strong wind pushing its way through the steep mountain ravines, Castillo waited in his isolated ranch near Esquinapa, Sinaloa, with two beautiful young girls from the area. They had already drunk three bottles of Dom Perignon Brut Rose Champagne, 1996. Each bottle cost $7,500 dollars. Castillo had very expensive taste, not only in liquor, but also in women. What the hell, he was making a fortune and was hoping to expand his business into other countries. He had access to tons of cocaine and was producing his own methamphetamine and heroin. If it weren't for Lisa Rochin, he would be sitting on top of the world. But he knew that the drug business was unlike any other. It was the type of enterprise where you had to sleep with your eyes open. Trust was not in a drug lord's dictionary. Power, in his opinion, was also synonymous with treachery.

The sudden crack of thunder startled Castillo. He stood

up and peered through the window. He could see streaks of lightning in the sky and it was getting dark fast. One of the girls, now naked, grabbed him by the arm and pulled him back to the sofa. She fell on the white carpet and giggled hysterically. Castillo laughed and picked her up and grabbed the other girl with her, and took both of them into his bedroom. He was again startled when there was a loud knock on the front door. He ordered the two girls to stay in the bedroom and slammed the door. One of his men opened the door and in walked General Martinez in a green, plastic military poncho. He dripped water all over the floor and carpet.

Castillo asked, "Espero que tengas buenas noticias? What was so important that it couldn't wait?"

The General, with blinding speed, drew his sidearm and shot the two bodyguards in the room. He then pointed it at the head of Castillo. Automatic gunfire could be heard outside, then a deafening silence. Castillo yelled, "*Que chingados*? What the fuck is wrong with you?"

"I have been offered twice the money you were going to pay me by Lisa Rochin. She told me to tell you that she hopes you enjoy hell."

The General pulled the trigger and a bullet drilled a hole in Castillo's forehead and came out the other side pulling a large amount of brain matter behind it. One of the General's men entered and told him that they had killed everyone outside. Castillo's men were outnumbered and outgunned. They never knew what hit them. A search of the house ensued and the soldiers found over ten million dollars in cash in one of the closets. They also discovered the two girls hiding under the bed. They were terrified and choked back their tears. The General told them to dress and he would have his men drive them to their village. He gave each one of them a stack of ten thousand dollars and told them never to return or tell anyone of what had happened. They nodded their heads that they understood.

CHAPTER 11

Narco Politics

The U.S. began to enter its worst drug epidemic in history and it was having a massive impact. In one year, over sixty thousand people died from drug overdoses and most were from opioids. The number of deaths in this one-year alone exceeded all of the U.S. military personnel killed during the entire Vietnam War. Americans were consuming eighty-five percent of the opioids being produced in the world. They were either in a lot of pain or there was horrific abuse taking place. Doctors caused much of the problem by overprescribing opioid drugs that were being pushed by the greedy pharmaceutical companies in the U.S. Many who became addicted later turned to heroin, since it was the cheaper alternative. This fueled more violence in Mexico as cartels fought for opium producing areas in the south, such as Guerrero.

Also complicating the problem was China. They produced eighty percent of the world's synthetic opioids such as fentanyl and carfentanyl. Fentanyl was fifty times more powerful than heroin and carfentanyl was a thousand times stronger. The latter was used to tranquilize elephants and a few grains could kill a person.

Three months earlier, David Fields had been elected President of the U.S. He was a wealthy land developer. He was tall, blond, and lied about virtually everything. Villa had watched the campaign and never in a million years expected Fields to get into the White House. Villa was concerned about the policies Fields had promised to accomplish if he became President. One was the pledge to build a wall along the two thousand-mile U.S./Mexico border. Villa knew that it would be a complete waste of time and money. The traffickers would easily punch holes in it or fly over it with ultra-lite aircraft that looked like flying lawnmowers. Also, the border was completely riddled with tunnels and more were being built each day. Fields announced that his first international visit would be to Mexico to meet with President Imelda Maestas. She thought he was a moron, but knew it was important to maintain relationships as they related to trade, anti-drug efforts, immigration, and many other political and economic issues.

The meeting was cordial and President Maestas was well versed and discussed many issues with great clarity. Fields bumbled his way through the meeting and seemed like a fish out of water. He didn't even have a clue as to the history between the two countries and the need to work closely together on a multitude of issues to include national security.

Less than twenty-four hours after returning to Washington, D.C., Fields gave a long television interview calling Mexicans rapists and murderers. He reiterated his stance on building a wall, but stupidly commented that Mexico would pay for its construction. This created a firestorm in Mexico, which Villa thought was totally unnecessary. Villa knew that it could have negative political consequences, especially cooperation on counterdrug efforts.

President Maestas called Villa late one Sunday and wanted to see him. Both had been swamped with work and had not spent time together in over a month. Villa loved being with her and bouncing ideas off of each other. Her laughter was infectious, but what he liked most was her genuine nature. She was always in a good mood despite the great stress that her position created.

Less than an hour later, she arrived and parked her car near the front door. She was dressed casually in blue jeans and tennis shoes. As soon as Villa closed the door, she grabbed him and they kissed with more passion than most people felt in a lifetime. She held him saying, "You have no idea how much I have missed you. You are always on my mind."

"I know, because I feel the same way about you. You are very special to me," replied Villa.

They sat on the living room couch and held each other. They comforted each other and shared secrets about their lives and work. President Maestas, or Imelda, as Villa called her was a truly dedicated public servant who wanted the best for her country. She, however, knew that ominous political clouds loomed on the horizon with Fields becoming President.

"President Fields has already created a difficult situation in Mexico with his rhetoric. I want to continue the close relationship with your country, but many oppositional political parties here are hardliners. They want to stop security cooperation with the U.S. and even some members of my party agree. It is becoming an untenable situation that may bubble over," divulged Imelda.

Villa added, "Yes, he is causing many, many problems with many of our strongest allies. He is literally denouncing the value of NATO and existing trade agreements that have worked well for a number of years, to include the North American Free Trade Agreement."

Imelda replied, "Instead of building alliances and political bridges in today's world of uncertainty and terrorism, he wants to build walls to move the U.S. into isolationism. It is not a good thing for anyone."

Villa changed the course of their conversation, "Well enough about politics. Let's toast with a shot of tequila to better days and a safer world. Salud." He put his arm around Imeda and kissed lips that had a hint of peppermint. They kissed over and over again in a tight embrace. Villa then grabbed her hand and took her to his bedroom where they made love like the world would end that night. Later, when Imelda left, he felt a tremendous loneliness. He knew he was madly in love with her.

The pollution levels in Mexico City were horrible and getting worse by the hour. Many people walking alongside the road were wearing white gauze masks in an effort to reduce the caustic contaminants in the air. Villa looked at them with great curiosity and wondered if the masks actually worked. He was skeptical. He drove slowly, in the rush hour traffic, towards the U.S. Embassy. As he approached Chapultepec Castle, Villa observed plumes of white and gray smoke high in the cloudless sky. He chuckled and thought Popocatepetl, the volcano, which was still active and located in the states of Puebla, Mexico, and Morelos was rearing its ugly head. Although it was about seventy kilometers from Mexico City, it was so huge that it could easily be seen.

After what seemed to be an eternity, Villa reached the Embassy. As he entered, his secretary Ursula handed him a pile of teletypes that had just arrived from Washington, D.C. He rushed into his office and got settled. A few minutes later his extension rang. Ursula said softly, "One of your sources is on the line and says it is urgent that he speak with you."

Villa picked up and heard a raspy voice and immediately recognized it. "Sammy, que sorpresa! It has been a while since I heard from you. I didn't know if you were still walking among the living."

"Ya no la chingas! I have been busy taking care of my mother who passed away a week ago from cancer. Que Dios la bendiga!"

Villa expressed his condolences then added, "Sammy, I know you called for a reason. What can I help you with?"

"As you know, Lisa Rochin took over the Cartel of the North after the death of Albino Romero. She is one smart fucking woman and has been expanding her empire very rapidly. I learned through a brother-in-law of mine, who works for her, that she is planning on flooding the U.S. market with Ecstasy."

Villa responded, "What the fuck? Ecstasy, huh? Surprising, but not shocking the way Mexican cartels evolve and change tactics and patterns."

Sammy continued, "She apparently is in the process of ordering a ton of it in pill form from an underground laboratory located somewhere in the Netherlands. She is paying three cents per pill and can sell it in the U.S. for thirty dollars per pill. Now that is a hell of a profit."

"Wow, I am familiar with the drug and we refer to by its acronym MDMA. It is a synthetic drug that changes a person's mood and perception. It is chemically similar to both stimulants and hallucinogens. The DEA has made it a Schedule I controlled substance, in other words, it has no legitimate use. Sammy, this is a fucking dangerous drug that has killed many kids in the U.S."

Sammy laughed, "My brother-in-law mentioned that it will be mislabeled as something else and shipped by air to the airport in Toluca. Some of the Customs people have been bribed to let it pass through without an inspection. Allegedly, the load is supposed to arrive in about three days. I will know more by tomorrow as they finalize their plan." With that, Villa and Sammy exchanged well wishes and hung up.

Villa sat quietly on his desk pondering the expansion of Mexico's largest and most powerful cartel into "Ecstasy" distribution. Actually, it made sense. It was popular and extremely profitable. Villa during various assignments in the U.S. had worked a few ecstasy cases. He knew that it was a popular drug in 'rave clubs' associated with electronic music. The effects gave the users a sense of euphoria and confidence. It also increased sociability and feelings of communication. Some would have a sense of closeness with others. The short-term effects were dehydration and hyperthermia. Prolonged use caused depression, loss of cognitive skills, and loss of appetite. Villa knew that many young kids had lost their lives through the use of ecstasy and knew the massive infusion of the drug into the U.S. market would be catastrophic. He knew that they had to act quickly before it established a trend with the Mexican cartels that would be difficult to reverse.

Villa was aware that he was up against one of the most cunning and intelligent drug traffickers in the history of Mexico. Lisa Rochin was the most formidable foe that he had ever faced on any continent. He could not afford to make a single tactical error with her and survive. Regardless, it made his adrenaline rise to a new level and he welcomed the challenged.

The next morning, Villa was giving dictation to Ursula regarding the large increase in violence throughout Mexico. He wanted to send a Teletype with wide distribution that included headquarters and all the border DEA divisions. It was important to keep them in the loop as to what was occurring in the country. He was almost done when the telephone rang. Ursula leaped up from her chair and picked up the receiver. Covering the mouthpiece, she whispered that it was Sammy calling.

Villa answered, "Hola, buenos dias! What do you have for me?"

Sammy replied, "I have a lot more. The ton of ecstasy will arrive tomorrow at the Toluca Airport at six in the evening on Aero Mexico flight 2017 from Amsterdam. The drug will be in steel drums, but it will be in powder form, instead of pills as my brother-in-law had initially reported. A truck will be used to transport the barrels to a cartel warehouse. Lisa

Rochin has bought several pill presses and plans to convert it into pills here in Mexico. That way it will not attract the attention of law enforcement and no one will know it is actually ecstasy unless they do a lab analysis. Each pill, as you know, sells in the U.S. for at least thirty dollars. Do the math and it is fucking amazing. The Cartel of the North has the ability to do a hell of a lot of damage to the U.S. unless you stop them now."

Villa thanked his informant and gave him instructions, "Thanks, Sammy! Please call me on my cell phone if anything changes. I will let you know how things go tomorrow. Keep a low profile and don't say a word about this to anyone, no one!"

Villa then called Comandante Florentino Ventura of the Federales. Both of them were like brothers and the danger they had shared on many occasions had bonded them even more. Villa stated, "Florentino, I have some reliable information that a ton of ecstasy is coming in from Amsterdam tomorrow and will be arriving at the Toluca airport tomorrow at six in the evening. It is being imported by the Cartel of the North. It will be in barrels and will be labeled as something else, but we have to be careful since Customs officials may be working with the cartel."

"Chingados, that airport is becoming a hub for drugs coming in and money going out. I will be at your office in an hour so we can come up with a plan. Nos vemos," replied Ventura.

Toluca was only 70 kilometers from Mexico City, and many flying into the Mexico City area were starting to recognize the convenience of going through Toluca since it had a lot less traffic.

Later, Villa was on the phone when one of his extensions rang. It was post one, the marine security detachment at the front of the embassy. The marine informed him that Ventura was there and needed an escort to come and get him. Villa took the small elevator to the ground level and pushed open the heavy, reinforced door. Upon seeing Ventura he gave him the traditional Mexican abrazo. Ventura asked, "Didn't a KGB agent gain entry into the embassy a year ago, and was caught wondering around freely throughout the entire building?"

"That is an absolute fact," laughed Villa, "It just goes to show how easily security can be circumvented, especially by foreign intelligence services."

Villa and Ventura both decided to try to follow the ecstasy once it left the airport to its final destination. It would be difficult, especially through the heavy traffic in the city. Damn near impossible was more like it. Villa recommended using a single engine aircraft that Ventura had at his disposal. Ventura chimed in and said he would have one of his men near the area where the ecstasy would be off-loaded. He added that he would have several cars with his men to follow the truck away from the airport. Villa and Ventura would be in another car. Villa really loved working with Ventura because he was also a strategic thinker.

Villa, at the last minute, asked Ventura to get a marine helicopter gunship to use in the operation. His instinct told him that they better have one just in case. After over three decades of counterdrug work, Villa had developed a sixth sense and it had just kicked in, big time.

Ventura looked surprised, "Miguel, isn't that a little bit of overkill? I can get it, but we will have quite a few men out on the operation and they will be heavily armed."

"Trust me on this! For some reason, I have it in my mind that we may need it. If we don't, the marines will get some good training, right? I would rather be safe than sorry."

Ventura smiled, "Esta bien, hermano. I will call General Diaz. He is an old friend. Anyway, let's plan on meeting tomorrow for at least three hours, before the plane arrives."

That night, Villa stayed up late thinking of all the details that needed to be taken care of for the operation. He had a glass of wine and thought of Imelda. It relaxed him and he finally went to bed and dozed off within minutes. Tomorrow, he and Ventura would roll the dice and hope they didn't come up craps.

The following day, Villa and Ventura met for an early lunch to go over the final details of the operation. They both ordered their favorite food, tacos made with chopped carne asada in corn tortillas. The salsa was spicy and hot.

The cilantro put it over the top in terms of flavor. They ate quickly and then drove to the airport. On the way, Ventura contacted his men by radio and all of them were waiting at the prearranged location. All inbound cargo at the Toluca airport had to go through inspection and there was only one exit. Ventura's agent would be pivotal since he would see the barrels taken from the aircraft and put into the truck that would transport it out of the facility. Everyone sat tight and waited and waited. Less than three hours later, Ventura's radio crackled and then hissed with a little static. Ventura quickly turned it off and then on again. The static was gone. The Federale inside the airport reported that a forklift was in the process of loading the barrels into a tractor-trailer truck. He described the truck as black with orange stripes. The doors of the truck bore the name, Transportes Chihuahua in white letters. Ventura then communicated with the single engine aircraft that was airborne a few miles away to give them a heads up. The ground surveillance would have to tail the truck from the airport until it could pass it off to the aircraft.

The radio sputtered, "Mi Commandante, the truck is moving and is on its way towards you. It is moving slowly and there are three men in it. I didn't see any weapons, but we have to assume that they have them."

Ventura replied, "Perfecto, muchas gracias! Okay, everybody, we have to stay close to the truck and not lose it until our plane can take over. After that we can follow at a distance."

A few minutes later, the truck rolled slowly out of the airport. Villa and Ventura took the point and began relaying information regarding the direction and speed of the truck to the other surveillance units. The traffic, as usual, was horrendous and cars zigzagged with impunity across the traffic lanes. One came within inches of hitting Villa's car. They stayed close to the truck like flypaper to a fly. Ten long miles down the road, one of the pilots came on the radio. "Okay, we have it. Great job in not losing it in that chaotic traffic down there."

As always, Murphy's Law always found a way to inject itself in some way into all operations and this was no exception. Ventura's radio suddenly went dead. Reacting quickly, he called Jairo using his cell and asked if anyone had an extra one. Jairo, luckily had brought a couple more. In minutes, he maneuvered his car within inches of Villa's and made a hand off to Ventura. It was pinpoint driving while both cars were traveling about sixty kilometers per hour. They were back in business.

The truck finally cleared Toluca and began to head north. As surveillance followed some would break off and refuel and then catch up to allow others to also gas up. Surveillances were difficult even with a plane providing assistance. It involved skill and logistical planning, especially the greater the distance. In Mexico, they were much more difficult because of the wild Mexican drivers that never adhered to traffic laws. The surveillance cars changed positions constantly to avoid detection. The drivers of the truck, who rotated the driving from time to time on this long trip north, were undoubtedly checking their rearview mirrors to see if they were being followed.

The truck kept moving north and only stopped to refuel. At the southern edge of the state of Chihuahua the truck turned into a narrow dirt road. The lead surveillance car, which had Ventura's agents, Julio and Patricio, in it, then made a tactical error and followed the truck rather than allowing the aircraft to report on its movements. Julio and Patricio soon came up on the truck, which was now stationary. The truck was at a dead end and so were they. Instead of getting out of their car and pretending to urinate, a legitimate excuse for being there, they turned around and headed back to the freeway. Not good!

Everyone pulled off the road and waited. Thirty minutes later, the pilots reported that it was moving again and going slowly towards the highway. It was on the move again. About sixty kilometers from Chihuahua city, the surveillance cars came to sharp right turn on the road and immediately noticed ten cars move into position effectively blocking them. Another eight to ten cars came up behind them blocking their retreat. Dozens of men jumped out and began firing at the agents.

Villa quickly moved his car next to another one, positioning them side-by-side, pointing in the same direction, so they would be shielded on both sides by the aligned car engines. Bullets ricocheted everywhere and pounded the cars. The agents returned fire. Yells and screams could be heard over the continuous gunfire. Two gunmen, in a crouch and carrying AK-47's, ran towards Villa and the Federales. Villa pointed his 9mm Beretta at them and fired from a distance of ten meters. They died instantly and crashed to the pavement and tumbled over each other.

Minutes later the sound of a rotary aircraft could be heard approaching. It was the Apache helicopter that Villa had requested. It flew over at a fast rate of speed and turned back quickly. It then unleashed a horrific shower of lead pellets. The M134 Mini-gun, a six-barrel rotary machinegun, was firing six thousand rounds per minute. Villa and everyone hugged the ground while bodies and cars were being ripped apart by the lethal downpour.

Seven cartel gunmen began running towards a wooded area about fifty meters from the road. They couldn't out run the speed of the Apache helicopter and even less, the velocity of the bullets. The mini-gun fired a few thousand rounds at them sending them flying like paper dolls in a hurricane force wind. The helicopter, minutes later, disengaged from the immediate area, and caught up with the truck carrying the ecstasy. It was quickly immobilized by peppering its engine with bullets. The helicopter landed and several marines were able to take the three passengers from the truck into custody. They also seized the ton of deadly ecstasy.

Back at the firefight, Villa and Ventura stood up from the asphalt and looked at the dead bodies on the road. They looked like meat put through a grinder. Bodies with their heads blown away, arms and legs were scattered everywhere. One body had a hole in its chest large enough to put a basketball through it. The smell of burning tires and gasoline filled the air. Villa counted twenty-eight dead men including those that tried in vain to escape death through a desperate and hopeless run into the woods to escape the carnage. The scene was mind numbing and a couple of the Federales vomited uncontrollably on the side of the road. Villa asked that they write down all of the serial numbers, make, and model of the weapons so he could give them to his friends at the Bureau of Alcohol, Tobacco, and Firearms (ATF). They would be able to trace ownership, which could yield valuable evidence.

"Miguel, you must be a mind reader," exclaimed Ventura. "Had you not thought of using a military helicopter, we would probably all be dead by now."

Villa and Ventura surmised that the individuals driving the truck called for reinforcements when they detected they were being followed. Both of them understood that no operation would ever be perfect and mistakes occurred in all of them.

Fortunately, none of the Federales were injured or killed and that was the only thing that was important.

Villa told Ventura, "It is a great day, my friend. We prevented a ton of a very dangerous drug from entering my country. I know it would have killed thousands of people. You and your men did well and we also have to congratulate the marines."

Ventura replied, "Miguel, these operations are becoming more dangerous by the day and our joint planning and sharing of information is even more critical now. We will always work together despite your crazy President Fields and his stupidity. Esta bien loco!"

Ventura's words turned out to be prophetic as President Fields, despite Mexico's concerns, moved forward with building a wall on the border. He failed to heed the advice of experts who told him that most drugs were being smuggled through established ports of entry. The U.S. Congress that approved thirty billion dollars for the ridiculous project had obviously drunk from the same delusional Kool-Aid as the President.

One dark, moonless night, after only ten miles of the wall had been built, a series of loud explosions rocked the Tijuana/San Diego border area. When the U.S. Border Patrol responded they were shocked to find that the entire length of the wall had been blown into large chunks of twisted metal and concrete. They found a large sign that said, "Eres un pinche maricon Fields. If you want to build a wall do it around your fucking fat ass. But if you want us to pay for the wall, we will do it and incorporate all of the territory that the U.S stole from us under 'Manifest Destiny'." President Fields was persistent and tried two more times and each time the wall was blown up. He finally relented and blamed it on the Democratic Party. As far as anyone knew, it was the only good thing the drug cartels had ever done for Mexico.

A month later, Fields began to again bash Mexico in the media and accused them of being a failed state. He ordered the Department of Homeland Security, specifically the agents from Immigration and Customs Enforcement, to begin rounding up undocumented workers. Their homes were raided in the middle of the night and families who had committed no crimes were separated from their children with some being deported into Mexico.

A special session of the Mexican Congress was convened and it was ultimately decided that their security forces would make no effort to impede the flow of immigrants from Central America through their country. They would be allowed to travel to the U.S. unimpeded. When Fields became aware of the fact that ten immigrants crossed into the U.S. for each one he deported, he became enraged. He called President Maestas to complain.

He said, "President Maestas, this is President Fields calling from the White House. I'm concerned about the number of undocumented migrants coming into our country from all over Latin America through Mexico. It has become a huge problem."

"Buenos Dias, President Fields," responded Maestas. "Why is it such a big concern? These poor people are only seeking a better way of life. They pick your crops at less than slave wages and live in miserable conditions. Don't be delusional; they are not taking jobs from anyone there. No one in your country wants to do that type of hard, manual labor. And even if they did, you would be paying ten dollars for an orange instead of one dollar."

"But, but, but," stuttered Fields.

"Have a good day, Mr. President," President Maestas stated, as she hung up the phone on Fields. She turned to her aides and said, "Que hombre tan ignorante."

Three weeks later, Fields was giving a speech to several hundred people near Nogales, Arizona about the technology he was going to provide that would help secure the border with Mexico. He was standing behind a podium on a small wooden platform just a few yards from the border. All eyes were on him as he disparaged Mexicans as being a drain on the U.S. economy. No one noticed the two teenagers wearing baseball caps walking on a small dirt path close by on the Mexican side. As they got within twenty yards of Fields, they lobbed two fragmentation grenades high into the air. As they bounced next to the president they detonated in a huge, simultaneous blast that shot him into the air in bloody fragments. People screamed and fled in panic. The teenagers disappeared into a nearby village and were never identified. Both Mexico and the U.S. collectively breathed a sigh of tremendous relief with the abrupt and violent departure of Fields. He had been an immoral and disruptive force globally and caused enormous damage in every area that he touched. No statutes or memorials were built in his honor and he was effectively erased from history. He was not even a bad memory.

CHAPTER 12

The Cartel of the Suns

After the brutal killing of Mario Castillo, the head of the Blood Alliance Cartel, a short period of uncertainty gripped the rank and file of the criminal organization. However, it was not long before a new leader emerged. His name was Jairo Alvarez. He was a tall, muscular man with premature white hair. He had been a regional boss for the cartel for over ten years and was respected by everyone. He had proven himself in the ongoing cartel wars by engaging in brutal violence when the situation required it. People feared him and never took him lightly. Most of his criminal associates didn't challenge him for control of the cartel. They knew that the head of a criminal network meant that you would be the lightning rod for law enforcement efforts. It was best to get rich and try to stay in the shadows as much as possible. Most cartel leaders had a short shelf life and ended up going to jail or being killed. Most in the business wanted to avoid that situation at all costs, but some were willing to gamble and sought the top job in the cartel hierarchy.

Alvarez knew that the Blood Alliance Cartel had taken many severe blows to its leadership and was severely crippled. He had a great challenge in front of him and he wondered if he would be able to revive it. Apart from having to mend it internally, he had to contend with the regular attacks from the other now more powerful cartels and the security forces of Mexico. He would have to maneuver carefully because the slightest misstep could mean the death knell for the cartel and maybe even him. He decided that until he was able to rebuild his organization it was wise to establish an alliance with the Cartel of the North.

Through one of his men, Alvarez reached out to Lisa Rochin and requested a meeting with her. Two days later, he was told that she would meet with him in Hermosillo, Sonora. He would be told when and where within the next two days. Alvarez was apprehensive and caution was always wise as far as he was concerned. But, he knew that he had little control since it was he that was calling for the sit down. He hated to deal from a position of weakness, but it was now necessary since the cartel he now led, the Blood Alliance Cartel, had lost most of their drug smuggling routes, sources of supply for cocaine, and the corrupt politicians who provided necessary protection.

The following evening word was received that they would meet at a ranch near Hermosillo. Alvarez would be allowed to bring two of his men with him, but they would all have to be unarmed. On Friday at noon, they were to meet some of Rochin's men in front of the Catedral Metropolitana de Hermosillo and they would transport them to the ranch where they would meet with the feared head of the Cartel of the North. Friday was two days away and it didn't give Alvarez much time to plan his agenda. He also knew that he would have to trust Rochin not to snuff him out like a fucking candle. He selected Felipe and Santiago to accompany him. They were two of his most trusted and ruthless sicarios. When he told them of what was about to occur, they looked at each other with a sense of dread. "No weapons?", they thought to themselves. This is a fucking suicide mission, but what choice did they have in the matter? Alvarez was their boss and they were obligated to follow his orders.

On a sweltering, hot day, Alvarez and his two men drove into the city of Hermosillo situated in the middle of the Sonoran Desert. Traffic was light and they had a couple of hours to kill so they decided to have breakfast. They went to a small restaurant at the Valle Grande Hotel, which had seen better days. A beautiful young girl, with long dark hair and dark eyes, wearing a very short black dress greeted them at the entrance. "A table for three?", she asked. The men were taken to a table in the corner. Being quite hungry, they quickly ordered steak and eggs with a plate full of flour tortillas. The salsa was hot, but they didn't like it any other way.

Felipe and Santiago expressed their concern about walking unarmed into the so-called mouth of the lobo. Felipe spoke first, in a low voice, to not be overheard by anyone, "Jefe, you know Lisa Rochin has killed many of her rivals and is not above killing us. She is more cunning and ruthless than any man I have ever known. Are you sure that you want to go through with this?"

Alvarez whispered, "Look, I know we are taking a chance, but we have no choice. We are very weak right now and we need to grow and get stronger. I just want a temporary alliance with Rochin until that happens. We can then break off from her and continue down our own path, understand?"

"Bueno, Jefe! We are here to support you," said Santiago.

After enjoying their hearty meal, they drove to the Catedral Metropolitana. They sat in their white sedan and admired the baroque, neoclassic design as they watched worshipers go in and out. The soft breeze made the heat palatable. They sat and waited. Sharp pangs of fear stabbed at their stomachs. Now they wished that they hadn't eaten so much. The wait was not long before they saw two black Mercedes Benz's enter the square and go around twice. They were searching for anything that seemed out of place. One of the cars finally approached and parked next to Alvarez. The other car remained about twenty meters away. Two men who looked like ranchers got down and walked slowly towards them. They were wearing straw cowboy hats, blue jeans, and plain boots. As they approached one of them spoke up, "You have to be Alvarez. We are here on behalf of Lisa Rochin. Leave your car here and come with us."

When Alvarez and his two men entered the back seat of the Mercedes Benz, a man placed black hoods over their heads so they couldn't see where they were being taken. One of the men said, "Don't worry, we are just taking security precautions. We would expect you to do the same. We are not far from where we are going so relax and enjoy the ride."

Felipe and Santiago were now breathing heavily and sweating. The moisture was pouring down their necks like a waterfall. They had killed many men in their lifetime, but it was very different when you might be the victim. No one spoke in the car and the deadly silence heightened the anxiety levels of Alvarez and his men. One of the drivers finally turned on the radio and Vicente Fernandez's voice came blaring out with one of his popular corrido's called "Los Mandados." Felipe was having trouble breathing and worse was acutely claustrophobic. He twisted and fidgeted restlessly. Someone spoke, "Aye chingado. What is the matter with you? Oh, I understand." He loosened the hood and Felipe felt much better. He relaxed for the moment. They traveled for about half an hour and then the blindfolded men could tell that they had gotten onto an unpaved road as it got rather bumpy. Alvarez felt a sharp pain in his right lower back and his spinal herniated disc began to shoot throbbing pain throughout his body. He felt like screaming, but that would be a sign of weakness. He clamped his jaw as tight as he could and remained silent.

After what seemed like an eternity, the car slowed down and finally came to a stop. The hoods were lifted and Alvarez and his men winced as the bright sun flickered in their eyes. One of Rochin's men ordered, "Vamos, they are waiting for us." Alvarez noticed at least twenty men standing around a house that looked out of place. It looked like a Swiss chalet. It was made of wood with a heavy, gently sloping reddish roof. There were only two small windows in front of the house. Tall palm trees surrounded it and a small patch of grass was off to one side.

Alvarez and his men entered the house and were escorted to a room in the back, which had a large mahogany desk with an intricate design. The three of them sat on one side of the table and waited under the watchful eye of five men armed with long gold-plated weapons. Five minutes later, Lisa made her grand entrance and stared at them warily. Alvarez was taken aback, he had heard of her legendary beauty, but it was much more than he had imagined. Lisa extended her hand and shook hands with each of them, while stating, "Senores, it is a pleasure. I'm Lisa Rochin. Mucho Gusto. I was told that you had something you wanted to discuss with me."

Catching his breath, Alvarez uttered, "Es cierto. As you know, I have taken over the Blood Alliance Cartel, which has been your rival for a number of years. My plan is a simple one. I would like to work with the Cartel of the North and expand our distribution markets together. We can be much more powerful as one, rather than fighting one another and disrupting each other's flow of drugs into the U.S. We only lose money, and that is not a good way to run a business."

Listening intently, Lisa spoke, "Maybe you are right, but what guarantees do we have that you will adhere to an alliance? Right now, you are very weak and you wouldn't be able to wage an all-out war with us. We could destroy you in the blink of an eye."

Alvarez, measured his words carefully, "That is true, but you are facing a strong enemy in the Invincible Jalisco Cartel and they are becoming stronger by the day. We can help you fight them and together we can get rid of those perros."

Lisa was pensive, "I accept your offer, but I will kill you if you betray me. For a fee of fifteen percent of your profits, you will receive protection from us and you will be allowed to use our drug routes into the U.S."

Alvarez thought for a second, "Muy bien, we have a deal. You will have to trust me, as I have to trust you. Let's toast to a new beginning and together we can conquer more territory and poison more pinche gringo putos."

One of Lisa's men poured tequila into shot glasses and everyone hoisted them into the air and simultaneously proclaimed loudly, "Salud!" After downing the shot, Alvarez grabbed the bottle and poured himself another glass. He tilted it and the liquid went down his throat smoothly, but with a warm sensation. He let out a loud, satisfying, "Ahhh!"

Before Alvarez left, Lisa made it a point to tell him that on a day-to-day basis, he would report to Gonzalo, her trusted second in command. She also announced that she had created "The Council" that was comprised of her plaza and regional bosses. It would now also include the head of the Blood Alliance Cartel. It would meet every month, or more often if required, but instead of having everyone physically travel to a meeting site they would use telephone conferencing equipment. Everyone would be given a code name, and a list of code words that would be changed for every meeting. The system would be encrypted and almost impossible to intercept. But it was always a good idea not to speak openly about criminal activities. Lisa wanted to use "The Council" to discuss cartel matters and strategy. She wanted her subordinates to feel like they had a say on important matters and that would make them more loyal. They would also be more motivated in carrying out orders and accomplishing cartel objectives. Everyone thought it was a great idea.

Under Lisa's profound leadership, the Cartel of the North now controlled sixty percent of all drug distribution in the U.S. Their tentacles reached into just about every rural and urban area. The death toll from drug overdoses became an epidemic. More people were dying each year and consumption continued to increase. The moronic politicians continued to have town hall meetings to discuss the problem, but as usual offered no solutions. It was obvious that they wanted important sounding titles, but certainly not the responsibilities.

One day, one of Lisa's regional bosses, Luis, came to see her. He was one of her most loyal and competent leaders. Luis was always unkempt and wore dirty blue jeans and scruffy cowboy boots. He excitedly said, "Lisa, I was contacted by a man who says he represents the leaders of the Venezuelan Cartel of the Suns. They have a business proposition for us and would like to meet with you."

Lisa had heard of the cartel and was surprised with the request for a meeting. She knew that the Cartel of the Suns consisted of high-ranking Generals of Venezuela's military, primarily the National Guard. Their name came from the sun symbols their Generals wore instead of stars like in the U.S. It piqued Lisa's interest and she wanted to see what they had to offer. She replied, "Bien, arrange the meeting and I will travel to Venezuela to meet with them as long as they give me safe passage."

"Si Jefa, I will call him and make all the arrangements.

I will let you know when everything is ready. Any other instructions that you have for me?"

Lisa replied, "No, just let me know where they want to meet. Tell them I will be bringing Gonzalo with me. He can watch my back. There is a lot of turmoil in Venezuela and the socialist government has fucked up the entire economy. It is close to being a failed state."

Luis shook hands with Lisa and left as abruptly as he had arrived. Lisa told one of her guards to get Gonzalo, who was outside playing cards and having a few shots of tequila. A few minutes later, Gonzalo came in and quickly uttered, "Lisa, a sus ordenes! What can I help you with?"

"Gonzalo, we will probably be going to Venezuela in the next few days. I just spoke with Luis and it appears the Cartel of the Sun wants to meet with us. Obviously, they are interested in some sort of business arrangement. We will meet with them and see what they have to say."

Gonzalo said with a smirk, "Well, they say that the women there are guapas. Who knows, I may find a girlfriend over there."

Lisa playfully slapped him on the side of the head. "Be serious! I am hoping that this will open up more opportunities for us."

Early the next day, Lisa was in her bathrobe having a cup of steaming hot Colombian coffee. She looked out the window and saw her brother, Armando drive up to the front of the house. Watching him as he got out of his car, Lisa knew him well enough to know that he was concerned about something by the worried look on his face. He walked to the front door with a slow, tired stride and his chin was almost resting on his chest. Armando made a weak smile and gave Lisa a hug.

She immediately said, "Armando, what is wrong? You look like someone died."

"Hermana, for the last four days, I have been trying to reconcile all our accounts and ten million dollars is missing. I have done several audits and it still comes out short. One, or several of our people who launder our money stole it,"

"I don't need this headache right now. Who do you think did it? I will kill them," stated Lisa.

Armando responded, "There are only eight people who have access to those accounts."

Lisa thought for a moment and then said, "I want you to set up a meeting with all eight of them here. Let's do it tomorrow in the early afternoon. Whatever you do don't tell them what it is all about. Let their imaginations run wild. I will handle the rest. Trust me."

"Ok, I will arrange it, Hermana," replied Armando, as he kissed Lisa on the cheek and gave her a long embrace. It was not often that he saw her. Most of their interaction was by telephone. Armando felt much better as he walked back to his car. He knew his sister could handle any problems and was happy that he had her to rely on. Family ties meant trust and confidence to Armando. It was everything to him.

A storm moved into the area the next day bringing light rain and a strong wind. Lisa could hear the wind rustle through the trees. She felt like taking off her clothes and running through the mountain trails. It would be liberating and she could cast aside all her problems and responsibilities, if only for a moment. After having huevos rancheros for breakfast, she heard cars drive up. The crunching of the tires on the rocks and gravel could be heard above the whoosh of the wind. She peeked from the window and saw Armando's car and a second one park in front. Several men began getting out of the cars and walking towards the house. Lisa had ten of her sicarios in the large living room, all brandishing AK-47's. She wanted them to immediately create an atmosphere of intimidation during the meeting. Armando and his group of money launderers were escorted into the house. Most of them had a perplexed look on their face since they had never met with Lisa. The look of surprise was quickly replaced with one of abject fear when they saw all of the evil looking gunmen. After they had taken a seat, Lisa entered the room with a supreme air of confidence.

She got right to the point. "I have been told that ten million dollars of our money is missing and the only ones who could have taken it are in this room, one or several of you. I want to know who stole this money."

Francisco, one of the money launderers, spoke up, "I can only speak for myself, I have never taken a single penny of your money. For one of us to have stolen that much money would be suicidal."

No one admitted to taking the money and this went on for about five minutes. Lisa finally got tired of toying with them and called Gonzalo on one of her secure cell phones and put him on speaker. Gonzalo then placed the mothers, fathers, sons, and daughters that had been kidnapped less than an hour earlier from their schools or homes on the phone. They were all crying hysterically.

With the seriousness of a heart attack, Lisa said, "Whoever took the money has one minute to confess or we will begin killing everyone's family members one by one. Then we will begin killing you."

The room went deadly silent and the seconds ticked by. The hostage's screams became progressively louder. As Lisa was about to give the order to kill everyone, Fernando, one of the money launderers, yelled, "I did it! It was me who took it! Please, don't hurt anyone. I'm sorry. I developed a gambling habit and began betting big money with offshore sports sites. It was so easy, and I could bet on games, horseracing, and casino games. Sadly, I thought I could win it back, but I only got deeper into the hole."

Lisa glued her eyes on his and commented, "Gonzalo, let everyone go. All of you, except Fernando can leave. Let this be a lesson to all of you. If you steal from us, you will die. There will be no exceptions."

The other seven money launderers scurried out of the house. Lisa nodded her head to Armando to go with them and he lowered his eyes and left. She looked at Mochomo, one of her most vicious killers, and said, "You know what to do, but do it away from here, understand? Take a few of the men with you."

Fernando began to plead for his life, but to no avail. Tears started to streak down his cheeks. Mochomo hit him on the shoulder with the wooden butt of his AK-47. Fernando screamed loudly and fell face first on the white tiled floor. He was lifted off the ground and dragged out of the house.

The ten million dollars to Lisa was nothing more than a drop in the bucket. The Cartel of the North was making that much money each hour of the day. Regardless, she knew that if she didn't make an example of Fernando others would do the same. It was human nature and the only thing people understood and feared was violence and death.

Early the next morning, Lisa was still sound asleep when her phone rang. It was Luis. He spoke animatedly, "Jefa, it is all set. They will receive you tomorrow at the Simon Bolivar International Airport. When you land they want you to taxi to the military section of the airport, away from prying eyes. You will not have to go through Customs or Immigration. General Molina will meet you."

"Esta bien, Luis," replied Lisa. "Have they told you yet why they want to meet with me?"

Luis informed her, "They are interested in doing business with you. I was told that they are moving over two hundred tons of Colombian cocaine through Venezuela each year and they want to expand their business into Mexico. They are involved with the Colombian insurgent organizations such as the Armed Revolutionary Forces (FARC) and the National Liberation Army (ELN) and other networks that run cocaine through Venezuela."

Lisa muttered, "Okay, I'm sure the meeting will be interesting. I will let you know how it turns out."

It was still dark when Lisa and Gonzalo left early the next day. Storm clouds had started to move into the area again. The dirt road they were on was still muddy from the recent rainfall, but their four-wheel drive SUV easily navigated the treacherous road. It took three hours before they reached the Abraham Gonzalez International Airport in Juarez, Chihuahua. They took a side entrance that was only used by security personnel and airport officials. Everyone there was on Lisa's payroll and she had carte blanche in terms of circumventing security protocols. The young security guard looked into the vehicle and upon seeing Lisa, he said, "Ah, perdon! Please, go ahead. Be careful! A few days ago, the army was here snooping around. I haven't seen them for a couple of days though."

Lisa smiled and handed him a few hundred-dollar bills. She asked him to take care of their vehicle and that they would be back in a couple of days.

The guard responded, "No hay problema. I will make sure it is safe and no one will touch it."

Lisa and Gonzalo drove to a large hanger on the southern side of the airport and met with two of their pilots who were waiting. Both Jairo and Dario had been working for the Cartel of the North for about ten years. They had worked together at Aero Mexico and when the airlines started losing money, they were laid off. Shortly thereafter, the cartel hired them to fly their fleet of Lear jets.

Jairo spoke, "Buenos dias! I hope your trip here was uneventful. We have filed our flight plan and are ready to go."

Gonzalo removed their luggage from the SUV and Jairo stuck them in the plane's cargo hold. Minutes later, the jet taxied out of the hanger and they were immediately cleared for takeoff. Once airborne, Gonzalo opened a bottle of tequila and poured a shot for Lisa and him. After downing several shots of tequila, Lisa reclined her seat and fell into a deep sleep. She had been working nonstop for months on making changes to her cartel and she was beyond exhausted. The trip took over six hours, but to Lisa it seemed much shorter since she slept soundly most of way there.

She woke up when one of the pilots, Dario, announced on the intercom that they were beginning their descent and would be landing in about twenty minutes. Lisa quickly got out of her seat and went to the small restroom to freshen up. Returning to her seat, Lisa fastened her seatbelt and told Gonzalo, "Let's see what kind of deal they offer. We will negotiate to ensure it is advantageous to us."

The landing was hard and Lisa grabbed the arms of her chair. As they taxied to the military side of the airport, Lisa looked out her window and saw a vast assortment of aircraft such as C-130 transport's, F-16 fighters, and military helicopters. Russian SU-30 MK2's were neatly lined up near a large metal hanger and mechanics dressed in blue were working on their engines.

The Lear jet finally came to a stop and a minute later the pilots shut off the engines and opened the door for Lisa and Gonzalo. As they climbed down the narrow stairs and onto the tarmac, they saw three military officers all of whom appeared to be Generals. They all had several sun insignias on their military shoulder boards. They were surrounded by dozens of soldiers in camouflage uniforms and all carried AK-103 assault rifles. One of the officers, a short, squat man with dark skin approached with his hand out. "Bienvenidos a Venezuela, I am General Molina," he said with a smile. "I hope your trip was enjoyable."

Lisa held her hand out, "Gracias, the trip was good and I was able to get some needed sleep."

With an even broader smile, General Molina introduced Generals Macias and Cruz. Once the introductions were done, the entire group walked to a large conference room in a building close by, which contained military administrative offices. There was no small talk. Molina got to the point, "May I call you Lisa? I know you don't mind. We wanted to meet you for quite some time to discuss a business proposition. If we are able to reach an agreement it will make all of us rich beyond our wildest imagination."

Lisa, kept her best poker face on, and replied, "What is it that you have in mind?"

Molina grinned, "We have formed an alliance with most of the larger Colombian cartels, including the FARC and the ELN that are also trafficking tons of cocaine through our country. We allow them to operate in Venezuela and provide them with protection. In return, we get paid huge amounts of cocaine. You are the leader of Mexico's largest cartel and we can supply you with as much cocaine as you want."

Lisa, looking squarely in his eyes, commented, "I already have a great source for cocaine. What can you offer that would make it advantageous to me?"

"Well, how much are you paying per kilo?", Molina countered.

"Let's cut to the chase. What is the price you have in mind? If it is beneficial to me than we might have a deal," said Lisa.

General Macias spoke, "We will cut a thousand dollars per kilo from what you are currently paying. We can either deliver the cocaine to you, but that will cost you more. If you pick it up in Venezuela, we will allow you to use our military airports or naval bases and provide complete protection."

"Perfecto, we have a deal. I would be loca not to accept it," Lisa said softly. "I will be able to move all the cocaine that you can give me. One more thing, I want a Venezuelan passport for Gonzalo and me. It will help me travel throughout the world and avoid detection."

"Consider it done," chuckled General Cruz. Everyone shook hands. Lisa had just made a deal that would increase her profits tremendously. Later that night, the Generals hosted Lisa and Gonzalo at El Cine Restaurant, a five-star establishment where they enjoyed lobster and steak. It was beautifully appointed, with small white tables and shiny metal chairs. After dinner, Lisa and Gonzalo checked into the Renaissance Caracas La Castellana Hotel. Early the next morning, they were picked up by a platoon of soldiers and taken back to the airport. Fortunately, the pilots had already filed a flight plan and had refueled the Lear jet. After their takeoff, Lisa reclined her seat and smiled. She had just pulled off the deal of the century.

CHAPTER 13

The Struggle

Jaime Santana, the head of the Invincible Jalisco Cartel, was sitting next to his large pool in the shape of a handgun in Puerto Vallarta. His men surrounded the home and they continuously walked around its perimeter, communicating with each other through radios. Santana was having fun with a handful of beautiful girls who wore skimpy bikinis. They laughed and pushed each other into the pool. Bottles of wine, hard liquor, and a couple of kilos of beluga caviar were on a large glass table. Several ounces of cocaine were in a solid silver bowl with two beautifully sculpted figures of parrots on each side. A small coke spoon was in the middle of the white powder. The girls preferred the cocaine to the liquor and snorted it every ten minutes. They were flying higher than a kite.

An hour later, José Trujillo, the second in command of the cartel arrived at the house. He was a short, unattractive man with coarse brown hair. He walked with a noticeable limp, a reminder of an old wound when he had engaged the Mexican army in a gun battle in the rugged mountains of Sinaloa. He had singlehandedly killed five soldiers before making his escape into the dense brush in the area. A bullet had severely damaged his right leg, but he had not felt it at the moment since his adrenaline was pumping at optimum levels. When the adrenaline subsided, the pain set in and the sharp throbbing pain in his leg caused him tremendous agony until a village doctor removed the bullet using rudimentary tools.

Upon seeing José, Jaime yelled, "José, take your clothes off and jump in the pool. These beautiful women want to have some fun. Help yourself to the food and stuff on the table. I am glad you came, otherwise these women would have probably killed me. I cannot handle all of them by myself."

"Ay, Jaime, I am surprised you are not dead yet, not from a bullet, but from all of the Viagra you take every day."

"Is everything all right?", asked Jaime. "I have been spending too much money on security since it seems that the government and the Cartel of the North want to kill us. It is eating most of our profits."

Just then they heard the sound of automatic weapons fire nearby and everyone froze. Again, more explosive bursts. In a panic, Jaime and José, with the girls following right behind, ran into the house. As they entered, several men armed to the teeth subdued them. The girls were crying and screaming adding to the chaotic scene.

Jaime shouted, "Who the fuck are you and what do you want? Do you know who I am, do you know who the fuck I am?"

The response came from a feminine voice, "They know who you are, or should I say who you were!"

Seated on a sofa in the living room was the Narco Queen herself, Lisa Rochin. She looked regal and exuded power from every pore in her body. She smiled and told the girls to go into the kitchen and wait there. Lisa then stared at Jaime.

Then she told him, "You are a treacherous snake who stupidly decided to make me an enemy. Did you really think that I would allow you to live and continue to be a thorn on my side? You will now pay the ultimate penalty."

She nodded to Gonzalo, who quickly walked up to Jaime and put a bullet in his head. Jaime's eyes grotesquely rolled back in his head and he fell backwards onto the expensive, white Italian tile. José was now covered in sweat. His eyes, showing abject fear, were focused on Lisa. He was convinced that he had but a few seconds to live. His hands shook uncontrollably and his knees were close to buckling.

Lisa stared at him, "Don't worry, I am not going to kill you. As of this moment, the Invincible Jalisco Cartel will be nothing more than a component of the Cartel of the North.

I will make you the leader and your first order is to talk to your people and convince them that it is in their best interest to come with us. The can make more money with us. Jaime was a greedy bastard who kept most of the money and paid his people very little. Are you in agreement?"

José quickly answered, "Of course! It will not be a problem. The only concern our people have is making as much money as possible. They don't care what master they serve as long as they are taken care of. I will handle it. Most of them didn't like Jaime anyway."

Lisa smiled, "That is what I want to hear. But beware, I don't tolerate treachery and you will pay with your life if you even think about it. You are now free to leave, but you will get together with Gonzalo in the next few days to iron out all the details for our new merger."

José left the house and made the sign of the cross with his right hand as he walked to his car. He had come close to death and was lucky to still be among the living. He made it a point to never cross Lisa, not even in thought.

Lisa, had accomplished the near impossible by conquering the rival cartels and incorporating them into the Cartel of the North. It was now, without a question, the most powerful cartel in the world. Very few heads of state were stronger than the Narco Queen.

Three weeks later, Lisa had a council meeting at a secluded ranch on the outskirts of Hidalgo de Parral, Chihuahua. All her cartel leaders were present. Lisa did not start the meeting until all of the council members had arrived. She wore a tight-fitting, black pantsuit with a red silk scarf around her neck. Before speaking, she looked everyone in the eye.

"Buenas tardes," she said. "I called for this meeting to tell you that things could not be better for the Cartel of the North. We are the only cartel in Mexico, now having incorporated all of the others into our ranks. But, despite our power and money, we are still being pursued by the DEA, especially Miguel Villa. He is like a cat with nine lives and has survived many attempts on his life. We need to eliminate him once and for all. Gonzalo, I want you to take care of him. Understand? It is time to eliminate all of our enemies once and for all."

Gonzalo frowned, "That is a very risky move. If we kill him they will come after us with a vengeance. You know the U.S. will pressure our government to attack us until they kill or capture us."

Lisa responded, "I understand that, but they are doing that already for the most part. It is Villa who is now our biggest problem. He is as cunning as we are and maybe more ruthless, at least in his pursuit of us. I consider him more formidable than the cartels that we have fought against in the past."

Gonzalo replied, "I will follow your orders, but want you to know that there will be consequences."

Villa was having lunch with Ventura at the Restaurante

Diana, near the U.S. Embassy. Villa loved the elegance of it. The huge red Afghan carpet, large wooden tables and the beige leather-covered chairs made it cozy. But, the massive wine rack in the dining area impressed him the most. They were in the middle of conversation when Villa's cell phone went off. It was Ursula, his secretary.

"Mr. Villa, sorry to bother you, but I have Arturo on hold. He says it is imperative that he speak with you now."

Arturo was one of Villa's most important informants. He always provided accurate information and didn't make up shit like some of the others. Arturo had been an independent drug trafficker, but had friends throughout the drug trade that trusted him. They would share information with him, never realizing that he was passing it on to the DEA. He was tall, gaunt, and had white hair. He always dressed in expensive suits and to Villa looked more like a diplomat.

"Not a problem. Go ahead and pass him through."

"Miguel, this is Arturo. Hope you are doing well? I have some important things to tell you. Lisa Rochin has taken over all of the cartels in Mexico by killing their leaders. She is now a very powerful person. I heard through a friend that she has put out a contract on you, so be very careful."

"*Gracias*, Arturo! I appreciate the info and will be careful. See what else you can dig up."

"I will try and will keep in touch with you."

Villa hung up the phone and became pensive. Now he

knew that they were coming, but had no idea as to how or when. He would be vulnerable and this was not a good thing. Ventura noticed the change in Villa's demeanor.

"What the hell was that call all about? You look like your thought process went into overdrive. Is everything all right?"

Villa explained the details of his conversation with Arturo. He told Ventura that he would have to be totally on guard since Lisa Rochin had put out a contract on him. This also worried Ventura because he knew the drug traffickers never forgave or forgot.

Ventura commented, "Mi amigo, we must take precautions. I will have some of my men provide you with twenty-four-hour protection. You will not survive without a large security escort."

"Thank you, but I would prefer to be very discreet. If I am seen with a large number of bodyguards it will only call attention to me. Believe me, I will not be complacent and it is a good thing that this was brought to my attention. But at the same time, I am not going to hide or bury my head in the sand. This is a dangerous business and risk is part of the game."

Ventura cautioned, "Just be careful, the Cartel of the North always carries out its threats and they have an army of sicarios."

Miguel knew that a way out of this situation was to simply request an immediate transfer to another country or even back to the United States. Miguel was not one to run from danger and he was not about to start now.

During the next several weeks, Villa requested three million dollars from the U.S. State Department's Narcotic Assistance Unit (NIU) in order to establish a wire intercept center for the Federales. The center would be under the command of Ventura. Villa didn't tell the NIU representatives that most, if not all, of the wires would be *extra-legal*. This would make them squeamish. What they didn't know would not hurt them. The DEA was identifying a lot of suspect numbers that could be used to develop important information on the Cartel of the North. The wire intercept center was developed very quickly and to avoid compromise and prying eyes, Villa and Ventura rented an apartment near the downtown area. The center was equipped with pen registers to record incoming and outgoing calls from targeted numbers from both hard lines and cell phones. It would operate 24/7 with three separate shifts of personnel. More importantly, it had the capability of monitoring a hundred phones at the same time, which would be more than enough.

Slowly, they began to intercept the phones of family, attorneys, and associates of the cartel. As they monitored the calls and analyzed the pen register information they were able to identify other numbers that they began to intercept. The operation began to collect valuable data.

One day, a call was intercepted between two cartel plaza

bosses discussing the amounts of money they were making from drug sales in the U.S. One of them was visibly drunk and slurred his words. He mentioned that a big shipment of money was going to be smuggled into Mexico from the U.S. the following Wednesday, which was three days away.

He boasted, "The money is being put in secret compartments of ten cars being transported from Denver, Colorado, in a large auto carrier. All of them will have money, but they will never find it since it will be well hidden between the rear seats and the trunks in specially built compartments. Don't say anything, but it will be crossing from El Paso into Juarez."

Both men laughed and continued to talk about their sexual exploits and other non-relevant issues. It didn't matter, since the beans had already been spilled. Minutes later, Ventura called Villa and told him of the money shipment. Villa was elated and recommended trying to follow it to its destination. He knew it would be difficult, but it would be worth the effort. Again, they would have to rely on the Mexican single-engine aircraft to follow it through traffic and the maze of narrow streets and alleys.

The following morning Villa along with Ventura and one of his elite groups took Avianca flight 6754 to Juarez. Once they landed, they walked through the airport bumping into people who were distracted and not paying attention to where they were going. Separately, they rented several run-of-the-mill sedans and drove to the Hotel Lucerna. Villa was impressed with the large pond and tall palm trees in front of the hotel. The hotel had valet parking that was a great convenience. To maintain operational security, everyone registered individually. After lugging their bags to their respective rooms, they slowly filtered into Ventura's room. It was crowded, but Villa and Ventura explained the plan in detail and the role everyone would play. That afternoon, the Mexican single-engine aircraft arrived at the El Paso Airport. Villa had earlier made the arrangements with the DEA office in El Paso.

A few hours later, Ventura received a call on his cell from one of his men at the wire intercept center. He excitedly told Ventura, "Mi Commandante, a call just came through and they mentioned that the money shipment will arrive early. It will cross the border into Juarez at about noon tomorrow. Thank God that you decided to go there early, otherwise we may have missed it."

Ventura replied, "Thanks for passing that piece of information quickly. I want you to call me on anything that you collect from the intercepted phones. It doesn't matter if it sounds unimportant. Understand?"

"Si Jefe, I will keep you posted at all times."

Ventura called for another meeting in his room to advise them of the latest information. He instructed them to have dinner and go to bed early. Tomorrow could be a long day and he wanted everyone well rested and alert.

Villa went to his room and ordered some tacos. After watching a crazy game show on television, he went to bed.

The next morning, everyone was up at the wee hours of the morning. Two of Ventura's men went to the port of entry and established surveillance from a small park nearby. They had a good visual of all the vehicles entering Mexico. Everyone else was nearby and the pilots were already at the El Paso Airport waiting for the word to launch. Villa and Ventura sat in the same car and made small talk about their lives, romances, and plans for when they retired. Both agreed that nothing would ever compare to the experiences of chasing after some of the most dangerous criminals on earth.

Villa jokingly said, "Maybe we should open a chain of taco stands throughout Mexico and the U.S. after we pull the plug."

Ventura laughed, "You must be crazy! With your love of tacos, you would eat all of our profits. We would end up being paupers."

It was slightly past noon when the radio came alive. The carrier with Colorado license plates had just been spotted and it was in fact carrying ten cars. Ventura's men were following it closely until their plane could take over the surveillance. Villa and Ventura saw the carrier pass slowly and fell in behind it. Thank God the traffic was light and the road was free of the regular accidents, which would choke the movement of cars. Before the surveillance plane was even off the ground, the carrier pulled into a ranch on the east part of town. Everyone pulled off momentarily, then the decision was made to move in quickly. The Federales and Villa moved in a small caravan at a high rate of speed down a narrow dirt road. Dust billowed into the air and made it difficult for the cars following to see ahead, but they plowed forward.

When they were about fifty yards from a sprawling ranch house, they came under heavy fire. They swerved the cars as they came to an abrupt halt, so they were perpendicular to the road. They jumped out, hiding behind the engines, improving their chances of surviving the incoming high velocity bullets. They immediately opened up with their own barrage of gunfire. Within milliseconds it sounded like a military battle with bullets flying all over. Villa noticed that a man ran out of the house and was trying to reach the carrier parked nearby. Villa took careful aim with his .9mm pistol and shot him in the arm and chest. The man fell face first into a patch of dry weeds. After a few minutes of torrential hot lead, the whining sound of a helicopter could be heard nearby. Suddenly, a Bell 206 helicopter lifted into the sky from behind the ranch house. It hovered for a second, high in the air, and Lisa Rochin leaned out and threw everyone a finger signifying "Fuck you." The aircraft then sped away in a southerly direction.

Once Rochin had made her escape, the six traffickers in the house surrendered and were taken into custody. A search of the property led to the seizure of half a ton of cocaine and just over two hundred kilos of methamphetamine. The true prize however was in the cars on the large carrier. A total of sixty million dollars was found in secret compartments. Four traffickers were killed in the exchange and fortunately none of the Federales ended up as casualties. It was a good day's work. Once they returned to Mexico City, Villa invited all of the Federales who participated in the Juarez raid out for a steak dinner and several congratulatory shots of tequila. The celebration was an enjoyable one and, to Villa, it was important to create a strong comraderie between the DEA and the Mexican counterparts. It paid significant dividends.

Less than a week later, Villa left the embassy late in the evening. The night was illuminated by a bright, full moon. He was tired and wanted to get home for some quiet time and relax for a few hours before hitting the sack. As he drove, his eyes darted in different directions looking for anything unusual that might pose danger. As he turned onto the quiet street leading to his house, he heard a massive explosion before his car was sent flying several feet in the air landing upside down on its top. The explosion was the result of the detonation of an improvised explosive device. Villa was in shock and his eardrums were throbbing and he did not have a clear head. He knew that he was in serious trouble and struggled to regain his senses. Villa instinctively unfastened his seat belt and quickly lifted himself out of the car. As he did so, he noticed four men approaching quickly with pistols in their hands. He breathed a sigh of relief that his handgun was still in his waistband. Ducking behind the car, he began firing. The men charged him and he quickly shot and killed three of them. The last one came within five feet when Villa shot him in the left eye. The bullet penetrated his brain, turning it into the consistency of watery Jell-O. He was later identified as Lisa's right-hand man, Gonzalo.

CHAPTER 14

The Final Reckoning

Lisa Rochin was beside herself when she learned that Gonzalo had been killed. She could always count on him to watch her back. Now, she would have to be more careful than ever before. The money and the drugs she lost in the raid in Juarez could easily be replaced, but a loyal and trustworthy friend was a horse of a different color. Regardless, she was gaining tremendous respect for Villa, his tenacity and ability to survive assassination attempts were nothing short of amazing! Lisa realized that he was definitely her equal intellectually and both were very methodical in everything they did. It was almost as though they had the same DNA.

She would tell her people, "Can you imagine if Villa worked with us? The Cartel of the North would be unstoppable. Sadly, he is too principled to engage in criminal activities. I would pay him millions of dollars to help us. He would be well worth it. He is as cunning as a leopard in the jungle and maybe even more than me. One day, I know we will collide like two hurricanes with such a monstrous force that maybe neither one of us will survive that encounter."

A couple of weeks later, one of Lisa's spies within the cartel, Pablo, called and told her that he had some important information, but preferred not to talk about it on the telephone. Lisa told him that she would meet him the following day on a small dirt road an hour's drive south of Juarez. She described a large sign next to it that advertised Volkswagen cars. It was an ideal location since the road was no longer in use and was covered by weeds and large trees would shield them from prying eyes. She would arrange for the area to be surrounded by security. Nothing would be left to chance.

The following day, as the sun beat down on the scorched Chihuahuan Desert, Pablo arrived in a small, blue Ford sedan. Lisa, who was waiting a few miles down the road, was immediately advised by radio that he was at the location. Lisa had an escort of over fifty of her best sicarios. Finally, she got word that it was safe to approach the area. She was driven by a carload of armed men to the area where Pablo stood outside his car. The loud sound of doors opening could be heard and Lisa made her grand entrance with five men brandishing a large arsenal following behind her.

She gave Pablo a hug, "Mi amigo, what is it that is so

important? I hope that everything is well with you and your family."

"Claro, I heard some things that you need to know. Ever since Jairo Alvarez took over the Blood Alliance Cartel, which is now nothing more than a component of the Cartel of the North, he has been bad mouthing you."

Lisa retorted, "What are you talking about? I consider something like this as treachery and it will not be tolerated!"

Pablo continued, "He has been telling people that the only reason he joined forces with you is to grow more powerful, but when the time is right he will leave your cartel and become one of your rivals. He is a treacherous man and you need to get rid of him."

"Pablo, you have never given me bad information and I have always considered you a trusted friend. Thank you for bringing this to my attention. I will deal with the matter. Go in peace and we will talk soon."

Pablo stated, "Gracias! If I hear anything more, I will call you right away. Be careful."

Lisa pondered the information she had just received. She understood that treachery was part of the drug business, but wished it wasn't so prevalent. Everyone was making a lot of money and no one had anything to complain about. People were not happy with just becoming rich, they always wanted more and were willing to betray associates, friends, and even family for money. Now she knew why Alvarez was so willing to become part of the Cartel of the North. He wanted to lay the foundation for becoming a strong cartel, once again, and then splinter away from Lisa's organization. Alvarez would then, undoubtedly, become a powerful enemy. He was like a fucking rattlesnake. He was using her and in the end would go to war with her for domination of Mexico's drug trafficking underworld.

On a cloudy evening, as the wind was gaining momentum, Alvarez arrived at one of Lisa's safe houses, which was located close to the U.S. border in the Mexican state of Sonora. He brought four of his men as security. He wondered why in the hell she wanted to meet with him, but didn't suspect any danger. He was confident that she trusted him, but unfortunately perceptions can be wrong.

Lisa was sitting on a large, white leather couch when Alvarez walked in the door. His men waited outside.

Lisa said, "Thank you for coming. I hope your trip was pleasant. Do you know why I had you come here?"

Alvarez was perplexed and answered, "No, I don't! I assume it has to be important business. Please tell me how I can serve you?"

Lisa said, "I hear that you have been trying to undermine me by saying lies and that you and the Blood Alliance Cartel joined us so that you can grow strong, only so you can be a threat to us. Is this true?"

Alvarez raised his voice and in anger shouted, "No, it is

nothing but a bunch of fucking lies. Who is the dog that has been spreading bullshit about me? I will kill him with my bare hands!"

Lisa did not back down. She told Alvarez, "It is you who are a liar! I wanted to make sure that the information against you was true and therefore some of my men wiretapped your phones with some very sophisticated equipment that I bought recently. Do you want to hear some of your conversations?"

Beads of sweat began to form on Alvarez's brow. His hands began to tremble noticeably and his mouth went completely dry. He didn't expect to be accused of treason and was not prepared to defend himself. Worse, they had him on tape and how could he refute this type of evidence. He decided to confess hoping that Lisa would spare him.

"A la chingada, it is true. What can I say? We have always been rivals until recently, but bad blood is hard to get rid of and it takes time. I also have a problem answering to a woman. It has always been my belief that women should not be involved in a business that has always been controlled by machos with balls."

Lisa, as quick as the lethal strike from a rattlesnake, pulled out her handgun and pointed it at Alvarez who was now soaked in sweat. It had seeped into his eyes that were now painfully burning. Large tears poured down both his cheeks and dripped to the floor from his chin.

Alvarez started to say, "Don't---!"

He heard a loud explosion and felt a hot object slam into his chest with the force of a sledgehammer. As he fell, he felt a rush of tremendous pain. Once on the floor, he felt something warm and sticky pouring from his mouth. Suddenly, he realized that it was his blood. He began to choke. Panic set in, as he was unable to breath. Alvarez stared wild-eyed at Lisa and then everything went black. Lisa had killed him. She knew that treachery had to be dealt with quickly and with lethal force. One could not be weak in these types of matters. Brutal examples kept people in line and discouraged anyone from being an informant or from attempting a hostile takeover of the organization. Alvarez knew the rules of the game better than anyone and he paid the ultimate price for ignoring them.

The four men who came with Alvarez were marched in at gunpoint to where Lisa sat near the body of their former boss. They too began to sweat as they were lined up in front Lisa. She looked at them one at a time.

Lisa spoke, "Muchachos, as you can see your former boss is dead. He caused his own downfall by being disloyal and the penalty for treachery is a violent death. Do you prefer to follow Alvarez to hell or do you want to continue working for me? It is now in your hands."

All of them spoke simultaneously that they wanted to continue working for Lisa and they pledged their undying allegiance to her and the Cartel of the North. They knew to do otherwise would be an immediate death sentence. Lisa gave each one ten thousand dollars and shook each man's hand. They retreated hastily from the house and prayed to Santa Muerta for letting them walk the earth a few more years. Hopefully!

A few days later, Lisa invited her siblings, Anita and Armando, to spend some time with her at one of her many hideouts. This one was located in the small town of Batopilas, Chihuahua. It was in the Sierra Madre Occidental Mountains near the border with Sinaloa. Lisa loved the beautiful glens, rivers, and the exotic flowers and birds that flourished in the area. It was a magical place with its beautiful plaza and its nineteenth century aqueduct that once formed part of the silver route. The sleepy town's homes and buildings were painted in vibrant colors that were pleasant to the eye. People sat in front of their houses and looked forward to talking with anyone who walked by. Lisa felt safe there and donated large sums of money for the building of schools and had also started a scholarship fund for the children to go to college. She built parks and soccer fields and was admired by the citizens of Batopilas. The small police force was in her pocket and dropped everything to protect Lisa when she was in the area.

Lisa had a large colonial style house about three miles from the town, which was surrounded by several hectares of orange trees. All of the fruit was donated to the entire village that harvested them. Prior to the arrival of her brother and sister, Lisa had the house cleaned and decorated with fresh, fragrant flowers. She also had more than fifty of her men providing security, just in case. Several cooks were hired and lots of food and drink were brought in for the occasion. Lisa wanted everything to be perfect. She wanted to spend some quality time with Anita and Armando and wanted to get away from the violent world that surrounded them. She had them transported to a dirt airstrip near her house and some of her most trusted men picked them up and drove them to the house.

When they entered the house, Lisa ran and gave them a big hug. She felt calm and more relaxed when they were with her. It was because she knew that they were safe with her. She would protect them with all the power that she now possessed.

Lisa cheerfully welcomed them, "It is so good to see you. Thank you for coming. Please give your bags to my men and they will put them in your sleeping quarters. Come on out to the back and we will have some frozen margaritas."

They followed Lisa to a large wooden deck at the back of the house. It had a large wooden table with a bright blue and yellow deck umbrella. The chairs had matching blue cushions. A crystal pitcher full of frozen margaritas with slices of lime was in the center of the table. One of the cooks, a short, dark-skinned woman, with several missing teeth, slowly filled their glasses.

Lisa commented, "To family, love, honor, and trust. The three of us will always be there for one another. Nothing is stronger in this world than blood. We are all one, are we not?"

Anita added, "I pray for you both at night and day and know the spirits protect you from the evil that is in the air at all times."

Armando added, "Yes, I have been looking forward to spending time together with you. It is difficult to sometimes get away, but we need to try to see each other at least three or four times a year."

After a couple of drinks, the three of them went to their rooms to freshen up. The sun was beginning to set behind the spectacular mountains and one of the maids lit up hundreds of round paper lanterns in the backyard. The purple, blue, red, orange, black, and yellow colors created a festive mood.

As Lisa and her siblings returned outside, a twelve-men mariachi band began to belch out "El Rey." The music, lights, and the beautiful moon were making it a sensational night. A rectangular table with expensive blue lapis inlay was brought out. Huge trays of lobster, steak, rice, beans, and warm, homemade tortillas followed it. After feasting on the succulent food, they laughed, joked, and sang along with the mariachi group at the top of their lungs.

The next day, the three of them went for a long hike to

burn off some calories. A well-armed escort followed them. The sky was a turquoise blue, and the warmth brought out the strong scent of the wildflowers that quilted the area. Lisa, Anita, and Armando bonded by talking about their younger days and the pranks that they would pull on each other. They enjoyed reminiscing. As they topped each other's stories, it sparked hysterical laughter. They would stop momentarily along the hiking trail, to hug each other time and again. This visit was something that Lisa needed for her soul. Anita and Armando needed to feel this closeness as well. Lisa felt a great sense of comfort. Lisa only wished that Anita and Armando could be with her always so she could protect them. Unfortunately, she knew they had their own lives and were no longer children.

All too quickly, the time came for sad goodbyes. Lisa called her siblings into her bedroom and sat them down. She told them that the times were becoming very dangerous and didn't want them involved in her business anymore. Lisa opened her purse and took out two checks in their names. Each check was for twenty-five million dollars. Lisa handed them to Anita and Armando. It brought tears to their eyes. The checks were from a shell corporation out of Panama, one of many that Lisa used to launder drug money. The checks could never be traced back to her. She hugged both of them before they left. Lisa felt tremendous emotion because she didn't know if she would ever see them again.

Hours later, Lisa also left and flew to a clandestine airstrip on one of her many ranches near Juarez, Chihuahua. She felt refreshed and was now ready to throw herself into the business at hand with a vengeance.

Two days later, Lisa was at her desk looking at her financial statements from accounts spread around the world. She had just tallied them at slightly over eighty billion dollars, when her secure phone rang. It was General Molina calling from Venezuela.

"Hola, Lisa! I hope you are doing well? My colleagues, Generals Macias and Cruz, and I want to come see you in Mexico to begin sending some huge shipments of cocaine that we have stockpiled. It is imperative that we move it soon. We just want to check out things there to make sure our merchandise is going to be safe."

Lisa responded, "Of course! That would be great. When are you planning on coming? It would be best if you came on a private plane so you can land at one of my ranches. I will send you the coordinates."

General Macias replied, "Muy bien! That will be fine. You can expect us day after tomorrow. Please send the coordinates quickly. We look forward to seeing you again."

Within hours, Lisa sent the coordinates and arranged for heavy security to be in place while the heads of the Cartel of the Suns were in Mexico. She was pleased they were coming so she could show them how secure and sophisticated her operation had become in a few short years. Lisa knew that moving drugs through Venezuela was important, especially since the entire government was involved in one way or another.

Two days later, a blue and white Beechcraft King Air made its approach and descended rapidly onto a dirt airfield at one of Lisa's sprawling ranches. Over twenty men guarded the area and Lisa stood nearby as the plane turned around and finally shut its engines off. The three Generals exited the plane, followed by the two pilots. They walked over to where Lisa was standing and each one kissed her hand in homage to her power and wealth.

"I hope your trip was enjoyable," said Lisa. "Mi casa es su casa! Please follow me. My men will bring your bags."

General Molina replied, "Gracias, muy amable. We ran into some severe turbulence about a hundred kilometers from Venezuela. It felt like we were riding a bucking horse. But the important thing is that we are here."

After settling in, the Generals sat in Lisa's living room. The room was impressive, with white Italian tile, red sofa's and expensive paintings adorning the walls. Bottles of the finest liquor were neatly lined up on a round coffee table, along with a solid silver ice bucket. With drinks in their hands, they began serious discussions.

General Molina commented, "Lisa, as you are aware, we have provided protection to Colombia's largest drug trafficking groups to include the FARC. As a result, we now have access to more tonnage of cocaine than ever before, but we still have to be careful with the people we deal with. We trust you and wanted to see if you can handle additional tons of cocaine through your organization."

Lisa assured General Macias, "Of course, I can do it. I have a huge infrastructure and more importantly it is a fact that the gringos are now consuming more drugs than ever, especially cocaine. Tomorrow, I will take you and show you some of our warehouses and the routes we use to get our merchandise across the border."

Molina grinned, "That will give us peace of mind. We get the cocaine on consignment from the Colombians and if we lose a load it will be our necks on the line."

Lisa answered, "I understand completely, but keep in mind that we do have a lot of government and law enforcement officials in our pocket, both here in Mexico and on the other side of the border, that provide us with protection and assistance in moving the loads across the border."

It was a windy morning when Lisa and her visitors drove from the ranch in a silver Mercedes Benz, followed by three black Jeep Cherokee's full of deadly sicarios. Lisa gave the Generals a tour of the border area and showed them many of the large warehouses where the cartel's drugs were stored; the border crossing routes and some of the sophisticated tunnels that had been built; and the fleet of light aircraft used to fly the drugs into the U.S. The Generals were more than impressed with what they saw. Lisa only gave them a small glimpse into her organization. She was smart enough to know that everything was on a need to know basis even with close associates. Lisa was aware that people could turn on you like rabid dogs in the blink of an eye.

That evening, as the sun was setting, Lisa held a huge party for her guests and invited many of her top leaders. The trumpets blared slightly over the loud violins and guitars as the Mariachi's del Sol played uplifting music. Several roasted suckling pigs were prepared and placed in a beautiful arrangement on several tables covered with red linen.

The festivities had just gotten underway when a small drone silently flew over the ranch. It was equipped with a sophisticated camera system that was sending valuable information to a large group of Federales and Mexican marines about a mile away. Villa and Ventura looked at the images carefully and determined that security north of the house was weak. There were hardly any guards for some reason. Villa also observed a small barn close by. The day before, a telephone call had been intercepted from a member of the Cartel of the North. He told his girlfriend that he was at a ranch preparing for a party Lisa was having for some visiting Venezuelan officials the following day. Reacting quickly, Villa and Ventura began to use sophisticated equipment to triangulate and obtain the coordinates of the phone and that was what led them to the ranch

Villa gave the order to move forward and a small army of plainclothes Federales and uniformed marines moved in unison over rocks and rolling hills. As they were about fifty yards from the well-lit house, one of the marines tripped on some weeds and accidently let off a round. In a nanosecond, automatic weapons fire broke the still of the night. Villa had everyone move forward, making sure that the house would be surrounded rapidly, preventing anyone from escaping. The flashes from the intense gunfire were everywhere. As Villa came closer to the house, he felt a sting above his right ear. He knew a bullet had creased his head and could feel warm blood running down his neck onto his shirt. He crouched low and continued to run forward. Villa could hear men scream in pain. He fired at three men that came running from inside the house and killed them as they raised their weapons. He quickly moved towards the barn that had a light on and entered it cautiously. Once in the barn, he moved slowly, checking each individual stall. Suddenly, someone jumped out from behind a large wooden column. It was Lisa! He was awestruck and had never gazed upon a more beautiful creature in his entire life. Consequently, two of the most formidable adversaries in the world stood pointing guns at each other from a distance of ten feet. Villa finally lowered his gun and then Lisa did the same. Recognizing Miguel Villa, she smiled and blew him a kiss. Like a ghostly ripple in the air, Lisa stepped out into the dark night and disappeared.

Villa stood alone in silence in the barn. It dawned on him that despite being a criminal, he respected Lisa for her incredible intelligence, beauty, and ability to control the most powerful drug trafficking organization in the world. He just could not bring himself to kill such a magnificent creature that had captivated him for so many years. She, too, could not pull the trigger and end the life of Villa. They would meet again, maybe under different circumstances. Villa also put it into perspective. She was no worse than the corrupt politicians in her country or in the U.S. for that matter. U.S. Congressional leaders took millions of dollars from pharmaceutical companies, which created drug epidemics, based on greed. He looked forward to continuing the cat and mouse game with Lisa. As he thought about the chase to come, his adrenaline began to flow like a tsunami.

During the operation, twelve traffickers were killed and thirteen were taken into custody. Five Federales and two marines had been mortally wounded. The three Venezuelan Generals were arrested and their hands were handcuffed behind their backs. Venezuela immediately requested their return. The U.S. also wanted them on pending conspiracy charges for cocaine smuggling. Mexico told Venezuela that they would accept their request via a diplomatic note. They placed the Generals on a commercial flight to Venezuela with a transit stop in Tucson, Arizona where a group of DEA agents waited to take them into custody. Venezuela would have to wait.

About The Author

Michael S. Vigil, born and raised in New Mexico, earned his degree in Criminology at New Mexico State University where he graduated with Honors. He later joined the Drug Enforcement Administration (DEA) and became one of its most highly decorated agents. He served in thirteen foreign and domestic posts and rose through the ranks to the highest level of the Senior Executive Service.

Mr. Vigil received numerous awards during his elite career, such as law enforcement's most prestigious recognition: The National Association of Police Organization's (NAPO) Top Cop Award. Many foreign governments have honored Mr. Vigil for his extraordinary service in the violent struggle against transnational organized crime. He was made an honorary General by the country of Afghanistan and China bestowed him with the "Key to the City" of Shanghai. The President of the Dominican Republic also presented him with an Admiral's sword. He is mentioned in numerous books and appears on documentaries and popular television programs such as *Gangsters: America's Most Evil, Manhunt, and NETFLIX'S Drug Lords.*

He is a contributor to the highly regarded Cipher Brief. His highly acclaimed memoir, *DEAL*, was released in 2014. *Metal Coffins: The Blood Alliance Cartel* is his first fiction novel and many of the scenarios are derived from his experiences as an undercover agent.

His current novel, *Narco Queen*, is a sequel to *Metal Coffins: The Blood Alliance Cartel.*

Printed in the United States
By Bookmasters